The Experiment of Dreams

Brandon Zenner

Cover Design: James goonwrite.com
Formatting: Polgarus Studio polgarusstudio.com

ISBN-13: 978-0692355138
ISBN-10: 0692355138

Library of Congress Control Number: 2015904214

Dedicated to my wife Mallory,
For her unwavering love and support,
A million dedications would never be enough.

Chapter 1

Ben cut across the empty parking lot of the Annapolis Foundation for Sleep Research, picking at the dried paste plastered to his scalp where the electrodes had been attached to his head the previous night. He enjoyed an odd sense of pleasure in removing the paste, like finding pockets of sand buried deep in his hair after a day at the beach.

It was shaping up to be a warm day, and as Ben neared his car, he flung his jacket over his shoulder, letting the sunlight warm his hospital-cold skin. Ben pulled his keys from his pocket, and a business card that Dr. Wright had given him slipped away and fluttered over the pavement on a light wind. Ben jumped to catch it, but it danced over the parking lot in a gust and was lost from sight.

Not a problem, he thought. Dr. Wright had given Ben the same business card three times already and had been urging him to call the doctor—whose name was on the card—for over a month now. He explained in detail how important it was for Ben to meet the man.

Ben fiddled with his keys, found the alarm button, and unlocked his car. He flicked away the dried paste left stuck to his fingers, brushed his hands off on his pant legs, and climbed into the driver's seat. The reflection gazing back at him in the rearview mirror was not flattering. Nights at that lackluster hospital made him feel so disheveled. His face was gaunt, his eyes were bleary and red, and the stubble on his face was in desperate need of a shave. He rubbed the side of his cheek, enjoying the sensation of the coarse hairs against his palm. The stubble gave off a silvery-hue that reminded Ben that he was getting older. Even the hair on his head was now speckled with grey, like someone splattered a brush with drying white paint all over his head. He looked like his father, or rather how he remembered his father.

He turned his gaze from the mirror and put the car in drive.

Ben yearned for good coffee—not the sour crap they served in the hospital that tasted like the Styrofoam cups they served it in. The clock on the dashboard read 11:37. With any luck, he would be home in an hour— that is if he didn't stop along the way for coffee, and maybe some breakfast. And of course, if the traffic around I-95 wasn't particularly unbearable. But the chances of the circle around Baltimore's Inner Harbor being anything but hellish during lunch hour were slim to none.

He hated that circle, loathed every car that sped along the pavement, cursed it with every breath in his body. As soon as he merged with the traffic, his life was put in imminent danger. Cars and trucks sped between lanes, weaving this way and that, coming dangerously close to hitting one another—inches from disaster. When Benjamin Walker moved to Baltimore, he named I-95 "Maryland's Inner Death Circle," and the name became more relevant with each passing day.

As bad as driving I-95 was, driving the streets of New York was not much better; Ben was glad his commute was no longer between Baltimore and New York City. Currently his drive between Baltimore and Annapolis took a little over an hour, and outside of the harbor, the drive was not bad at all. It was a good thing Dr. Wright left the city to take the job in Annapolis. His loyalty to the man might have eventually worn out. The commute was not worth the money, unless the doctor started paying substantially more, which of course, the hospitals would never agree to. Ben's fees and rates were set in contract, per test, and rarely—if ever— changed in the slightest. Compromise and negotiation were out of the question.

Nevertheless, Ben knew in his heart that he would miss the old doctor if he ever stopped participating in his tests and experiments. Not exactly like missing an old friend, though Stuart *was* an old friend, but more like missing a well-accustomed routine. Or like missing an old tree in the backyard after watching it grow over the years. The tree could be replaced, but it would never grow the same branches.

Lately though, the work with Dr. Wright was good. The money was all right, and the sessions were regular enough that Ben considered it a real job. He could endure the old man's stale breath as he hovered over Ben's face attaching sensors and wires to his forehead and scalp. He could endure the sleep deprivation studies, the food abstention trials, the unknown medications presented in white Dixie cups, and the incredibly tedious paperwork and questionnaires he constantly had to fill out.

The biggest problem Ben dealt with over the last few years was not the pay or the long commute. It was the lack of anything new—anything exciting. The original tests, back when he was a teenager, were groundbreaking. At least they were to him. Over time, they became repetitive. The *same* sleep deprivation studies, the *same* food abstention trials, the *same* melatonin and B-12 supplements, over and over....

However, he could endure the boredom if the price was right. If the money kept rolling in, he would put up with it—and lately the money was rolling in.

Ben's curiosity was stirred, however, as they were wrapping up the sleep deprivation study earlier that morning.

Dr. Wright had paused, then said, "Ben, I have something for you. I'm not sure how to do this, so I'm just going to go ahead and do it." The tall doctor scratched the light fuzz on the side of his hairless head, wrinkling his trimmed mustache. "I want our working relationship to stay as professional as always."

"Sure, Stuart, so do I. What's up?"

"Here." He handed Ben a white envelope. "There's five-hundred dollars in there."

"Wait, is this all I'm getting? This study lasted over a month, I'm contracted—"

"Your check for the study is in the mail. This is a little something extra, a bonus. We appreciate your years of work at the hospital. This is just a little something to show our gratitude."

Ben thumbed open the envelope. *Our gratitude?* Five crisp, one-hundred-dollar bills were stacked inside, all facing the same direction. The money smelled new—starchy and fresh. Ben scratched his head. "Is this your way of firing me, like a pension or something?"

"No, no, Ben." The doctor shook his head. "Nothing of the sort. Not long ago we received some private funding at the hospital from some very generous donors. These individuals are following your work and dedication to the hospital; in return, these donors would like to show their appreciation by giving you a bonus. That's all there is to it. Just a bonus."

Each payment Ben had ever received over the many years working with Dr. Stuart Wright came in the form of a check written out to the exact amount. Ben even declared the earnings on his income tax, on a 1099-MISC form. Cash was never an option, never mentioned. Neither was a bonus. Hospitals do not run like that. Doctors get bonuses, but test subjects do not.

"This is cash, Stuart."

"I know it is." Dr. Wright's mustache moved with his sigh. "I think you can understand why we need to keep this … to ourselves. These are *private* investors, Ben, and it's just a bonus." He patted Ben on the shoulder. "We've been working together for a long time now, and you deserve a few extra dollars every once in a while. Don't think so hard; you'll give yourself a migraine. Just say 'thank you,' and take the cash." He smiled, wrinkling the furrows on his bald forehead.

Private investors rolled around Ben's head. He stared at the money—cash money, five hundred dollars, tax-free. Ben had worked in the bar business for most of his life; even owned a small place in upstate New York that did quite well while it was open. It wasn't unusual for a few dollars here and there to slip through the cracks and not get reported to the IRS. This was normal in the bar scene. But from a doctor, from a hospital? Perhaps the less he knew the better. He folded the envelope and tucked it inside his jacket pocket.

"Tell them 'thank you.'"

"I will, Ben. I will."

This conversation played over in Ben's mind as he eyed his jacket lying on the passenger seat, where the five hundred dollars were folded inside. He shook his head.

Strange, he thought.

Rent money, he assured himself.

Ben survived "Maryland's Inner Death Circle," certain that several of the other drivers were trying to kill him, and found a space to park less than two blocks from his door. Walking past a flower-store delivery van that lately always seemed to be parked around his block, he arrived at the entryway of the four-unit apartment building—an old, converted row-house that he called home.

At the top of the staircase on the second floor were two apartments with their front doors mirroring each other on opposite sides of a small landing. Ben's apartment was the door to the left. He unlocked the deadbolt, turned the handle, and hurried inside, happy to be back in his own space with his own bed and comfortable couch. The apartment was not much to look at—just a narrow one-bedroom flat—but the interior had a bit of character. The living room wall opposite the front door was solid brick and ran the length of the room. It was open to the kitchen and a dining-room nook where Ben stored unopened boxes from when he first moved into the apartment. Ben liked the brick wall, liked it very much. It probably drove the rent up an extra hundred dollars a month, but he didn't care. It gave the place a touch of personality.

Ben tossed his keys on the kitchen counter, grabbed the bottle of dish soap from the sink, and walked straight to the bathroom. He changed out of his hospital clothing, burying the dirty garments deep in the hamper. Anything he wore in hospitals during trials and tests absorbed that antiseptic hospital stench—that sterile smell that reminded Ben of the color white—and lingered on his skin for hours after.

A hot shower removed more of the electrode-crust plastered in Ben's hair and scalp, but whatever the stuff was that the doctor used, it never cleaned off completely with soap and water. After years of trials, Ben found that dish soap worked the best. Now clean and fresh—the hospital smell scrubbed from his skin—Ben put on his old well-worn robe and collapsed on the couch.

His body was sore, his mind exhausted. He needed a few hours of rest before heading to his shift at the bar. He wished he had never agreed to work that night, but filling in shifts was why the bar hired him. Ben was obliged to work when an employee was sick or went on vacation, or when someone just wanted the night off. A few shifts a week always popped up.

It was times like these—these lazy afternoons—that Ben wished he had cable TV. The old square box on the shelf wasn't even plugged in. Why he didn't just get rid of the thing, he didn't know. Of course, he could plug it in, look for the antenna in one of the boxes in the dining room, and maybe pick up a few channels, but there was nothing on TV worth watching. Besides, he wasn't even sure if TVs still used those old-fashioned antennas. Instead, he just sat there, gazing at the stack of books on the coffee table, debating whether he was too tired to read anything at all. The only books on the coffee table were philosophy—Nietzsche, and the like—all books that he started reading at some point or another and never finished. In his current frame of mind, he couldn't handle philosophy.

He looked up from the books, his gaze wandering, until the solitary painting hanging by the front door stole his attention. It was the only painting created by his beloved wife Emily that he still owned. It was the only thing remaining from his old life in upstate New York.

It was a small painting, about a foot and a half square.

The swirls of paint were still vibrant, still brilliant. It was a painting of the cabin in the woods, the cabin they hiked past dozens of times. A small wooden building hidden among the towering pines. A whisper of smoke trailed from the chimney, hinting of the cabin's warm and cozy interior, sheltered from the blustery air. Snow covered the ground in half-melted patches, with stale, dead grass poking out from beneath. Clouds soared in the blue sky, illuminated by swirls of creamy zinc and titanium white paint. The sun was barely visible in the corner, brought to life by yellow and orange swirls, twisting and turning with various shades of red. This painting, out of the many paintings in Emily's studio—the landscapes, still-lifes, and portraits—had always been his favorite. The scene was realistic in detail, yet she used her own flair of artistic imagery to turn it into a surrealistic figment of her imagination. The sky swirled in shades of blue and purple never found in nature, yet her artistic ability was subtle enough to make these irregularities easy to overlook at first glance. It was not until you spent time absorbing the painting in full that the irregularities became apparent to see. It was genius.

At least it was to Ben.

This was the only painting he had taken from her studio. He left the others neatly stacked in the corner of her paint-flecked room, exactly where Emily had last touched them.

After she died, Ben could not be around her things—not even the house they lived in. He could not sleep in the bed they'd shared for the eight years of their marriage, side by side. He couldn't look at her clothes, or her shoes—the leather boots she just polished and left out to dry—or her toothbrush balanced on the corner of the sink. He couldn't look at her watch with its coiled black-leather strap, sitting on the bedside table where she had last taken it off.

When he stepped into that house for the first time all alone, straight from the hospital, he was still wearing the same clothes from the night before, speckled with blood—her blood. The quiet and stillness all around him was maddening. It took a considerable amount of strength just to step away from the front door. He wanted to be outside, to run as far away as possible. These things, *her* things, were causes of great pain—not relief, not comfort, nor gentle remembrance, just pain.

She was everywhere in that house. She was still in her studio, standing in front of her easel with her back facing him. Her image on the large plate-glass windows reflected the focused concentration of her creased brow as she applied a stroke of color with her brush. He saw her applying her makeup in front of the bathroom sink, her face an inch away from the mirror. He smelled her in the almond-scented shampoo and the little jasmine-scented bars of soap with the Chinese writing on the packaging. Everything in his home reminded him of her. Emily had seeped into the very walls, fibers, and structure of their home. It was impossible that she was gone, absolutely impossible—she couldn't be. She was everywhere in that house, around every corner, and in every room.

But she wasn't there. She was gone.

Taken from him like all the rest.

A simple accident. A stupid fight at the bar. Two drunken patrons fighting over something. Anything. Nothing. Sports, maybe. A girl, perhaps … it didn't matter. Words were spoken and punches were thrown. By the time Ben heard the commotion and ran out from the kitchen, it was over. Stunned customers were circling about. The two men stood slack-jawed and in shock, all of their anger deflated. Emily lay on the ground bleeding, the knife by her side. She had tried to stop the fight, tried to get between the two men.

That was it, an accident. No sickness, no long hospitalization. She was healthy and vibrant one moment, dead the next.

Ben left New York, left their old home and sold it all, leaving everything behind but for one thing: the painting of the cabin in the woods.

As time passed, his decision to abandon Emily's possessions caused countless nights of regret and anguish. Those items, however painful they were at the time, would have been most welcome as the years went by and the reality of her being gone truly sank in. The longing to possess anything and everything of hers became an obsession, a comforting need, and an endless source of torment and sorrow. How could he have left everything? Why? He had to smell her, hold her, squeeze one of her shirts in his hands, smother it against his face. Breathe in lungful's of her fragrant scent lingering on one of her silk shirts—but it was all gone. Ben called the agent who sold the house and contacted the current owners in an attempt to track down any of the paintings left behind, but to no avail. All of Emily's possessions were gone, and all Ben had left were his memories.

These thoughts and needs raced through his mind in endless waves of guilt as he stared into the swirls of paint in the sky above the cabin in the woods. Feelings pierced his mind like sharp blades, slashing away without consequence, sinking their cold metal teeth deep into the flesh of his brain.

The painting brought back memories both beautiful and horrid. He saw his wife painting, her reflection in the plate-glass window, her forehead furrowed in concentration, paint smeared and dotted all over her hands, forearms, and face. He stood in the doorway, just looking, not wanting Emily to see him looking at her. Just enjoying the pleasure of watching her work, doing the thing that made her most happy … and *that,* seeing her smile, was what made him happy … so happy ….

Ben got up from the couch. The bottle of Jameson on the counter was calling his name. The thought of a drink made his stomach rumble and his mind swirl, but he could not let the rest of the day be consumed by dwelling on the past. It was too easy to spend hours staring at the painting while drinking to oblivion, as if the painting held some great divinity that he desired—the answers he needed, and the cure for the pain he both longed for and resented.

He licked his lips. His head throbbed. The yearning for a stiff drink stung at his mind, made his mouth salivate. His throat had a dryness only alcohol could soothe. A twinge of pleasure was released at the very thought of taking a sip of whiskey—a foresight into the relief the alcohol would have on his body and mind.

He turned away from the bottle and went to the bedroom, setting the alarm. Sleeping in the middle of the day was tough, but he needed some rest before work. Three hours should do it. He grabbed his blindfold from the bedside table and accidentally brushed off the business card hiding beneath. Bending over, he retrieved the card from the floor, noisily exerting himself from the strain. Printed across the center of the card was the name, *"Dr. Peter Wulfric"* followed by a telephone number underneath. Dr. Wright had emphasized to Ben that Dr. Wulfric was working on a very exciting project and was looking for a client. He paid very well. Ben had put the card in his pocket and then on the bedside table, then forgot all about it. The same went for the other two.

Then Dr. Peter Wulfric had called him.

The man was happy and pleasant and urged Ben to meet with him. Ben shied away, telling the doctor, *'I can't get out of town … I've got a lot on my plate right now.'* Dr. Wulfric volunteered to travel to him, to Baltimore, just so they could talk—a quick lunch. Perhaps it was intrigue, or perhaps curiosity when Ben asked what hospital the doctor worked for and the doctor said, *'We can discuss that when we talk face-to-face,'* that Ben's interest grew. He conceded to a meeting. Dr. Peter Wulfric was coming to Fells Point in two days, and hopefully he would pick up the lunch tab.

Ben tossed the card back on the bedside table and pulled the covers up to his chin. The blindfold was fastened tightly over his eyes, shielding away the intense rays of sunlight penetrating through the blinds. He took a deep breath and relaxed his mind. Sleep was not going to come easily.

Thoughts of the painting along with visions of Emily flashed in his mind: her dark-curly hair bouncing on her shoulders as she laughed, paint on her face, cheeks, and hair. He saw his own finger dip into a pool of dark blue paint from the pallet and watched his finger move to smear her nose. She shrieked with laughter, grabbed at his palm and fell backward. She was laughing too hard to resist, and his finger found her nose, rubbing it all over with the oily blue paint.

She shrieked, *'Stop, Ben!'*

He heard his own laughter as they kissed. She grabbed him close, not letting him go, holding him by the ears and smearing her paint-covered nose all over his face.

He saw this as it happened, in that paint-speckled studio of hers. He heard the laughter and felt the warmth of love in his heart. His blindfold grew warm with the onset of tears.

Chapter 2

Dr. Peter Wulfric called Ben as soon as he turned off I-95. Although Ben lived in a safe neighborhood just a few blocks from Fells Point, the seeming underbelly of Baltimore was just a stone's throw away. Dr. Wulfric was an avid fan of *The Wire,* and the last thing he wanted was to get lost outside the safety of the Inner Harbor or Fells Point.

The phone rang several times, and then a voice rasped in the receiver, "Hello?"

"Ben, is this Ben?"

The voice cleared the sleep from his throat. "Yes—yes, this is Ben. Dr. Wulfric?"

"I'm sorry, did I wake you?"

"No, no. I'm up. Just closed my eyes for a second."

Dr. Wulfric thought he could hear a shower being turned on in the background.

The doctor checked his watch; it was almost noon. He wasn't early. Dr. Wulfric knew Ben bartended nights, so twelve in the afternoon was like seven in the morning to him. What he did not know was that Ben, like many other bartenders, had a few drinks at the end of his shift. And then a few more when he got home. Whatever time it was when Ben finally fell into bed, the sun was already up.

Ben reconfirmed with Dr. Wulfric the directions to a coffee house a block away from his apartment—the Still Life Roast. One of these days Dr.

Wulfric would start using the GPS on his phone, but whatever the reason might be, he liked to rely on old-fashioned technologies—like a map.

"Okay, Ben; I'll see you there."

He hung up, picturing Ben scrambling to brush his teeth to get ready for their meeting.

Guess I'll take my time, he thought. *And try not to get lost.*

***

Dr. Wulfric paced before the coffee house, his hand stroking his white beard.

Did he say Still Life Roast?

A moment or two passed, then he saw Ben walking toward him from down the street. He waited until he got closer, then waved and called out, "Ben, It's nice to finally meet you."

"Likewise." Ben extended a hand and the two men shook. Ben's hair looked wet and his eyes were puffy.

I woke him up. I must have.

"Let's get some coffee," the doctor said. "Are you hungry?"

"I could eat."

It was a beautiful day, and Dr. Wulfric was glad the waitress sat them outside on the sidewalk. Ben removed his windbreaker, and Dr. Wulfric unzipped his brown leather jacket. Under his coat, Dr. Wulfric was wearing his typical attire: a collared shirt and generic tie. Nothing fancy. He had been in a bit of a rush that morning and felt that his hair and beard might look a bit unkempt. *I look like freaking Jerry Garcia,* he thought. In the rush, he didn't realize he had put on an old shirt that was too small for his growing girth, and when he sat, he was cautious not to pop a button.

The waitress brought them coffee, a bagel for Dr. Wulfric, and a blueberry muffin for Ben.

"Ben," Dr. Wulfric began, blowing steam from his coffee, "Ben, do you know why I've been trying to meet you? Did Dr. Wright tell you anything about us—about the project?"

Ben shook his head. "No, he gave me your card and told me to call you. Several times. He said you're working on an exciting project and need someone with my … skill set. I've worked with some of Dr. Wright's associates in the past, so I didn't think much of it. Now I have to say, and I mean no disrespect, but this is all a bit strange, don't you think?"

"What do you mean?"

"Well, I've done a million tests with Stuart—umm, Dr. Wright. I've done clinical trials for hospitals, clinics, and private research companies all over the East Coast. I'm practically on the payroll at the Annapolis Foundation for Sleep Research. A doctor has never taken me out to lunch, or driven out of their way just to talk to me. Trials are always set up the same way—with the same fast-talking receptionist calling to schedule a time and the pay. Sometimes I get a letter in the mail offering fifty dollars to test some new medication, or whatever. That's how it has always been done. So, I'll give you this—you have my attention. But all the same, this is quite strange."

"We understand." Dr. Wulfric pointed at himself. "… *I* understand. This is a little strange, even for us—me. I'm not used to hand selecting participants, but we have never before needed a person with, say, your abilities."

"And what abilities are those?"

"The way you sleep, Benjamin. The control and vividness you have over your subconscious. Dr. Wright and I have been colleagues since grad school—did he tell you any of this? He was a few years behind me in school, but we were good friends, and remain so to this day. He personally recommended you for my project, and after seeing some of the tests you two have accomplished over the years, I can honestly say that he was right to recommend you. I couldn't have picked a better participant if I had spent months trying."

"Okay," Ben said, "I get it. Let's cut to the chase: what hospital do I need to go to, and what's the pay?"

Dr. Wulfric chuckled. The coffee seemed to be waking Ben up. "Aren't you a bit curious about the experiment?"

"Honestly, no … not really. Whatever it is, I'm sure I've done it before, or something similar."

The doctor leaned over the table, almost whispering. "I can assure you, you've never done anything quite like this before, Ben. Not by a long shot."

"Okay, well … what is it then?"

"I think it would be best for you to see our facility for yourself, with your own eyes. It would be impossible to simply explain it to you. I've put together a short presentation back at the lab that I think you would enjoy seeing. However, before we get to that, let me backtrack. There are a few things you need to understand."

"All right …"

"My employer would—"

"How are we all doing?" The waitress appeared out of nowhere, sneaking up behind Dr. Wulfric, who nearly jumped out of his skin. His hand shook, and a small wave of coffee jolted out of the cup.

"Oh jeez, I'm sorry, sir! Didn't mean to creep up on you like that. Let me get a towel."

"No, no. It's okay. I'm fine, dear; thank you."

"You're sure? It's no problem."

"Absolutely. As you can see, my nerves don't need the extra caffeine anyway." He gave her a big smile and she walked away, returning with a stack of napkins.

"Well," Dr. Wulfric said, "that was fun."

"You burn yourself?" Ben asked.

"Oh, I'm fine."

They were quiet as Dr. Wulfric cleaned the mess, then he heard Ben's voice crack. The boy was laughing.

"I'm sorry, I'm sorry! I wasn't trying to laugh."

Dr. Wulfric felt his own face form into a smile, and he started laughing as well.

Good, he thought. *That ought to lighten the mood.*

"Now," Dr. Wulfric cleared his throat. "Where was I before I embarrassed myself … our employer. He wants you to know that he appreciates any work you may choose to do for him. Whether or not you decide to go forward with the project is completely your own decision."

"Um, right … I would hope so."

"He is truly thankful for the work you've done at the hospital and hopes you are happy with the bonus Dr. Wright recently offered you."

"Right, that … so it was your *employer* who gave me that money?"

"Yes, in a way. Our employer recently made some very considerable contributions to the Annapolis Foundation for Sleep Research, and he is now on the board of directors as a silent partner. It's more of a title than anything else—he doesn't do any hands-on work. He's not even a doctor … anyway, you could say that the money came from him, the hospital, and all the doctors and staff. The man is, well, a bit of an eccentric. He has many interests both at home and abroad. He contracted us—my assistant and me—not very long ago to continue work on a project we had begun at Johns Hopkins."

"If you started the project at Johns Hopkins, why not finish it there?"

"Finances, my boy, finances. We ran out of them. Johns Hopkins cancelled the funding for the project. Then, a few months later, our employer approached me with an offer to continue the project under his directive. This project, this work—is too important to simply give up on. We're onto something big, and when I say big, I mean huge. Enormous."

"And you're not going to tell me, right? I have to see it for myself."

"Until we show you the lab, yes. I think that would be the best course of action."

They were quiet, sipping their coffee and eating their food. Dr. Wulfric finished eating and folded the napkin over his plate.

"This lab," Ben went on, "I'm guessing it's not an ordinary lab, like in a hospital."

Dr. Wulfric nodded. "By traditional standards, no. Technically, it's one of a kind. There's no other lab quite like it anywhere in the world. I'm sure of it."

Ben nodded. "And the money?"

"Our employer is a generous man. He would like to pay you just to come see the lab, for taking up your time. He knows that you're a busy man." Dr. Wulfric doubted Ben was busy at all, but he was not about to say anything.

"Where's the lab?"

"The Hamptons."

"The Hamptons? Like, the Hamptons in New York? That's, what, four hours away?"

"Three and a half, with no traffic."

"Christ. Well, when does he want me to go? And what's the pay?"

"He will pay you one thousand dollars for the day. You can drive yourself if you want, or he is willing to have you driven there and back."

"A thousand dollars just to check it out? That's nuts!"

"Cash."

"This is fucking sketchy, pardon my saying so. You want me to get in a car and be driven several hours away to do some unknown, off-the-record experiment in some stranger's house?"

"Well," Dr. Wulfric shifted in his seat. He wished that Ben were still laughing. *Maybe I should burn myself again.* "I understand what you're saying, but let me explain something—and I would like to be completely honest with you." Dr. Wulfric put his cup down on the saucer, lacing his fingers. "We didn't choose you as a participant for your abilities alone, as extraordinary as they are. There are countless other people who can dream lucidly, like yourself. Many have experienced aura migraines throughout their lives as well, just like you. The similarities are extraordinary, although I don't believe the two are related. Your ability is indeed remarkable. I've never seen test results quite like yours, but you're not the only person on our list of participants."

"Right, I get it. So why are you choosing me?"

"Because of your willingness, Ben. Because you're sitting with me right now, contemplating, when most others would turn the other way. Over the years, you agreed to perform each and every test that has come your way. You never say no, no matter what the experiment may be. Your records prove it. It's how you make a good portion of your income. You are extremely easygoing." Dr. Wulfric paused, taking in a deep breath. *Here it goes,* he thought, and continued, "Now, I don't want to upset you, or cross any personal boundaries, but the fact that you live alone and work part-time at night leaves you with plenty of free time during the day."

"And the fact that my wife is dead?"

He's a smart lad. He knows we've done our research. "We—well, not exactly because your wife is deceased, but because you are alone, yes. We did our research; I'm not going to lie. It's all there in your personnel file at the hospital. You're a perfect fit. This experiment will require a lot of time, of which you have plenty. Your participation would be highly valued and appreciated. Not to mention that you passed our little test."

"What test was that?"

"You had no problem taking the envelope Dr. Wright gave you."

"Well, cash *is* king. So what is the pay if I choose to do the experiment?"

"That would be decided by Mr. Marcus."

"Mr. Marcus is your employer?"

"No. Mr. Marcus is my employer's associate."

They were quiet as Ben finished his coffee. Dr. Wulfric knew that Ben had never before been in a situation like this. It was absurd, completely nuts, absolutely out of the question … yet, Ben was intrigued. Dr. Wulfric could tell. Ben's mind was processing, trying to decide if he should accept the work, or if he would be nuts to turn it away. Dr. Wright had personally assured Ben that he could trust Dr. Wulfric. Never—even with all the crazy tests and experiments—had Dr. Wright ever put Ben in any serious danger. Dr. Wulfric knew Ben would trust Dr. Wright's advice and recommendations.

Dr. Wulfric was also privy to the conversation between Dr. Wright and Ben on the phone, just last night. The old doctor had some unfortunate news to tell Ben. He was set to retire in just a few, short months. Dr. Wright was officially throwing in the towel. That did not necessarily mean that Ben's work at the hospital would stop completely, but it would significantly decline—by nearly eighty percent. It was bad news for Ben, but good news for Dr. Wulfric. Ben would need a new source of income, and money was something Dr. Wulfric had at his disposal.

Dr. Wulfric could see the thought process churning inside Ben's mind. He was probably thinking about his conversation with Dr. Stuart Wright. Thinking that it was the old doctor's wishes for him to start working with Dr. Wulfric.

Ben looked squarely at Dr. Wulfric. "All right, I'm in. You're right. I live alone, I don't give a shit, and I take cash. I am the perfect fit for some crazy experiment like this."

"Oh, that's great, Benjamin. You're making the right choice. You won't be disappointed. I assure you, this is no *crazy experiment,* so to speak. The science we are creating is revolutionary. This project will change your life. It's going to change everyone's life. You'll be a part of something big."

"A thousand dollars will change my life, sir, that I assure you. I'm sorry I called it crazy. I don't know a thing about it. Can you at least tell me who I'm working for?"

"On the way, Ben. We have a long drive ahead of us."

"Wait—you want to go now, like, right now?"

"Well, yes. Sorry, I assumed you knew. We would like you to start immediately if possible. Is that okay? Our limo is waiting a few blocks away. We can leave whenever is good for you. You're more than welcome to take your own car if you prefer."

"A limo?"

They were quiet.

Oh no, I pushed the envelope.

"I see that's a bit sudden for you. Why don't you take some time to think it over?" Dr. Wulfric said.

Ben nodded.

"You'll receive five hundred dollars up front, either when you arrive at the lab or when the limo picks you up. The remainder will be given to you after the presentation."

"Cash, right?"

"Cash."

"And lunch is on you?"

Dr. Wulfric laughed. "Of course. I wouldn't have it any other way." He motioned to the waitress for the bill by signing his name on an imaginary piece of paper in the air.

"Well, then," Ben said. "I have a lot to think about."

Chapter 3

Ben conjured up images of the lab in his mind. Questions circled his brain, specifically: *What the hell is going on in the Hamptons?*

Dr. Wright had shared some unfortunate news with Ben just a day ago: the old doctor was retiring. This was a huge blow to Ben, both financially and for his own mental well-being. Ben needed the stability—the scheduled tests and rigorous sterility of the hospitals. No matter how laborious the experiments seemed at the time, the hospital was his life outside of his real life. And lately, his real life was nothing special.

Ben went back to his apartment after his meeting with Dr. Peter Wulfric. He walked to the center of his living room and looked around. The unpacked stacks of boxes in the dining room corner were still there from when he moved in. He didn't know what was in most of them. The kitchen cabinets were empty, except for a few cans of soup. The refrigerator was the same. He even stopped buying milk because it went bad before he could finish it.

His life was boring. And as he looked at the seat on the couch where he always sat— looking up at the painting across the room as he drank more, and more, and more—he became more solemn.

When was the last time I had people over? Have I ever had people over?

Ben got the bottle of Jameson from the kitchen counter and rinsed a glass in the sink, dirty from the previous night. It was early, but he needed a stiff one.

This experiment, this test, whatever it was, did have one thing going for it: it was exciting. Ben had no idea what it could possibly be about, but one thing was certain, it was *not* a simple sleep-deprivation test.

As the booze sank in and his mind calmed to a gentle flow, he rationalized his thoughts, reflecting back to his childhood … and how it all began:

As a child, Ben suffered from extreme and somewhat unusual migraines. Not only did he often get the usual pain and nausea associated with the headaches, but he also suffered from a condition called *aura migraines*. They would strike without warning, starting out as a small blur in the corner or center of his vision—like looking into a bright light bulb then looking away, with the afterimage of the bulb still burned in his eyes. The small blur would grow, spreading fast, until it took over most, or all, of his field of vision. Bright and blurry colored lights, in an array of lightning-bolt fractal patterns, would consume his sight. His vision would return about a half-hour later, but the world would look like he was viewing it through a piece of smoky glass.

Vertigo, nausea, and confusion followed, ranging in severity from a mild nuisance to near disablement—not being able to read or understand words written on a page. The experience could last anywhere from a few hours to a couple of days. Oddly enough, the pain was typically mild during these episodes, making it difficult for doctors to make an initial diagnosis. Information on aura migraines was sparse when Ben was a child.

Ben's parents, and then foster parents, took him to specialist after specialist—each doctor trying to determine the cause and trigger for these strange headaches. Some doctors believed they were strokes, the symptoms being similar, although not nearly as severe. Other doctors believed they were purely diet related. Some even suggested they were not neurological whatsoever, but caused by torn retinas in his eyes. Ben went on restricted diets, endured CAT scans, MRI's, vision exams, and hearing tests.

As he grew older, the aura migraines became less frequent—attacks occurred maybe once a year, sometimes the respite lasting as long as two to three years. The trigger for these migraines was never determined, with all the initial tests done in vain.

An acquaintance referred Ben and his foster family to Dr. Stuart Wright when Ben was barely a teenager. The then forty-something-year-old doctor was making a name for himself in the field of Neurology with a particular fascination in sleep related sciences. Dr. Wright was the first doctor to diagnose Ben's condition as aura migraines, ruling out the possibility of strokes or a diet related allergy. This was a huge relief for Ben and his foster parents. Now they had a name for his condition.

Dr. Wright worked with Ben to make the tests as stress free as possible. He believed the constant transition from specialist-to-specialist and test-to-test was compounding the stress on Ben's mind, further fueling his condition. Dr. Wright explained to Ben in a friendly and factual manner the science behind his condition: it was a chemical and electrical response between nerves in his brain, made worse by a sudden onslaught of blood throughout his head.

Ben was finally able to understand what was happening as it happened and not panic, which normally compounded the effects. He could feel and identify the areas in his head where the blood was congesting as the aura migraine was twinkling before his eyes. The pressure started at the base of his neck, where his spine and skull met, and worked its way up to the crown of his head. It felt like small bubbles inflating against his skull, ready to burst, then suddenly deflating.

It was during these initial tests, after talking to Ben about his sleep patterns and irregularities, that Dr. Wright had told Ben that he had much more going on in his head than just aura migraines. These peculiar observations further fueled Dr. Wright's own research, and grew to consume the majority of his professional career.

Ben's dreams were vivid experiences. He could remember his dreams in full detail, hours after waking. He was aware he was sleeping while he was sleeping, and eventually, with plenty of practice and understanding, he could control some or all aspects of his dreams down to the smallest detail.

Dr. Wright had been familiar with similar studies done on lucid dreaming prior to meeting Ben. The subjects in those studies reported the experience being just as realistic in touch, taste, smell, and clarity as when conscious. Ben told the doctor that the environments he experienced around him while dreaming lucidly were brighter and entirely more vivid than they were in real life—somehow more realistic. His senses were heightened and extremely sensitive. Experiences came straight from the brain, bypassing the physical body and world. Ben felt textures: grass under foot, bumpy brick walls, and sunlight on his skin throughout his body in a stimulating rapture. Sexual intimacies were full-body, euphoric experiences and highly addictive, especially when Ben was a teenage boy.

After some initial tests, Dr. Wright deduced that Benjamin's brain reached the REM phase of sleep faster than normal, and the activity in his brain during REM was much more active and alive than any person previously recorded.

With this knowledge, the working relationship between Ben and Dr. Stuart Wright took off, even blossoming near friendship levels.

Their relationship further increased after Ben's foster parents died in a freak car accident coming home from a Halloween party. Their car skidded off the highway and hit a telephone pole. His foster mother died instantly, while his foster father survived halfway to the hospital.

The accident might have happened because the roads were icy that night. It might have happened because they were drinking at the Halloween party, or because they were driving over the speed limit. Whatever the case, the accident *did* happen, and his foster parents *did* die within an hour of each other.

Ben's estranged grandmother agreed to take him in while he was still a minor under the stipulation that Ben abide by her strict living conditions. Unbeknownst to Ben at the time, she had only agreed to take him in so she could declare him as a dependent and receive a tax break. His grandmother, a woman he barely knew, had no business supporting a teenager—or anyone for that matter. She could have taken Ben in when he was eight years old, when his birth parents died in a boating accident while he was at

Sunday school, but she didn't. Ben's foster parents told him that his birth mother was given up for adoption by his grandmother when she was just a baby. His birth mother and grandmother didn't meet until later on in life. Ben never questioned his grandmother about his real mom and doubted she would tell him much if he did.

Ben was young when his birth parents died, but he could remember the details of that day clearly. He had been in Sunday school, sitting on the ground playing with wooden blocks. Two uniformed police officers walked into the classroom with their caps in their hands. All the kids stopped playing to stare at the police officers. His teacher, Mrs. Hughes, stood with her palms over her mouth as the officers spoke to her in hushed voices. The crackling noises from the radios on their belts cut through the stillness of the classroom.

The official report stated that his father had a freak heart attack while steering his boat when out for a leisurely afternoon cruise. He lost control, and the boat veered wildly before flipping over the surface of the water like a skipping stone. A gash on his mother's head indicated she was most likely knocked unconscious before drowning.

That was all there was to it.

Ben's grandmother only agreed to take him after his foster parents died since he was already a grown teenager and would be out of the house as soon as he turned eighteen. She never shared with Ben any benefit of the tax rebates she got from Uncle Sam, but rather made Ben pay rent while he was under her roof. He was an incursion in her life, an unwanted thorn in her side, and he knew it. Ben was a stranger, merely a lodger in her neat and weathered little home, and he did not want to be there.

It was during this time, while Ben was living with his grandmother, that Dr. Wright gave him the best possible support he could offer: he gave Ben a job, a purpose in life. Ben no longer had to pay for office visits, but rather received pay to volunteer as a test subject.

A year later, with money also coming in from waiting tables at The Pit Boss BBQ, he was able to move out from his aging grandmother's house, leaving her alone to wallow upon her recliner in angry solitude, drinking glass after glass of cheap boxed wine. He moved to a small one-bedroom apartment that he rented for a couple of years. That time of his life was painful and confusing— blurry even, as if the essence of time did not pertain to those cloudy years. There was no one around to help him become a man, to see him through the difficult process of becoming an adult and dealing with the loss of his parents and foster parents. He moved farther upstate soon after to distance himself from the pain of his childhood and to begin a future as a man.

The only happiness he received came from the hospital—from hearing Dr. Wright's voice—or his receptionist—on the phone to set up another visit. The doctor's voice meant money, and money meant rent, food, and paying bills. Money equaled adulthood. His mind relaxed when he heard the phone ring. If he could, at nineteen, he would have worked at the hospital day and night. During a few of the trials, he nearly did.

The early studies and tests were exceedingly enlightening for Ben. He was an experimental subject in everything from simple sleep deprivation studies to the testing of pharmaceutical-grade sleeping pills—everything from mild melatonin to zolpidem tartrate.

In a way, those early tests were genuinely fun to perform. He learned about his mind, how sleep patterns worked, and how his brain waves changed during different activities and times of the day. He learned that his mind cycled from beta waves during normal day-to-day activities to alpha waves when he became calm, relaxed, or meditative. These brain waves were much higher in frequency than the theta and delta waves, which occurred during sleep.

With his increased knowledge and awareness of how his mind worked, Ben was able to take control of his lucid dreaming on a scale never before seen. There was one milestone test Ben completed where he was able to respond to questions using eye twitches while in a deep sleep. Ben could hear Dr. Wright's voice from within his subconscious and decipher a rational decision on how to respond.

The hospital recognized Ben's eagerness to participate in these tests and experiments, making them more frequent, and increasing his pay. They recognized his ability to truly flex his mental capabilities while under the influence of mind-altering medication. Thus began the long relationship between Dr. Stuart Wright and Benjamin Walker, and the many years of tests and experiments that followed.

As the years passed, the jobs rarely changed in frequency.

Ben took a lull in the testing during the eight years he was married, but then greatly increased his participation after the accident that left his wife dead and his business in shambles. Although his friendship with Dr. Wright was more on the professional side, the man was always there for him. When Ben needed money and asked the doctor for work, Dr. Wright always had some new experiment, some new drug, or a new sleeping pattern to offer.

At present, Ben did not care how long or strenuous the assignment might be. He just wanted to work and keep his mind active. When he was alone with his thoughts without his dear wife Emma, drinking unaccompanied on the couch, his mind would veer to dark and dangerous places.

Ben swigged a mouthful of whiskey and sighed. What did he have to lose by going to see the lab? Even if he decided not to participate, he would be five hundred dollars richer; and maybe he would learn a thing or two. Judging by the stacks of unfinished books on the coffee table, *learning* was something he could use. Besides, it wasn't like Dr. Wulfric posed any sort of threat. If Dr. Wright trusted the man, then Ben could too. With Dr. Wright retiring, what choices did Ben really have? The bar wouldn't hire him full time. He was lucky enough to fill in on shifts when they became available.

An hour went by as Ben contemplated his prospects, and with the time went a quarter of the Jameson bottle.

He retrieved Dr. Wulfric's business card from the bedside table, and dialed the number. A man with a nasal voice answered the phone, identified himself, and said Dr. Wulfric was not in. Ben was talking to his assistant, Dr. Charles Egan, and Dr. Egan would *love* to set up a date for Ben to visit. Ben asked, "How about tomorrow?"

Dr. Egan answered: "Tomorrow would be great. Would you like the limo to pick you up, or would you prefer to drive?"

Ha! The Limo!

"The limo would be great, thank you."

After a few additional mouthfuls of whiskey, he found himself in bed early. He didn't get drunk and stare at the painting as usual—losing himself in loss and regret—but rather, his mind was preoccupied with his visit to the lab. Having something to look forward to was a strange feeling. A feeling he had not felt in quite some time.

A limo is picking me up!

Chapter 4

The limo stopped at the gated entrance to Stone Hollow. The driver lowered his window, leaned out to type on the security keypad, and the gates opened before them. The car continued along the narrow pebble-lined driveway, curving to the left and right past rolling sand dunes covered in patches of low scrub-brush. After a few twists and turns, the driveway entered a clearing. To the left was a two-story house with an attached two-car garage. The car stopped before the house and the driver got out to open the back door. Warm air, laden with the salty thickness of the sea, rushed inside.

Ben got out, stretching his legs and looked about. The house was rectangular, with the driveway leading to the narrow side so that the front of the house faced off to the right. This was strange, Ben thought, since he had never seen a house that faced the side of a property.

The house was large, but not the mansion he'd envisioned when told all about Mr. Timothy Kalispell, the owner of Stone Hollow Estate. During the long drive up, Dr. Wulfric told Ben that Mr. Kalispell was a multimillionaire, perhaps billionaire, who liked to spend his money on lavishness and luxuries, and sometimes oddities and obsessions. The house Ben saw before him had maybe four bedrooms.

"Is he home?" Ben asked Dr. Wulfric as the old doctor pulled himself out of the car.

"Mr. Kalispell? No, he's rarely here. This is his summer home. He brings his family here once in a while, but I haven't heard word of him coming down."

Ben could smell the ocean and hear it along in with the breeze, but all he could see were the rolling sand dunes and the wild thorn bushes and trees.

"This way, Ben." Dr. Wulfric started walking toward the house as the limo driver drove farther up the driveway. Ben noticed that the driveway swerved past the house and disappeared around a bend. Dr. Wulfric caught Ben's gaze and stopped, "Oh," he said, "Were you asking if Mr. Kalispell is here—in this house?" He pointed to the two-story building, the bottom half a façade of light oval stones, the second half wood-shingled in soft blue, almost grey, with three white bay-windows facing outwards, and one large half-moon window cresting out of the roof from the attic.

"This isn't the house, Ben; this is the guesthouse. Rather, it *was* a guesthouse. Now it's our lab. Originally it had a pool, I believe, but the pool was filled in long ago." The doctor laughed. "No, no, Mr. Kalispell wouldn't be here, his house is farther up the driveway."

They walked to a door on the side of the building. Dr. Wulfric found his keys, unlocked the door, and held it open for Ben to enter. The entryway looked more like a home than a lab, with a Persian rug on the ground and colorful sconces on the walls. The row of starched lab coats hanging on the wall contrasted with the cozy feel.

Dr. Wulfric exchanged his jacket for a lab coat, asking Benjamin to do the same. Immediately Dr. Wulfric looked like a scientist—a stereotypical mad scientist. His white hair and beard, combined with his glasses, white shirt and tie, changed him from a gentle old man into a serious doctor.

"Okay, Ben, this way." Dr. Wulfric opened a second door and searched a moment for a light switch on the other side. Overhead lights flickered to life, and Ben entered the lab.

It was a large open room with a long counter running the full length against the left wall, covered with vials full of colorful liquids and thin tubes that twisted this way and that out of glass beakers. Shelves lined the walls above and below the counter—everything neat, everything tidy, everything organized. Three tables were set in a row beside the long counter. Looking down at the room from above, the left side would resemble the letter E. Computer monitors, an unidentifiable box-like apparatus, greasy mechanical parts, and strips of wire covered the three counters in an orderly fashion—although, Ben had no idea what that order may be. Several cube-shaped machines, some four feet high with thick cords jutting out from random slots, sat heavy on the ground. Red and green LED lights blinked in random intervals from various parts. A CAT scanner, or what looked like a CAT scanner, sat large in the opposite corner. Thick black cords trailed from the back, connecting to a desk covered with computer monitors and blinking control panels.

"Welcome to our lab, Ben," Dr. Wulfric said, walking from desk to desk, turning on switches and bringing computer monitors to life.

"Nice lab," Ben said, not sure how to reply since he had no idea what he was looking at.

"Fortunately for us, our lab is in a house rather than a hospital. It gives the room a rather, well, warm feel. Wouldn't you say?"

Ben looked around. He noticed the same playful sconces lining the inside walls. They cast a reddish glow from their swirled glass covers along the room's highly detailed molding and trim. A light gray plastic—or perhaps rubber—mat covered the floor, but Ben could see hard wood along the edges. If it were not for the harsh fluorescent lights overhead, the lab would certainly resemble a sitting room rather than a lab.

"Yes, Dr. Wulfric, I have to agree with you. This is much better than a hospital."

"Please, Ben, call me Peter."

"Peter, does the lab extend back there?" Ben pointed to a set of double doors in the middle of the far wall, and one singular door to the left of it.

"Um," Dr. Wulfric began, staring at a monitor as it spewed numbers, "Not exactly." He looked up. "The one on the left goes to the second floor. The other leads to a separate room—nothing to do with the lab. Come, Ben. Take a seat."

Ben sat on a swivel-stool next to Dr. Wulfric. A moment later the single door on the left side of the room opened, and a tall man wearing a lab coat entered.

"Ben," Dr. Wulfric said, not looking up from the computer, "this is my assistant, Dr. Charles Egan."

"Nice to meet you." Dr. Egan shook Ben's hand.

"Likewise."

Ben recognized the nasally voice from the telephone call the previous day. Dr. Egan was a gaunt man with prominent facial bones and thick glasses. Under his lab coat, he wore the same generic button-down shirt as Dr. Wulfric, only his tie was plain and drab. Dr. Wulfric's tie, Ben noticed, was vibrant, resembling modern art.

Dr. Wulfric looked up from the monitor. "Dr. Egan," he said, "would you please lower the lights?"

Dr. Egan nodded and went to the light switch. The atmosphere immediately became subdued. Fluorescent lights gave Ben a headache—not an aura migraine—but a headache nonetheless. Plenty of natural light came in from the high windows bordering the ceiling.

Dr. Wulfric typed something on the keyboard, and the numbers disappeared from the computer screen, replaced by a still image. "Here we are," he said. "Sit back and enjoy the show."

Dr. Wulfric hit *play*, and the images on the screen came to life. Whatever they were watching was shaky and fuzzy. It looked like a home movie from the '80s—like something his father with no photography experience would have taped when he was a child. There was a small pond, with maybe … something moving … birds, perhaps. Yes, definitely birds, distorted and pixilated. They flew upward. The camera panned along the horizon, following them until they disappeared out of view.

Then the screen flashed and displayed just a jumble of colors and thick pixilated shapes. Ben squinted. It was nonsense. There were people on the screen, lost behind distortion and blur, oddly shaped and almost impossible to make out. Someone walking away—no, not walking. Gliding? Yes, gliding. Now turning to smile at the camera. Suddenly, the image became sharp. It was a young girl, a child maybe six or seven with long blonde hair. She was smiling at the camera while waving and talking, although there was no sound. Ben thought she looked familiar, but then again, all cute little blonde children looked alike to him.

Suddenly the camera veered to the right, and in a flash, the scene cleared, and focus and clarity popped in great detail. It was a roller skating rink with people skating in circles. Only the people now were fuzzy and stick-like. The shiny pine-colored rink, the bright blue and red waist-high wall that encircled the rink, and the rotating disco ball flashing different colors and casting them about the room in a circling array—those colors were vivid, in amazing clarity and detail.

The scene seemed limited by the resolution of the monitor. Ben could practically hear "YMCA" playing in the background. It looked identical to the roller skating rink his parents took him to as a boy. The colors coalesced with such force, the room so realistic and nearly three-dimensional, that a spike of pleasure—a sudden release of endorphins and adrenaline—went off in Ben's brain, trailing down his spine in a shiver. The hairs on his skin stood on end.

The camera swung back to the blonde child, skating away on small uncertain legs, her arms stretched out from her body like a tightrope walker. The hand of the camera operator waved to the little girl. She turned again to face the camera, only her face had become blurred, the features no longer crisp.

"What is this?" Ben asked.

Dr. Wulfric paused stroking his beard. "Just keep watching."

The scene disintegrated into a swirl of pixelated color. It reminded Ben of one of his aura migraines. Images resembling buildings and people appeared among the swirling sea of pixilation, only to drown back down in the tide of colored noise.

"Just a moment," Dr. Wulfric said, using a swivel knob on the keyboard to fast-forward the scene. He stopped as the images cleared to what looked like mountains; only they were very blurry. Then the image again snapped into unimaginable clarity, the brightness of which startled and entranced

Ben. His brain let loose a sense of euphoria that swept through his body. The camera was high in the air—in an airplane or helicopter—flying above a colorful mountain range or deep valley, perhaps the Grand Canyon. Ben didn't know.

"It's beautiful," Ben said. "Is that the Grand Canyon?"

"I'm not sure."

Patches of brush in the far distance appeared in such detail that Ben doubted that he'd be able to see it any clearer if he were there himself.

Suddenly the camera dropped, diving straight into a massive gorge. The plane barreled down, and then quickly leveled itself, going faster and faster—like a jet. Ben felt his stomach lurch as the camera swung straight up, hugging the wall of the canyon. It was so close to the rocky edge that whatever aircraft was taking these pictures was in serious danger of crashing into the wall. Flashes of dark brown, yellow, and orange whizzed past the screen at amazing speed, yet the image was never blurred; only his eyes couldn't process the speed in which they were passing. When Ben blinked and held his eyes shut, the exact image of whatever was flashing by on the screen stayed in his mind like a photograph—no streaking or blurring whatsoever. It was so fast—too fast. The scene swooped down and back up through the valleys and gorges, in unbelievable detail.

Ben's mind whirled. Dr. Wulfric hit a button and the screen went black. Ben shuttered his eyes, letting his brain rest.

"So, what did you think of my video?" Dr. Wulfric asked.

"I don't know. Those colors … I've never seen colors that vivid on a TV screen. What is this, some new high-def system you're testing?"

"Not exactly." He chuckled. "The little girl was my daughter, although she's no longer a child. The roller skating rink is just like the one we went to on her third birthday, maybe a little different. The mountains, though— I have no idea where they came from."

"Okay …"

"That, Ben … was from a dream I had a few days ago. I don't remember dreaming it, but that was indeed recorded from my dream."

Ben looked about the room—the CAT scanner, the computer monitors and blinking machinery, and the Pyrex beakers and other labware. "What exactly are you guys doing here? You recorded your dream? Is that what that thing does?" Ben pointed to the scanner.

"Sort of," Dr. Egan replied before Dr. Wulfric could answer. "What we have here are two separate technologies. We've created a serum that actively monitors the neurological activity in the brain during REM sleep and transmits the activity to that piece of equipment over there. That instrument is called a Frequency Responding Lucid Transmitter. The serum works off the electrical output of the brain, triggered in part by the release of serotonin in the pineal gland, which lies above the medulla—"

"Yes, Ben," Dr. Wulfric said, waving Dr. Egan down—who was pointing at the base of his head to his own medulla oblongata. "To answer your question without confusing you any further ..." He looked again at Dr. Egan, "that device can read and transmit the images from your sleep— from anybody's sleep. Presently, it can only transmit during the REM cycle, but that is about to change. This machine can record a dream in greater length and detail than the dreamer is aware when he's dreaming."

"That's just crazy," Ben said. "I mean in a good way. It's amazing. I'm starting to see where I fit in with all of this."

Dr. Wulfric smiled. "We would like to further explore the extent to which this machine can operate. We need someone who can utilize their REM cycle to its fullest potential. Someone like you, Ben."

"So, I would have to sleep in that thing overnight?" Ben pointed to the bulky machine, covered with cables and blinking lights. The bed was nothing more than a thin pad, and barely wide enough to support the width of a man's shoulders.

"We call that old girl Lucy, short for Lucid Transmitter, which is short for Frequency Responding Lucid Transmitter. Lucy sounds better."

"Right. Lucy, then."

"We've come up with an updated model—a much smaller unit that fits right over a bed frame. All you have to do is sleep. There's a bedroom upstairs. The test requires that you stay the night."

"And what was that about a serum?"

"Yes, the serum works to communicate information from your body back to Lucy. It transmits at a frequency produced by the neurons in your brain and sends that information to Lucy, where it is further processed. That's all I can tell you about the serum right now. I'm sure you understand, but until you decide to go forward with this project, there are certain things that will need to remain private. What I can tell you is this: the serum possesses no direct or indirect health threats or problems, whatsoever. It is not dangerous or toxic. In twenty-four to thirty-six hours after injection, the compound stops working, shuts down, and basically dies. It filters from the body the same way as everything else."

"You pee it out?"

"Among other bodily functions, yes."

"Okay, okay …" Ben was rubbing his temples. "This is a lot to take in."

This certainly was not a simple sleep deprivation test. Contemplating whether to accept this experiment or not could take some time. This was, after all, not the usual hospital setup.

Ben was about to say, *'Let me think this over.'*

But he didn't.

He could leave, go home to his couch and the bottle. He could spend the night drinking alone, staring at the painting, bawling and crying until he was blacked-out drunk. God knows he'd spent enough nights doing just that.

But if he left—if he walked out the door—he would never know more about Lucy or the experiment. Maybe one day he'd hear about it on the news. He would never know what it would be like to see his own dreams, the parts he could not remember, play out before his eyes. He would never know what Lucy was capable of doing.

Besides from his own curiosity, he had to remind himself that this experiment was what Dr. Wright thought was best for him, for his future. His employment with the doctor was over, and he would either need to pick up more shifts at the bar, or look for another job. *Another* bar. *Another* restaurant. The thought was not appealing.

So, what did he have to lose?

Money, for one. An income. Not to mention the loss of knowledge. To do something with his mind other than rotting it away with whiskey.

The serum did not bother him—he had taken so many mysterious drugs in the past that one more couldn't hurt. It probably was not much different from the stuff he'd been injected with before taking a CAT scan, the dye, or whatever it was. Ben never had a serious complication from any of the experimental medications, other than occasional nausea and headaches—but the discomfort was little in comparison to a bad hangover.

I can always leave, Ben thought. *If the test goes sour, I can back out.*

"All right," Ben said, sitting straight in his chair. "Let's skip ahead a bit, and talk pay."

Dr. Wulfric's eyes widened. "We'll have to get Mr. Marcus on the line. But what I've been told is that after the papers are signed, you'll be paid a thousand dollars for the first night—a sort of test night to see if future experiments will produce results. Judging from your previous work with Dr. Wright, I don't think we'll encounter any problems. Future tests will vary in pay."

"What's that about paperwork? I thought this was all cash."

"Yes, absolutely. However, Mr. Kalispell has to protect his interests—like this experiment; this is sensitive technology we're dealing with. And the potential for reading a person's dreams is ... well, limitless. The general public will be able to spend a night in a clinic and go home the next day with a copy of their dreams. Eventually, Lucy will be able to work in a person's home and have the dreams loaded instantly onto a PC or tablet wirelessly.

Imagine what people will learn about themselves, about the nature of the human brain, the nature of humanity, art, and philosophy. Psychologists, judges and juries could watch the dreams of serial killers and murderers, learn about the darkest corners of the darkest minds. Or perhaps the brightest corners of the most intelligent mind: a Buddhist monk, world-renowned artists and thinkers, cutting-edge scientists. The applications are huge, endless.

The paperwork is basic nondisclosure stuff. As long as you don't go public with anything you see or hear, there will be nothing to worry about. We have an opportunity to be part of something big, history in the making, the biggest scientific breakthrough of our lives. At the end of the day, we will all go home happy and wealthy.

"I can't say much about it, but I want you to know that Mr. Kalispell has some very exciting and lucrative business opportunities for you, as long as the first few tests go well. But again, judging from your previous work with Dr. Wright, I don't think that will be a problem. Mr. Kalispell, he's a, well … different sort of man. He has many interests and hobbies, and plenty of money to make his interests and hobbies become realities."

"Okay," Ben said. "Okay. I have to admit … I'm intrigued. So, the next step is talking to this Mr. Marcus guy? Why don't you get him on the line, and let's get this show on the road."

"I believe he's at the house." Dr. Wulfric turned to Dr. Egan, who was already picking up a phone receiver. "When do you think you could start? What's a good night for our first test? You would need to be free the next day, until about noon. We would have to give you a basic physical, mostly to get your weight and blood pressure. The experiment itself is basic, just some memory and observational tests. Then we'll show you images and videos and see if you can recall any or all of what you've seen while sleeping. Since we know that you have good control of your awareness during REM, we would be testing the clarity of your memories while sleeping. If you can get into a lucid state of dreaming, that is."

"That shouldn't be a problem. I've practiced getting into a lucid state for years. I can choose when and how long I want to dream. I can dream lucidly almost all of the time. My mind is very much awake soon after I fall asleep."

As long as I'm not drinking, he thought.

"Excellent! That is excellent. I have a host of acetylcholine-inducing supplements available if you feel inclined to use them. I believe you are familiar with several different nootropics—various memory and neuro enhancers. I have it written down here, somewhere, that you tested many with Dr. Wright."

"Nootropics, oh sure. Which brand you got?" Ben laughed.

"I, uhh, let me see here."

"I'm kidding, Doctor, I'm kidding. I'm familiar with them. I've tested more than I can count. Thank you, but I'm fine without any supplements."

Ben had undergone a long stint of tests with supplements designed to increase the brain's function and potential, called nootropics. The typical nootropic claims to increase acetylcholine levels, which are neurotransmitters in the human body with links to cognitive brain function and long-term memory. A common side effect of many nootropics—based mostly on claims—is that the drugs help the user enter a lucid dream state.

Along with the nootropics, Ben had gone on restrictive diets meant to further increase his acetylcholine levels, eating mostly meat, wheat germ and nuts. Some of the drugs he'd tested included GPC choline, phosphatidylcholine, acetyl-L-carnitine, vitamin B-5 and B-6, and L-Alpha glycerylphosphorylcholine—just to name a few. They were always dispensed to him as nondescript white capsules in nondescript white Dixie cups. Most of the time he did not know what he was taking until after the experiment was over, and he never cared so much as to remember any names.

The majority of the supplements he tested did little-to-nothing for him—no increased attention span, no shortcut to REM, no increased vivid dreams, no boost to his intellect. Perhaps his brain had more than enough acetylcholine to begin with. The results of those tests were inconclusive; however, many other test subjects claimed positive results. During the time of those tests, Ben was drinking heavily. It was impossible to know if a supplement was giving his brain an increase in focus and awareness when a hangover was making him sick and delirious. However, he did notice that some of the supplements shortened the severity of his hangovers, a fact he did not share with Dr. Wright since he wasn't supposed to be drinking during the trials.

Dr. Wulfric cleared his throat and continued speaking, "Lastly, we'll monitor the length of your REM cycle."

"Can't you just pull up some of my old tests with Dr. Wright? He's tested my brain wave activity during sleep a dozen times. More than a dozen times."

"Yes, we've seen them, and the results are amazing. However, these tests … are not like anything you and Dr. Wright have done in the past. So, that being said, what day is good for you to start? The sooner the better."

"Umm, how about …" Ben scratched his chin. He was off from the bar that night … that was for sure, and the next … He shrugged. "I'm here now, why come back later?"

"Ha!" Dr. Wulfric smacked his knee. "You're a sport, you know that, Ben? Dr. Egan, get Iain Marcus on the line!"

"Yes, yes." He rolled his eyes. "I'm on hold, Peter."

Chapter 5

Iain Marcus was a tall man with a wide, sturdy frame—yet he wore his strength well, like an athlete. He did not stand out as being particularly big; perhaps it was the black suit and tie with the crisp, white-collar shirt that masked his stature. His dark blonde hair was neatly parted to the side, and his face was clean-shaven. He looked almost familiar, maybe like a newscaster or someone Ben had seen on TV. Ben pictured him wearing a pair of dark sunglasses, and thought he would look fitting standing beside the president. However, the man was soft spoken, kept a thin professional smile on his face at all times, and moved his hands around the paperwork with the fluidity of an artist.

Not the law enforcing type, Ben thought.

The two doctors, along with Iain Marcus and Ben, sat around a cluttered desk going over a stack of papers Iain had removed from his leather briefcase. He outlined each sheet, reciting the confusing sentences and words in layman's terms.

"The 'persons' shall be acquitted of all responsibilities should they so desire under any given circumstance, keeping all monetary gain already established and set forth under contract with the governing party, with the governing party not liable for any future compensation … yada-yada-yada. This just says you can stop whenever you like and can keep whatever money was promised to you, but you're not eligible for any future compensations that may have been discussed but not yet agreed upon."

"Mm-hmm." Ben leaned forward, resting his chin in his palm. For the last hour, his head had started to hurt. His mind wandered to anything other than what Iain Marcus was talking about. It was the same when he bought and sold his old house, or when he bought and sold his old bar. All the lawyers and paperwork—a bunch of mumbo jumbo, written so that only a select few can understand a word of it.

He nodded along with Mr. Marcus and signed the papers at the bottom, seeing no red flags—although he doubted he would know if there were any. Liability forms and nondisclosure agreements were common at drug trials and tests. Ben had a vague familiarity with the proceeding.

Iain Marcus tapped the papers on the desk, straightening them out, and put them back in his leather briefcase. He removed a billfold from the inside pocket of his suit jacket, peeled away five crisp hundred-dollar bills from a thick-folded wad of hundreds, and handed them across the table.

"According to the contract, you will receive five hundred additional dollars at the conclusion of the test, tomorrow morning."

Iain straightened his shirt cuffs, adjusting the clasps of the cuff links, and stood. "It was a pleasure." He shook Ben's hand, then shook Dr. Wulfric and Dr. Egan's hands, and turned to leave. "I'll show myself out." He walked to the door with urgent footsteps and left.

"Well," Dr. Wulfric said, smacking his knees as he stood, "shall we proceed?"

Ben tucked the five hundred dollars into his wallet and stood. The bills were so crisp, so new, that they felt dry and tacky against his fingers. "Absolutely, Doctor."

Ben first endured the routine physical. They checked his weight, height, and blood pressure, along with a quick eye exam and hearing test. They played both loud and soft tones over earphones and had him raise his arm whenever he heard a sound. *Boring stuff*, he thought. He'd done it all before.

Then he was led to a chair opposite a desk by the 'E' shaped workstation.

"Now we get to the fun part." Dr. Wulfric went to a cabinet above the long table hugging the wall, careful that his lab coat did not brush up against the various glass flasks and tubes as he reached overhead. A light turned on inside the refrigerated cabinet as the door opened. Cold vapor pooled out, evaporating in the air as it drifted to the ground like a waterfall. He removed a tray full of vials, selecting one from the others.

"This, Ben, is the serum. The Nano Technological Neuron Frequency Transmitting Fluid. That's a mouthful, huh? We call it Nano." He sat on a stool beside Ben, gently placing the small glass vial on the table between them. Someone handwrote the number eleven in thick black marker on the stickered label. The fluid inside the vial was red—not quite blood red, but dark, with a slight silver shimmer when light shone directly on it.

"The fluid inside this container is revolutionary."

"What, like tiny computers or something?"

"Yes, sort of like tiny computers. These microscopic computers pick up the information your neurons transmit during REM and transfer the data to Lucy, where it is processed. It is quite simple really. The serum currently ranges in frequency to cover the beta, alpha, theta, and delta waves, however it only works at peak capacity during the REM cycle when the delta and theta waves are most active—as of now, that is. It picks up the transmissions from within the body and sends the information back to Lucy, where the information is analyzed and reassembled like a jigsaw puzzle. Of course, there is much more to it than that. The technology behind the serum and Lucy is astounding. I can go into much further detail, if you desire."

"Feel free, but I can't promise I'll understand a word you tell me. The most important aspect for me *isn't* the science behind this—although I admit that what you're accomplishing here is very cool—it's whether or not this is safe. Now, you did mention earlier that there are no health risks with the serum, right?"

"The serum crosses the blood-brain barrier and is designed to intercept the data being delivered through the neurons during REM, but not interfere with the neurons themselves. Simply observe and transmit. Kind of like turning on your radio and listening to what's being played. You do no damage to the broadcasting station, or the radio waves, you simply detect the transmitted signal.

You may feel an initial wave of nausea and lightheadedness, but that will pass. I used this exact serum on myself to record the images I showed you earlier, and from my own personal experiences, the unpleasantness is minor and short indeed. The liquid exits the body through the blood system, gets filtered through the liver and kidneys, and disposed of with the rest of the body's waste."

Ben looked at the liquid in the little vial. He shook his head. "Let's get on with it then."

"Excellent," Dr. Wulfric said. "Don't be nervous. Besides myself, we've tested the serum extensively on mice, and none of them have had any ill side-effects." He removed the small cap from the top of the vial and extracted a syringe from a sterilized wrapper—which reminded Ben of peeling the skin off of a banana—uncapped the needle, and slid the needle into the thin plastic membrane on the top of the vial.

Dr. Egan readied himself before a computer monitor on the desk.

Dr. Wulfric began. "Eight thirty-five P.M.—"

"Hold on Peter." Dr. Egan was typing fervently. "Okay, I'm ready."

"Eight thirty-five P.M., Nano batch number eleven. Subject: Benjamin Walker, age thirty-eight, weight one hundred and seventy-four pounds, height five feet nine inches." He pulled the syringe from the bottle and told Ben to put his arm on the desk.

"Just to warn you," Ben said, "I'm a bit squeamish with needles." He felt the blood drain from his face.

"Would you prefer to lie down? You look a bit pale."

"No, just …" He clenched his teeth, "I'll look away. I'm fine."

In Ben's past work, Dr. Wright made sure to avoid needles whenever possible.

"I promise to be quick," the doctor said. "If you feel woozy, let me know." Ben shut his eyes tight. "Three milliliters of Nano, batch eleven."

Dr. Wulfric tightened an elastic tourniquet around Ben's arm, tying it above the elbow. Ben could feel his pulse beating against the elastic band where it squeezed the vein. He smelled the pungent smell of rubbing alcohol, followed by the cold wetness of a cotton swab on his skin. The needle slid effortlessly into his vein. Dr. Wulfric's thumb pressed the plunger and removed the syringe. It wasn't painful in the least, but the sensation of his skin being penetrated made Ben's stomach drop. He felt the cool liquid enter his vein and spread throughout his arm, down to the tips of his fingers.

"Are you okay?" Dr. Wulfric asked.

Ben opened his eyes. There was already a cotton ball on the wound and the doctor was removing a Band-Aid from a package.

"Yes, yup, I'm fine." He took a deep breath. "God, I hate needles."

Dr. Wulfric laughed. "To tell you the truth, I'm not very fond of them myself."

The several hours following were devoted to memorization and problem solving exercises. Similar to basic IQ tests Ben had done in the past:

—Look at two nearly identical pictures and tell me if there are any differences between them.

—Look at this assortment of random shapes and tell me how to arrange them to fit into this one larger shape.

—Look at these lines of various symbols and pick from the list which new line of symbols would follow.

All the while, Dr. Egan typed away on the computer and Dr. Wulfric scribbled notes on a pad, keeping track of time with a stopwatch. The tests were laborious and boring, but Ben paid attention to them all. By the time he was finished, his head ached with exhaustion, and he yearned for a stiff drink.

At some point in the evening, Dr. Egan ordered a pizza, and they cleared a section of the table to take a short break. Ben's mind felt numb, but after a few slices of pizza, his thoughts began to unwind.

"Nothing too stressful, right?" Dr. Wulfric asked.

"No," Ben said, finishing the last bite of crust. "So far so good."

Dr. Wulfric glanced at his watch. "It's getting late. Let's wrap things up."

They cleared away the mess and moved back to the desk. Dr. Wulfric pushed aside the stack of cue cards they had been using and grunted audibly as he leaned over to open the bottom drawer on the desk. He pulled out two framed paintings, both about twelve inches by nine.

One painting Ben immediately recognized; it was a photo print of the *Mona Lisa*. The glossy paper glared under the harsh fluorescent lights. Ben did not recognize the second painting. The scene was that of an old wooden ship sailing on a turbulent sea, painted by hand—not a print like the *Mona Lisa*. When Ben looked closely, he could see the peaks and crests of paint from each individual brush stroke.

"I want you to examine these paintings one at a time. I want you to study them from afar and then look at them up close."

He looked at the *Mona Lisa* first. Dr. Wulfric held it across the desk and told Ben to absorb the painting as a whole and not focus on any one individual detail. They did this for a while, and then Dr. Wulfric placed the painting on the desk right before Ben. He told Ben to study it up close, from left to right in sections, like reading a book. Ben examined the pigment under her eyes, along her nose, and on her forehead, the swirls of color in the background that were perhaps trees, mountains, pathways and water. It was difficult since the painting was printed on a glossy sheet of paper, and the crests of paint that should be jagged were flat.

Dr. Wulfric then switched to the painting of the ship in the sea and pointed to the strokes of paint that swirled and crested to form the bubbling water where it crashed along the wooden side of the vessel. He then moved to the white and grey storm clouds in the sky. Ben was instructed to scan the painting in sections, from left to right, observe the various brown shades of the hull and the billowing sails that were stretched to their maximum expansion against the raging winds.

From up close, the swirling crests of paint made no sense, just one shade of color leading to the other. It was the same when he studied Emily's cabin in the woods. The painting was confusing when he stared at one small section—maybe because he wasn't an artist and didn't understand how colors worked—but when he stepped back and looked at the composition as a whole, the piece took shape, and the form and subject came to life.

Humans, Ben thought, *with the ability to produce and master art, use their minds in such ways that I will never truly comprehend.*

Ben studied every corner of the ship, up close, and far away. Finally, Dr. Wulfric put the painting down. Ben blinked his eyes back into focus. He was tired, not just from all the mental exercises, but because it was getting legitimately late.

"I want you to remember these paintings to the best of your ability when you go to sleep tonight. Try to get yourself into a lucid state of dreaming and picture each of these paintings as if you're observing them hanging on an art gallery wall. Look at them from afar, and then bring your eyes in close. Just like we did here. Examine each crest of paint, each line, each shade and crack."

Ben nodded. "I'll do my best."

"Good. Then that will be all for tonight."

Dr. Egan hit a few more keys on the computer keyboard then stopped. He leaned back in his chair with his arms stretched high, yawning.

"I'll show you upstairs. Charles, if you don't mind shutting things down?"

Dr. Egan nodded, removing his glasses to massage the tender area on the bridge of his nose.

Ben followed Dr. Wulfric to the small door on the far side of the room, beside the larger double door. It led to a small landing at the base of a stairway. At the top of the stairs the doctor flicked on a light switch to reveal a large and comfortable room. A small open kitchen took up the left side, with a fridge, sink, dishwasher, and a stove.

The opposite side of the room was more of a living space, with two couches facing a large flat-screen television. Books and magazines lay neatly arranged on a coffee table, and a small bookshelf beside the couch was fully stocked with an assortment of books. Two circular dining tables with chairs occupied the middle of the room.

"This is our break room," Dr. Wulfric said. "If you wake up before us, please make yourself at home. There's coffee in the cabinet, eggs in the fridge, and cereal in the pantry. Help yourself."

Behind the break room was a long hallway illuminated with the same wall sconces as in the lab and entry room below. They passed several doors on either side before arriving at the far end.

"Dr. Egan and I will be staying the night as well, in separate rooms. These late nights happen quite often for us."

"What does your wife have to say about that?"

Ben glanced down, seeing Dr. Wulfric play with the ring on his finger, stroking it unconsciously with his thumb.

"My wife passed away a few years ago. That's why I wear the ring on my right hand. Sort of an old custom."

"I'm sorry. I didn't know. You mentioned you had a daughter, and I saw the ring. I shouldn't have presumed."

"Please, don't apologize. It's fine, really. You should feel worse for Charles down there, whose wife gives him hell when he stays the night. I won't be in the same room with him when he makes that call."

They both laughed, relieving the tension. Dr. Wulfric opened the door at the end of the hallway to a bedroom. It looked like any decent hotel room: a large clean bed, a dresser, a desk facing a window, and a small bathroom.

"There are clean toothbrushes in the bathroom, shampoo in the shower, and pajamas in the dresser over there. Just put your dirty clothing in the hamper and put the hamper outside the door. Housekeeping will have your clothes clean before morning."

"Housekeeping? Are you serious? They're going to clean my clothes? I'm surprised you let a housekeeper in the lab."

"We don't. One of the doors in the hallway leads to a stairway going out back."

They heard heavy footsteps in the hallway. "Peter ..." Dr. Egan muttered between labored breaths. "Could you please?"

"Yes. Coming, Charles. Sorry."

Dr. Wulfric left, and then returned a moment later helping Dr. Egan carry a large, black case. It was the same type of case used by bands to carry speakers and equipment.

They lowered it to the floor, letting out a sigh, and Dr. Wulfric unsnapped the latches to let the case rest open upon its hinges. Two identical curved devices lay between protective foam walls, looking like two halves of a gigantic metal boomerang. They removed the two pieces and assembled them in the middle, making the boomerang whole. The two pieces together made an arch, maybe four feet long, with various cables emerging from one end.

They each held a corner and moved the device to the bed, where they placed it behind the pillows. Dr. Egan plugged one of the wires into the wall, and the other cable he connected to a small laptop. Dr. Wulfric typed a command on the laptop, and the machine came to life, making a fuzzy, static sounding noise, similar to the sound old computers made when turned on. After a moment, the device quieted to a gentle hum.

Dr. Wulfric fiddled with the computer, and then gave his attention to Ben. "That's it. All you have to do now is sleep. I'll turn the monitor off so the light won't bother you. Feel free to watch TV or read before you go to bed. There are plenty of books and magazines in the break room. If you're hungry, please eat. We'll see you in the morning. Have a good night."

"Goodnight, Doctor."

The two men left and Ben sat on the edge of the bed, observing the machine and letting his mind unwind.

What a day.

Checking out the books on the bookshelf sounded appealing, but he was too exhausted to read. He clicked on the TV and flipped through the channels, but there was nothing on that he found appealing. He washed his face, brushed his teeth, and put his dirty clothes in the hamper, then put the hamper outside the door as he was instructed. The dresser drawers were full of clothing, including several sets of pajamas, along with a drawer full of brand new underwear and socks, still in their original plastic packaging and in all different colors and sizes.

Spare no expense, Mr. Kalispell.

Ben tore off two small squares of toilet paper and fashioned them into earplugs. He found several folded handkerchiefs in the dresser and rolled one up to use as an eye mask. He was surprised there wasn't a sleep mask available, but he preferred to use a handkerchief anyway. The rolled up cloth covered his ears and kept the earplugs from falling out.

What a day.

Ben lay in bed under the canopy Lucy created over his head. Slowly, lying flat on his back under the blanket and sheet, he began the breathing exercises he used to calm his mind, relax his body, and prepare his brain for a lucid dream state. Through the makeshift earplugs, he could hear a gentle humming and metal ticking … louder than before, and different.

He opened his eyes and lifted his head so his ear was pressed against Lucy. The sound was not coming from the machine. He removed his earplugs, stood up, and pressed his head against the wall. The sound was louder with his ear to the wall, yet muffled. The noise was coming from another room. It sounded like the ticking of a taxicab meter, along with a sporadic humming and grinding, like machinery.

Whatever.

He put the earplugs back in and pulled the blanket up to his chin.

Hell of a day, he thought, and let his mind go dark.

Chapter 6

When Ben checked the laundry basket outside the door, his clothes were cleaned, folded, and placed gently back inside, just as Dr. Wulfric said.

What crazy hours these housekeepers must work, he thought as he got dressed.

He went to the break room where he smelled fresh-brewed coffee. A moment later, Dr. Wulfric appeared at the doorway to the stairs.

"Ah, Ben! You're up!"

Ben was sipping at a steaming cup of coffee.

"How did you sleep?"

"Good; slept good."

In the past, Ben participated in tests where he had slept on nothing more than an examination table with a thin white sheet. The room he slept in the night before was luxurious in comparison. He slept like a baby until this morning when the mechanical noises from the wall behind his room grew louder—much louder than previously.

"I would like you to know," Dr. Wulfric said, pulling up a chair across the table from Ben, "that everything went exceedingly well. We just started analyzing the results, and they're proving to be quite extraordinary." The doctor smiled from behind his thick beard, gleaming like a little boy. "Do you remember your dreams from last night?"

"Sure I do." Within the first several minutes of waking, Ben could remember his conscious and subconscious dreams very clearly. Typically, the images would fade throughout the day, unless the dream had some significance or effect on him. In a case like this, when he was truly focused, Ben could remember the dream as long as he liked. "I viewed the pictures just as you asked," he said. "First I looked at them from far away, passively. Then I scanned them up close as best as I could."

"Yes, yes," Dr. Wulfric nodded.

Ben smirked. He hoped he gave them a good show. In between his assignment, he took his dream on a little thrill ride. First, he flew into the sky like a bird, soaring over the tops of trees and sweeping down close to the ground, speeding down streets and alleyways inches above the pavement. He flew to the tops of skyscrapers to perch for a moment, only to dive back down, head first and recklessly fast.

Next, he swam—or more accurately, he walked—into a large body of water. His feet mired in the thick sandy bottom as he walked. He felt the tides pull and sway his legs. The water was warm, tropically warm. He looked at fish, coral, and an oddly fluorescent eel. His subconscious conjured up the details: the fish, the sand, the coral, the sky, and the climate—everything, really. All he had to do was think *beach,* and there it was.

Doing these things, like breathing underwater and flying, took years of practice, and he was no master. His initial response when presented with these impossible feats was fear and panic. It was difficult for Ben to separate reality from what was happening in his subconscious world, the land of his dreams.

Many dreams end abruptly with Ben waking in a state of near panic. He would hyperventilate while dreaming of drowning underwater. Or, his heart would practically beat through his chest after taking a sudden nosedive back to Earth on one of his high-altitude flights. While he is dreaming, he has to remind himself that in real life, he is lying in bed breathing fresh air, and that the water in his thoughts can't hurt him.

Breathing underwater was a difficult feat to master. Flying, on the other hand, was not as challenging. The flying part was easy; controlling where he went and how fast he wanted to go was another story. A person does not fly naturally, so there is no logical way to know how to direct and control the ability of personal flight.

Even after years of practice there were times when Ben would spiral out of control and shoot up into the air past the highest trees and tallest buildings, his body tumbling uncontrollably upward, his heart pounding wildly. The laws of gravity felt completely unreal. His mind and body responded to these events with the natural panic a person would experience if these things were really happening. Sensations felt during sleep—hot, cold, pain, and pleasure—were all just as vivid as in real life, and sometimes even more realistic and exaggerated.

He had developed a failsafe mechanism to get himself out of these predicaments—a last-ditch technique when a good dream went sour. It had started with a particularly frightening and frustrating dream he had one night. He was sleeping, completely lucid, then suddenly woke up. His room looked different. Things were not right. His bed was a twin, not a queen. The floor was carpeted, not hard wood, and the shape of the room was oddly rectangular. There was a poster on the wall so blurry he could not read whatever was written on it—and when was the last time he even owned a poster?

He realized he was still dreaming; he was dreaming that he had awakened from his sleep. This pattern repeated itself, perhaps a dozen times, and each time he was fooled into believing he was really waking up, only to find out he was not. Panic set in. Time had no precedent—perhaps hours went by, days even, or just minutes.

Am I stuck here? Are the sheets wrapped around my throat, cutting off the oxygen to my brain? Am I dying? Am I dead?

Suddenly his head began to spasm and twitch, the muscles in the back of his neck shaking, and he awoke to the real world. He was fine and safe, yet his head was sore, his brain overworked. After that dream, he could consciously do that "neck twitch" whenever he wanted, and it saved him from all sorts of dream-induced panic states and near-death experiences.

Dr. Wulfric cleared his throat, and continued speaking, "Ben, we would like to continue with the study, with you."

Ben laughed. "And I would very much like for you to proceed adding funds to my bank account." He had some money left from the sale of his old house and the bar, but not much. The bar's popularity plummeted after the incident that left his wife dead, and he barely made ends meet.

"Ha! That's excellent, excellent," Dr. Wulfric went on. "I have to call Mr. Kalispell this afternoon. He is anxious to hear the results. Feel free to make yourself some breakfast, and come down when you're finished. Mr. Marcus will be here soon to deliver the rest of your pay. We can schedule another appointment when he arrives. I'll call the driver to take you home whenever you're ready."

Dr. Wulfric stood from the table and walked to the stairway.

"Doctor?"

"Yes?" He turned at the top of the stairs.

"I was just wondering ... is it possible to see my dream, what you recorded?"

There was a pause. "We're still going through the data, cleaning things up. Let's wait until I speak to Mr. Kalispell." The doctor smiled widely. "I'm glad you're interested in the work we're doing. Mr. Kalispell will be pleased. Now, Ben, make sure you eat something."

Dr. Wulfric disappeared through the door. Ben thought about eating, but his stomach suddenly felt sour and his head had that far-away feeling.

A nap in the limo would be nice, he laughed to himself. *The limo! Emily, if you could see me now! Ha!*

Chapter 7

Ben pushed the front door open with his foot, careful not to squash the bags of groceries he held in his arms. The door to his apartment had a strong self-closing hinge that ensured that the door would always shut unless held open by something heavy. The door annoyed the shit out of Ben. The hinge violently slammed the door shut when he didn't want it to. He kept a brick nearby—that some kid had thrown though his window a couple months ago—to keep the door propped open, and he hopelessly searched for it now in the dark. He quickly released his foot and raced to the counter as the last ray of light shrank and disappeared with the slamming of the door. He felt for the edge of the wall with his foot and put the groceries down on the counter, then turned back to find the light switch.

In the living room sat a brand new forty-six-inch Samsung flat screen TV. It stood on the same stand as his old TV—the boxy old Hitachi with fake wood paneling that he'd bought as a teenager and somehow managed to keep working. At least he thought it might still work, it had been years since he had even tried.

With money coming in, Ben decided to splurge a little. He went home after his first visit to the lab with two thousand dollars, and three additional sessions scheduled—each at one thousand dollars. In a little over a month, Ben took home five thousand dollars, with the promise of more sessions to come. With that kind of income, Ben was able to tell the bar manager that he wasn't available to fill in any shifts that week.

He bought the Samsung on a whim after a drunken night of staring at the old Hitachi, gathering dust in the corner. That night, like many before, his gaze absentmindedly switched to his wife's painting on the wall. It was a pattern he'd grown familiar with over the years.

Thinking about the past was an obsession. Images swam through his mind, overwhelmed by Emily and his old house: she with paint on her cheek and forehead, standing before a canvas in the room with the large windows; he at the doorway looking in. He recalled the small bar they owned. He remembered the look of genuine joy and total fear on Emily's face as they signed the last of the papers, received the keys, and opened the door as bar owners for the very first time. That bar was their dream, their future. It was a place for their children to work and to learn the ropes of the business as they grew up. He imagined arguing with his kids as they grew from children to adults, they insisting the interior was outdated and drab and the menu in need of urgent updating.

He saw himself and Emily in their senior years—aged and stubborn—refusing to make changes to the decor or food, despite their children probably being right. Then, when they reached those final years—when it was time to view the world from rocking chairs on the front porch with thick blankets draping their legs as they sipped glasses of red wine—they would let their children run the place. Their children would hand the business down to their grandchildren, and one day to their great-grandchildren, and they would stay on that front porch for as many years as their bodies would allow, hand in hand, watching the sun set and rise.

Ben's mind created these warped thoughts and images, these events that would now never happen, as he stared at the painting of the cabin in the woods. He sipped from his glass of whiskey, taking slugs straight from the bottle between sips from the glass.

He saw his wife as she died, the shock and horror on the patrons' faces, the monsters pinned face down on the ground as the police tightened cuffs around their wrists. The blood, all the blood. Ben's own tears falling into the pools of that blood. The look in her eyes, the look in the eyes of the monsters on the ground craning their neck to see what was going on, the knife laying there in a puddle of warm blood, the hands of the medics ripping her away from him—swarming around her with respirators, gauze, needles, a neck brace.

They let him stay by her side holding her hand because he wouldn't let go—he would tear his own arm off before letting go. He stayed by her side in utter shock and solace for hours that felt like days. When he finally let go—had to let go—a huge amount of him died along with her.

He has tried his best to leave that world behind.

Then there was the painting of the cabin in the woods. Just glancing at it made everything come rushing back.

After these drunk and tormenting nights, he would wake up in the morning with his head on fire and his mouth stale and dry. Sometimes he would awake with the painting of the cabin locked in his clenched fingers like a vice. Other times it was thrown in the corner of the room—nearly destroyed in a rage of drunken delirium. However, the painting always made it back on the wall.

There was an odd and perverse sense of pleasure in his self-torment, an unwillingness to forget the past and erase Emily from his life and memory. There was pleasure in the pain, a pleasure in remembering Emily: her touch, her scent of jasmine, her warm embrace, her smile, her words, her skin, the way she was so suddenly taken out of his life.

His memories and the painting were all that was left to remember her by, and he refused to get rid of them—it wasn't right, it wasn't fair ... he couldn't forget her, couldn't let her go, it was just so ... unfair ....

The new television was a step in the right direction—a way to divert his thoughts from Emily and the past and steal his attention away from the painting. Only the day he bought it, he hung up after twenty minutes on hold with the cable company. Standing around his apartment listening to elevator music was maddening. He made a promise to try again later, when the line wasn't as busy. It would be stupid having a brand new piece of technology collecting dust in the corner of the room with the cord wrapped around the base, right next to the Hitachi. But he hadn't called back. And the TV still wasn't plugged in.

Earlier, as he was walking home from *Whole Foods,* he felt his phone vibrate in his front pocket. He adjusted the bags of groceries in his arms and pulled the phone out with two free fingers. There was a missed call from Iain Marcus on the screen. Back in the apartment, as he was putting the groceries away, he put his phone on speaker and listened to the voicemail. A recorded voice rang out: *You have one new message*—pause—*First voice-message.*

"Hello, Mr. Walker, this is Iain Marcus. This is just a reminder that we're scheduled to meet tomorrow afternoon, at the *Still Life Roast* coffee house. We'll be arriving at eleven. Please call me if there are any problems. We look forward to seeing you again."

This was the third time Iain Marcus had about the same meeting, since Ben finished his third session at the lab the week before. Ben held the phone, about to return Iain's call, but changed his mind and put the phone back in his pocket. The message clearly said, *'Call me if there are any problems,'* and there weren't any problems. There wasn't a problem the first time Iain called, or the second, and there surely wasn't one now. "This Iain Marcus guy has to chill out," Ben told himself, alone in the room.

With the groceries put away, Ben found himself sitting on the couch with a bottle of Jameson in one hand and his usual glass in the other. He poured the whiskey and sipped it. Then he swallowed it all. He closed his eyes as the warmth spread from his stomach to his head, giving him that 'Ahhh' moment, like a mother pulling the blanket up to her child's chin. *Everything's all right now. Shhh, relax.* He stared at the television thinking that maybe the cable company would still be open. Another shot of whiskey appeared in the glass.

Then the painting grabbed his attention, stole his eyes, flashed out from the other side of the room. He stared at it.

His emotions began swirling like the paint on the canvas, like the whiskey in the glass.

He looked at the Jameson; it was amber and beautiful. He screwed the cap on and stood up from the couch.

Not tonight, Ben. Not tonight.

He polished the remainder of the glass in one swig. Leaving it and the bottle on the kitchen counter, he walked to the bedroom, deciding to call Iain back after all. The cable company could wait.

***

The flimsy metal table wasn't large enough for the two doctors, Iain, and Ben to sit around comfortably. The legs wobbled on the cement sidewalk, even after Dr. Egan found a pack of matches to level the table out.

They talked about how beautiful the day was, the current Yankees lineup, and all sorts of things that didn't really concern Ben whatsoever.

The same waitress from his first meeting with Dr. Wulfric was working now, and she delivered four coffees on porcelain saucers. It still impressed Ben that a skilled waitress could deliver so many full cups—beer, martinis, coffee, whatever—on large platters without spilling a drop. After all of his years in the hospitality business, balancing a tray was not something he could do well.

"Anything else, guys?" she asked.

The four men shook their heads.

"No, thank you," Dr. Egan answered.

She left on quick feet.

"So, Ben, thanks for meeting us today," Iain began. "We have a few things we'd like to discuss."

Iain scooted his chair back from the table, picked up his leather briefcase, and opened it on his lap. He removed a manila folder that held three large photographs.

"Take a look at these, Ben." Iain passed the photographs across the table.

"Sure." They were three images of the *Mona Lisa*. He studied them. Two looked identical; the other was slightly off. A few shades didn't match and the left corner was distorted from the others.

Ben said, "It's the *Mona Lisa*. Again." At his third session, the doctors made Ben examine the two photos—the boat on the water, and the Mona

Lisa—again. It was becoming quite boring. As great as the *Mona Lisa* might be, it was not one of Ben's favorite paintings. Not by a long shot.

"This one here," Dr. Wulfric said, pointing to one of the identical photos, "is the same photo we showed you in the lab, only we took it out of the frame. This one, which is different than the others, is a printout from your first session—a snapshot from your dream that night. It's nearly identical, but with a few flaws. Now, this third photograph is from our latest session, the last time you studied the painting."

The hairs on Ben's arms stood on end.

I'm holding images from my dream, finally.

He looked at the two photos, examining the cracks in the old paint on her forehead and under her eyes, following the lines as they zigzagged and intersected. He compared the shades of paint, from light to dark.

There wasn't a single discrepancy between the two.

"I know you've asked several times to see what we've recorded, and I'm sorry that we haven't shown you anything sooner," Dr. Wulfric said. "As you can see from these two images, we've progressed significantly from our first session. We began producing identical images the second night. Which, and believe me," Dr. Wulfric leaned over the table, "is absolutely remarkable. Your mind is able to remember—or rather, store—details like taking a snapshot. Study the two photographs. They're identical."

Ben examined the photos. "Yeah," he said, "they are." He passed them back to Iain. "Can I see more?"

The three men looked at one another, and Dr. Wulfric said, "We're working on something to show you, I'm just editing out the blurry stuff, the nonsense."

"I don't mind seeing the nonsense. I would love to see it. I remember enough of my dreams to know they are not nonsense; I would like to see the rest."

Iain cleared his throat and spoke, "Being completely honest with you," he said, straightening his cuff links, "it's our employer's express wishes that the work being produced at this time remains under the strict supervision of Dr. Wulfric and Dr. Egan, alone. He does not wish for anyone, myself included, to view anything currently being produced. I hope you can understand; he's aware you would like to see the work, and I assure you he's taken it into serious consideration. He is enthralled that you have such an interest in the project. However, as of right now, it's still part of the research, and he doesn't want anything to hinder the progress we're making."

"Fine. I get it."

"So that brings us to our current business," Dr. Wulfric said, his voice bright, "Mr. Kalispell has an amazing opportunity for us. I think you will be very excited."

"What is it?"

"He would like to fly us to Paris, to conduct an experiment overseas."

There was a pause. "Paris? What would we do in Paris?" Immediately Ben envisioned himself walking the cobbled streets of France with Emily, arm-in-arm, and his initial reaction was to say that he couldn't go, shouldn't go. It was one of those trips they'd talked about since they met. Emily yearned to see the great museums and architecture of Paris.

One of these days, they'd say. *Next year when we save up some money, when we get staff that can run the bar without us …*

—No, Ben, no!

He thought, *She's gone; I can't deprive myself of having a life. She would hate me if I held myself back because of her.*

His stomach felt queasy and knotted up. He shouldn't go, couldn't. It wasn't possible … but he had no real excuse not to go, and deep down, somewhere deep inside, the thought of going to Paris set off a spark. It was a feeling he hadn't felt in quite a long time: excitement.

"We would be testing abroad," Dr. Wulfric went on. "We would be in Paris for four nights, studying various pieces of art at the Louvre, and then recording at night with Lucy."

"How do you plan to bring Lucy? I mean, as small as it is, you can't expect to get it on a plane. TSA will think it's a bomb."

"That's the cool part," Dr. Wulfric said. "We'll test our newest prototype, Lucy III; she's small enough to fit in a briefcase. I'm not worried about how we're going to get it to Paris; Mr. Kalispell will make the arrangements."

"Right, Mr. Kalispell seems capable of just about anything."

"Yes," Dr. Wulfric went on, "all we need is a time when you're available. You *are* available, right?"

"Shit, I can probably take off next week. I just have to make a few calls, make sure the bar knows I'll be out of town. This is incredible! I can't believe we're going to Paris." He looked at the three men. Dr. Wulfric was smiling under his thick beard. Iain had the same professional smile he always displayed—yet there was something playful under his stern demeanor. He was happy, Ben could tell. Dr. Egan, however, just nodded his head.

"Are we … all going?" Ben asked.

"Well, unfortunately Dr. Egan has to stay behind to mind the lab," Dr. Wulfric said.

They were silent for a moment, and then Dr. Egan spoke up, "Yeah, yeah. You guys have fun; bring me back some cheese."

They nodded.

"Fuck you guys," he added.

They all burst out laughing, even Iain.

"Okay, okay," Ben said. "Now, I have to ask—not that going to Paris itself isn't great—but what's the pay?"

"Of course," Iain said. "All of your travel and meals will be taken care of, naturally. Mr. Kalispell would like to offer you five thousand dollars for your time."

Ben tried to stop his jaw from hitting the table. He cleared his throat, "Five thousand … cash?"

"Yes, sir. All cash."

His head spun, "Well, I'm in. I'm game." The knot in his stomach loosened with excitement.

"There's a lot of work to do while we're there," Iain said.

Ben nodded, trying to focus through his excitement.

"Don't worry," Dr. Wulfric patted Ben on the shoulder. "We'll have time to sample some wine."

The waitress came over and handed Iain the check. The men stood, shaking hands. Dr. Wulfric told Ben he would call him later that night, after Ben called the bar. Ben left, walking home, and the three men waited as the limo pulled up to the curb.

"Well, that went well," Dr. Wulfric said, closing the door after they were all in. "We're going to have to show him some of the recordings soon. He's going to demand it eventually, you know."

Iain nodded, "We'll ask Mr. Kalispell after Paris."

"We can't show him everything," Dr. Egan interrupted. "We don't know the ramifications of showing a person the parts of their mind working independently from logic and control. It could change the results of our work, perhaps detrimentally. We're not ready to test that aspect of Lucy yet. In a few months we can reconsider, but right now we're making good progress—why risk ruining it so soon?"

"We would have to make significant changes to his dreams," Dr. Wulfric added. "We can't show him everything, that's a given. There's too much darkness inside him. We would have to remove that cabin he's obsessed with. It's come up in every test now."

"The one that looks like the painting?" Dr. Egan asked.

"What painting?"

"In his apartment, by the door. He has a painting of that cabin hanging on the wall. I could have sworn we've already discussed this."

Dr. Wulfric looked out the window, "I don't think we have. I never noticed a painting."

Iain interjected, "I agree with you—that cabin, with his wife ... Ben shouldn't see it."

Chapter 8

It was Ben's first time flying business class, and the slight increase of personal space helped the eight-hour flight go by much faster than he'd anticipated. He even caught a bit of sleep—something he would have thought impossible, flying coach. Nevertheless, the three men were exhausted when they touched down in Paris.

Outside the gate, a man wearing a suit and cap held a sign that read 'Kalispell.' He took their luggage to a waiting car to drive them to their hotel. Ben was in awe. He stared out the car window, fixated, like a child, watching the lights of the city flash before his eyes. It had been so long since he traveled—too long. He and Emily had gone to the Caribbean on their honeymoon, and the year after their wedding, they'd flown out west to Las Vegas, and from Las Vegas to the north rim of the Grand Canyon. Those were the only two items they had scratched off their list of places to visit in their lifetimes. Now Ben was scratching off another, only he was doing it alone.

The driver stopped the car before the hotel and spoke to Iain Marcus, who happened to speak fluent French, and got out to retrieve their luggage from the trunk. The sounds of the city flooded in: the mumble of words and laughter coming from the nearby bistros along the sidewalk; the cars speeding by on the *rond-point;* horns blaring; music emanating from somewhere, everywhere. It was indecipherable to Ben, a jumble of noise as thick as soup, and yet beautiful and poetic. He stepped out of the taxi and into the heart of Paris. The air was alive, electric, as smooth and delicious as the fluidity of the French language itself.

The hotel stood before him, a magnificent structure lit up like a Christmas tree, with floodlights mounted between each set of windows and all along the base—as bright and magnificent as any of the marvelous statues and fountains he had witnessed in a blur from the car window. The building sat on a corner where three busy roads intersected at a *rond-point* and was constructed so that the front angled 120 degrees at each corner. If Ben approached the hotel from any of the three roads, the building would appear to be facing him head-on.

Ben followed Iain past the doorman, who stood rigid in his starched uniform and white cotton gloves, holding open the immaculately polished massive brass handle of the front door. Ben could feel the heat emanating from the floodlights as he passed and wondered how the doorman wasn't sweating—or bursting into flames.

The hotel was made to accommodate the wealthy—the aristocrats, the important people of the world—not some lab rat working for a rich American businessman. A group of men passed on his right wearing tailored suits and wheeling designer luggage. The hotel staff dressed as if they were in a military parade, with crisp jackets, gleaming brass buttons, and colorful ribbons and stripes on their arms indicating job position and rank. Ben felt self-conscious and exposed as he looked down at the wrinkled jeans and button-up shirt he was wearing. His skin felt clammy.

He shouldn't be here, not alone, not without her.

He didn't deserve the good things in life.

The handle on Ben's luggage was becoming slippery, and he thought he could feel the eyes of the staff and guests all staring at him. They could tell he wasn't wealthy—that he couldn't afford to be in this opulent hotel among the rich and important people of the world. He should be a member of the staff, holding doors, carrying luggage, calling them Sir and Madam.

He saw Emily in his mind shaking her head.

Why do you do this to yourself, Ben?

Because I'm not with you, he answered.

She continued, *We'll be together again one day. You can't live your life in regret, waiting to die.*

He didn't answer.

She was right. Whatever voice in his head spoke for Emily was right—he should enjoy life when it was good.

Ben made his way to his room number and unlocked the door. His room was different from what he had imagined, judging by the building's exterior. The furniture and décor were rather modern and minimalist. He had envisioned a room with plush, ornate chairs and intricate old carpets and wallpaper—dark reds, purples and creams. However, the room was calm and cool.

He opened the set of double glass-doors that led to a small balcony, just large enough to stand on, and he breathed in the air from the city at night. It was dark, but the roads and buildings were well illuminated. His view from the balcony was of the two main crossroads in the front, both leading down long, busy streets with marvelous buildings on either side. Small parks took up the spaces between the roads, each with many trees and round tiered fountains. Directly below Ben's balcony was a small public square full of people going this way and that. A small kiosk, that Ben guessed sold souvenirs, along with magazines, newspapers, gum, and cigarettes, hugged the road. The kiosk was built to resemble the stunning architecture of the buildings all around.

So much goes into the tiniest of details, Ben thought.

Picturing the packs of cigarettes in the kiosk made him instantly crave one, and his forehead throbbed with the brief, blissful euphoria of what that first drag would feel like. He debated leaving his room to get a pack—along with a bottle of wine—and spend his first night in Paris alone on his balcony, drunk and chain-smoking cigarettes. It wasn't a bad idea.

There was a knock on the door. Ben turned from the balcony, and looked through the peephole at Dr. Wulfric. He opened the door.

"Ben, how's your room? Is everything okay?"

"Yes, absolutely. The room is nice."

"Good, good. I'm calling it quits for tonight; we have a busy day tomorrow. Feel free to go out and explore the city, but remember we have an early morning. The museum opens at nine, so let's meet for breakfast at eight. It will only take a few minutes to get there. We can walk. Sound good?"

"Yes, Doctor. Sounds good."

"Please, Ben. Call me Peter."

"Right. Peter, good night. I'll see you in the morning."

Ben closed the door and returned to the balcony. After a few minutes, he went back inside and locked the latch to the balcony doors. Twenty minutes later he was fast asleep.

***

Ben was stepping out of the shower when he heard a knock at the door.

"Just a minute!" he shouted, ripping a pair of pants from his luggage and hobbling to the door as he pulled them on. Dr. Wulfric was once again outside the peephole.

Ben opened the door. "Good morning, Doctor."

"Good morning. May I come in?"

"Absolutely." He pulled a shirt over his wet hair.

Dr. Wulfric entered the room carrying a shiny aluminum briefcase. He walked to the small table and placed it down. "This," he said, "is a Halliburton briefcase." He removed a key from his pocket and inserted it in the lock. "They're nearly indestructible." Ben recognized the briefcase from just about every spy film he'd ever seen. "Please sit down." Dr. Wulfric motioned to the chair besides him.

He opened the metal briefcase and removed a syringe and a small glass container with the odd red liquid that Ben had become so familiar with. Rows of syringes and glass vials lined the inside of the briefcase, organized in allotted slots in the foam walls.

"This just arrived, right on schedule. Now Ben, during this trip you're going to be exposed to a higher concentration of Nano than in previous experiments, and a slightly different formula. I'm going to check your vitals daily, and please tell me if you're in any pain or discomfort. Anything at all—a stomach ache, headache, dizziness, anything. Got it?"

"Yes, Doctor. Got it."

"That's Peter."

"What?"

"Call me Peter, please." The doctor smiled. "We're friends after all."

"Right. Peter."

"I'm sure at this point you won't need any, but again I have an assortment of nootropics available if you find it hard to get into a lucid state of dreaming, or if you need a boost focusing at the museum. Just let me know."

"Will do, thanks."

Dr. Wulfric tightened the elastic tourniquet around Ben's bicep and cleaned the crease of his elbow with an alcohol wipe. Ben didn't get as lightheaded during injections as he did before, but the process still made his stomach flutter.

"Almost over … there." He placed a cotton swab in the crook of Ben's arm and told him to hold it there.

"See you downstairs." Dr. Wulfric snapped the briefcase shut, and turned for the door.

Ben finished dressing, and met Iain and Dr. Wulfric in the hotel restaurant. After a heavy breakfast of warm crusty bread, thick croissants, amazingly rich butter, and fresh preserves, the three men made their way to the famous glass pyramid surrounded by the amazing Louvre Palace. They walked down the Champs-Elysées to the Allée Centrale—a straight path extending from the center of Paris to the Louvre, in the west. The path was lined extensively with statues and monuments, palaces, theaters, parks, and fountains. Ben remembered watching some TV show with Emily years ago, where an insanely rich middle-aged couple bought an apartment on the Champs-Elysées for an astonishingly high price. The host explained that this strip was the most expensive road in the world to buy real estate. Now that Ben saw the amazing architecture, monuments, and dazzling retail stores firsthand, he could understand why.

The Louvre itself was just as much a work of art as the collections it housed—an amazing structure built in a sort of 'U' shape, with the famous glass pyramid in the center of the courtyard.

Ben spun around, letting his eyes soak in the hundreds of stone and bronze statues of toga-clad and nude figures that adorned the building. The statues were everywhere. The grandeur was impossible to take in all at once. Like counting snowflakes, it was best to stand back and see the composition as a whole.

Iain Marcus led the way inside, acting as an interpreter, although every employee at the Louvre spoke fluent English. Ben was certain they were making their way to the *Mona Lisa*. So far, that small painting seemed to be at the heart of this entire experiment. Ben was surprised when they stopped, and it was not the *Mona Lisa* he was looking at.

"Okay," Iain said, looking over a folded museum map. "Here we are."

Ben looked past the thicket of people to the painting on the wall. It was another work by Leonardo da Vinci: *Saint John the Baptist.*

The painting was that of an effeminate-looking man with long, curly hair pointing to the heavens with his right hand. His facial expression was reminiscent of the Mona Lisa's, yet Saint John's smile was more pronounced.

"Ben," Dr. Wulfric said, "we're going to do this just as we practiced in the lab."

Ben stood beside Dr. Wulfric, shoulder to shoulder among the sea of tourists, until they inched their way as close to the front as possible. Dr. Wulfric unbuckled the leather satchel bag hanging from his shoulder and removed a sketchbook along with a folded cloth, which contained several pieces of charcoal, all whittled down in various sizes.

"We'll be here for a while," the doctor whispered. "It will look rather odd if we're not doing something."

"I didn't know you're an artist."

"I don't consider myself to be one; it's just a little hobby. Let's begin."

Dr. Wulfric took Ben through the same process as before. Ben studied the picture closely from corner to corner, focusing on detail, scanning from left to right one section at a time. He took in the strokes of brown paint, circular and shadowed to form the strands of curly hair. He observed the peaches, whites, tans, and browns that made up the soft flesh of John the Baptist's arm and hand pointing to the heavens. He then viewed the painting as a whole, both consciously and subconsciously.

He focused on the painting as his eyes wandered over it, and then again as his mind was elsewhere. Ben focused on the pleasant eyes, seeing the face and body together, the dark background, the animal skin he wore, and the cross in the background. The lines of white where the paint had been scratched and worn with age were clear and evident.

It was hard to stay focused under the conditions in the museum: the bustling crowds, hundreds of people nudging shoulder to shoulder, speaking various languages from every corner of the globe. Ben had to clear his mind and focus on his breathing more than ever. As they walked away from Saint John the Baptist, Ben found himself rubbing his temples. Nearly an hour had passed, and the sea of tourists around them had changed a dozen times over. Dr. Wulfric closed his sketchbook on a rather nice charcoal sketch.

"That's good," Ben nodded at the paper.

Dr. Wulfric smiled.

Iain Marcus was nearby with his back to them, talking on his cellphone.

"No, Michael, that's not an excuse." Ben heard him say.

Iain turned to see them. "I got to go. No. Okay, tomorrow. Bye." He looked at Ben, still rubbing his temples. "Are you okay?"

"I'm fine, I'm fine. This is just a hard place to focus. It's much louder than the lab."

Dr. Wulfric narrowed his eyes, "Ben, are you sure you're—"

"Yes, Doctor, yes. I mean, Peter. I'm fine."

Dr. Wulfric took Ben's blood pressure anyway and shined a penlight in his eyes to check the dilation of his pupils. Iain moved them to a quiet corner, avoiding the sea of tourists curiously gazing in their direction.

"All right," Dr. Wulfric said. "If your headache gets any worse, you let me know right away."

"I promise."

They walked about, taking a break to let Ben relax and ease the pressure in his temples. They spent some time looking at various statues, some so iconic that Ben recognized them instantly, like *Cupid and Psyche*, and of course, the *Venus de Milo*. They spent a short time walking through the Egyptian section before Iain finally led them to their next assignment.

They stood before the painting. "Oh God." Ben said.

Dr. Wulfric smiled. "Yes, this will be a bit more challenging."

Ben recognized the painting, although he didn't know the title or the artist's name.

"This is the *Raft of the Medusa*, by Theodore Gericault," Iain read from the brochure, before turning to leave.

Dr. Wulfric and Ben inched as close as possible.

The painting was a depiction of about a dozen people, twisting and straining in various elaborate positions as they struggled to board a makeshift raft on a turbulent sea. Whatever ship the men had been on must have recently sunk. Ben studied the various men in the composition, either dead or hanging on for dear life, clambering aboard the crumbling planks that made up the raft. Only one man in the group—with a naked corpse strewn over his knee—looked calm and resolute to the disaster that engulfed them. The rest of the survivors grabbed at each other in horror and dread of their impending doom.

"Oh man," Ben said, "this is going to take forever, isn't it?"

"Well, it may be more complex than *Saint John the Baptist* or the *Mona Lisa*, but we're going to study it in just the same way. We won't be here forever," he laughed, "just a long time."

"At least you picked an interesting piece."

Dr. Wulfric agreed. "Yes, Theodore Gericault was an amazing artist. To tell you the truth, the *Mona Lisa* is not one of my favorites."

"You don't say? I would have thought you were a big fan."

"I don't choose any of the paintings." Dr. Wulfric shook his head. "Mr. Kalispell makes the selections. However, I agree with you; this is a marvelous piece of art—just extraordinary. Now," he removed his sketchpad, flipping it to a clean page, "let's begin."

***

Dr. Wulfric returned to Ben's room later that night carrying a different, larger aluminum briefcase. This one had wheels and a retractable handle, the size of a carry-on bag. He turned the dial on a small built-in lock, removed a key from his pocket, and inserted it into a keyhole. The clasps snapped open.

"Benjamin, let me show you the newest development in our line of Frequency Responding Lucid Transmitters. This is Lucy III." He opened the case and removed a small, blue-gray, almost silver, device from a carefully molded foam inlay. It fit into the palms of his hands and appeared to be made of plastic rather than the metal-like contraption Ben had used in the lab. It was less than two feet in length and had a curve in the middle, similar to the larger machine—Lucy II. It still resembled a boomerang, only in reverse—as if the boomerang was flattened straight and then bent in the middle, so that the sleek side was now wide, and the wide side now sleek.

"It looks like a boomerang," Ben said.

"Ah, my boy, it does. Here, feel it." He leaned forward, offering to place it in Ben's palms. "Take it, take it. Don't worry. It's quite durable."

"It's light." Ben felt the slick curved plastic. The name LUCY III was etched on the side. "Looks like it belongs to a video game system. Or like some strange antenna."

"Ha! That would be quite a video game. Perhaps one day." The doctor smiled. "Here, let me show you how it works." He took the device from Ben's hands and walked to the bedside table, placing it so the curved side faced the pillows. He pushed on a small, hinged door on the back, nearly hidden, and it popped open. The open hatch exposed a USB port along with a small on-off switch and a round socket. Ben examined the smooth sides of the machine and saw two additional small doors: a long-thin opening on the top, and a round one on the side.

Dr. Wulfric went back to the aluminum box and removed a laptop and a length of bundled cable. "The device has rechargeable batteries capable of running about twenty hours, but we'll leave it plugged in. Just to be safe."

He connected a power cord to the round socket, and connected the laptop to the USB port. He opened the monitor and the screen came to life. "Good, good," Dr. Wulfric said, typing. "Everything's running fine. Nothing was damaged during shipment." He moved back to the Halliburton case, removed a pouch containing a vial of fluid and a syringe, and sat back down, placing both the vial and the needle on the bedside table.

Ben looked closely at the vial. The color was different from the reddish stuff he had been injected with so far. This liquid was black as ink and shimmered in the light. He looked at the needle. It was larger than the other hypodermics, much larger. This needle was thick and cruel, the width of a dull pencil tip. Ben felt a shudder go down his spine.

"Hey, Doc, I don't think I can do that."

Dr. Wulfric looked up from the monitor. Ben's focused intently on the large needle, his face went pale, his eyes wide.

"Oh, Ben, I'm sorry. No, no, no, this isn't for you. Don't worry. Here, I'll show you." Dr. Wulfric stood and flicked open the round, hinged door on the device, about the size of a nickel. Ben leaned in close to see what looked like a porthole of some kind. The material around it resembled a tight-fitting rubber washer, and the hole in the center looked airtight.

"What's interesting about this device is that it uses a compound similar to the Nano, only this serum works in reverse." He took the protective sheath off the syringe and punctured the membrane on the top of the glass vial, sucking out all the black fluid. He nudged the needle into the rubber grommet on Lucy and very slowly pressed down on the plunger.

"The fluid will course through the device, not unlike blood. Each tiny nanoparticle is just as important as any other. The nanoparticles communicate with each other to form a singular entity—the same as with the serum you are taking. This compound brings the device to life, instantly communicating with all its various mechanical parts, along with the Nano in your body."

Dr. Wulfric removed the empty syringe and closed the cap to the porthole. He flipped the switch next to the USB port and a tiny green LED light came to life. He sat down before the computer and watched as various numbers in different sequences and colors appeared on the screen. "That's it," he said. "She's fully operational. We were afraid to add the liquid before shipment; the pressure from flight could have caused damage, but she's working perfectly. All you have to do is sleep. Lucy can stay right here on the nightstand."

Ben stared at the silent machine. "I'm impressed."

Dr. Wulfric unplugged the computer from Lucy, shutting the laptop down. "You want to see something really impressive?"

"Umm, yes?"

"Check this out." He removed something small from the inside pocket of his jacket. It was a small plastic case that fit in the palm of his hand. He unsnapped the corner and took out a chip, displaying it to Ben.

"Looks like a memory card."

The doctor nodded. "Precisely. It *is* a memory card; it would fit in any digital camera. Only *this* memory card was specifically made. It has more gigabytes than you would find in any camera store." Dr. Wulfric flipped open the long, skinny, hinged door on the top of the device and placed the chip in the thin opening underneath, pressing it until it slid into place, and flicked the door shut. It fit perfectly. "There you have it. Lucy is up and running. Now, there's one last thing we have to do tonight."

Dr. Wulfric picked up a small leather satchel bag beside the aluminum case that Ben hadn't notice him bring in. It was a medical bag. Dr. Wulfric undid the clasp and removed a stethoscope and a blood-pressure cuff, placing them on the bed. He unwrapped the cords from the cuff and pulled apart the Velcro closure.

"Let's check your vitals." He continued removing medical devices until he came to the bottom of the bag. "And afterward, maybe you can help me sample this. One small glass won't hurt." The doctor removed a bottle from the bottom of the bag, handing it to Ben. Ben looked at the label: *Château du* … followed by words Ben couldn't pronounce. There was a picture of a huge estate surrounded by vineyards.

"Is it any good?" Ben asked.

Dr. Wulfric shrugged. "I don't know. I choose wine the way my wife taught me: find the prettiest looking bottle with the oldest year and the lowest price tag."

Ben laughed. "Funny, Emily did the same thing. I remember my grandmother doing that too, but she normally drank boxed wine. Think it's a girl thing."

Dr. Wulfric smiled. "It must be."

Ben looked around the room, to the counter above the mini-bar where two water glasses sat on a tray, still wearing the little paper lids the hotel used to keep them sanitary.

"Hope you have a bottle opener in that bag."

***

Their last night in Paris, Iain Marcus led Ben and Dr. Wulfric to a popular restaurant a few blocks from the hotel along the bustling Champs-Elysées. They sat outside under the bright red awning that extended over the small dining area hugging the front of the building. Ben could see the Arc de Triomphe in the distance, lit up so that barely a shadow was present. They ate and drank to their last night in Paris, offering cheers to a job well done. Both Iain and Dr. Wulfric seemed elated. The work was over and early the next day, the three of them would be flying home. Before they ordered their meals, they'd polished off a glass of wine each, and had happily poured a second. Iain undid the top button of his shirt, loosening his tie.

"Ben, have you ever tried *escargot?*"

"Yeah, once." He shook his head. "I didn't like it."

"I bet you never tried it in Paris. You'll love it."

"Well, I don't know about that, but if it makes you happy, I'll give it another try."

"Believe me, it's not like anything you've had in the States. Here, Ben." Iain reached across the table to refill Ben's glass.

They toasted.

"So, where did you practice law?" Ben asked.

A group of maybe twenty tourists passed, speaking a Slavic language akin to Russian. Iain cupped his hand over his ear. "What's that?"

Ben spoke louder. "Where did you practice law?"

"Practice law?"

"Right, like, what school did you go to?"

"No, Ben, I'm not a lawyer." The wine sparkled in Iain's eyes. "I handle many of Mr. Kalispell's interests, but I've never practiced law."

"Oh. I assumed … I mean, I thought … what are—"

"What am I? I'm Mr. Kalispell's eyes and ears. I make sure his interests are safe and secure and his wishes met. I'm a little bit of everything."

A waiter approached wearing a white button-up shirt, a black vest with bow tie, and a long apron down to his ankles. His face was set in a sour and aloof demeanor, as if nothing anyone could say, do, or order for dinner would surprise or interest him in the least.

"*Bonjour Monsieur,*" Iain began, then whispered to Ben, "I'm ordering *escargot.*"

***

By the time they left the restaurant, Ben's head was throbbing. The pressure headache he'd developed earlier that week from staring at the various paintings wouldn't let up no matter how many aspirin he took. The first glass of wine numbed his mind, made him feel good. The last made his head pulse, and pain soon followed.

Within minutes of returning to his room, Ben was asleep. The boomerang like device sat on the bedside table, silently working.

Ben fell into deep sleep, but he woke from time to time with a dry and scalding headache. The fragments of his dreams he remembered were strange, involving wine at nearly every turn. The color red permeated his memory of the dreams, soaked in his brain like a sponge. He saw himself drinking glass after glass, chugging the stuff like water—practically swimming in it.

The scene cut, and Ben saw his grandmother looming before him like a ten-foot statue. She stood in the center of the kitchen in her old house, her boxed wine nearby on the counter. The spout was wide open, and the red fluid was splashing to the ground like water from a hose. She was shaking her head in disdain, "That ain't a real job. You need to get yourself a real job."

"Grandma, the wine!"

"I done all I can do to see you get by."

Ben could only stare at the wine, flowing, pouring out, almost an inch on the ground already. The drab-grey nightgown his grandmother always wore was getting wet around her ankles. The air filled with the pungent, ripe smell of fermented grapes.

"Working in some hospital, doing crazy tests. Me, I worked in restaurants all my days. It would do you good getting your hands dirty, doing real work."

"Grandma, the wine is spilling! Grandpa! Do something!"

"Grandpa? He's dead. So am I … *so are you!*"

Ben woke up with a start.

His raw eyes blinked at the ceiling. The thought of wine made him sick. It had been so long since he'd had a dream about his family that when he tried to picture his mother and father's faces, it was difficult. His grandmother, though—he could picture her without a problem.

Such a strange dream, he thought. *Did I say 'Grandpa'?*

He'd never met the man. There were never any pictures of him, and when Ben asked his Grandma about him, she would say, "He was just some boy." Ben imagined that the man must have done well, or left her some money, because as far as he knew, his grandmother never worked a day after giving birth to his mother.

Whatever.

There was no point wasting time thinking about her.

The sun was coming up and Ben doubted he would fall back asleep, but he didn't want to move. His brain felt dehydrated, like a sponge left out in the sun. He needed a glass of water—definitely *not* a glass of wine.

***

They checked out early in the morning. Iain talked to the smiling receptionist at the front desk, signed a few papers, and paid for their stay.

"How are you feeling?" Ben asked Dr. Wulfric, noticing the redness of the doctors eyes.

"I'll be fine; just need some coffee. How about you?"

"I'm fine."

Ben's headache felt better, but it was still there. He didn't feel hungover, but his head was in the clouds.

On the counter of the front desk sat a tall flowering plant. The stem rose high from the planter then dipped back down like the neck of a swan. It had large broad-leafed flowers blooming along the way. The petals on each flower were a rich creamy white, as soft as pillows, with a slight hint of purple toward the center that turned to a vivid purple deep inside.

The flower fascinated Ben. His mind focused on the intensity and depth of the colors, focused like he'd been doing all week, yet with no effort on his part. The white seemed to brighten, and the purple pierced his eyes like a glowing sunset. It was so beautiful, intensely beautiful—too beautiful. The colors burned his retinas with impossible brightness never found in nature. The white was so bright, the purple so vivid that it dulled and blurred everything else. The only reality that remained was the flower and him. The colors and clarity pulsated, his eyes seared by the image, his ears seeming to hear inside the skin of the flower, the roots, the water and air …

"We're all set," Iain said, sliding several papers into his briefcase. "Ready, Ben?"

"Yeah. What? I'm fine." He turned away, blinking rapidly. The afterimage of the flower stuck to his vision.

"Are you all right? You look pale." Dr. Wulfric stared at him as they moved away from the front desk.

"I was just zoning out. That flower is pretty. What's it called?"

Iain and Dr. Wulfric looked over their shoulders to the desk.

"An orchid," they said in unison.

The image of the petals was still clouding his eyes, as if he'd been staring into a bright light. A shudder went down his body. He was on the verge of having an aura migraine. He could feel it at the base of his head, in his chest, his nerves sparking and twitching.

Breathe, Ben. Breathe.

Panic was setting in—and he couldn't let that happen. The only thing he could do was try to calm and focus his mind. He took several deep breaths … .

In through the nose, out through the mouth.

He counted each breath, feeling the air as it entered and exited his nostrils and expanded his lungs, pressing down to his stomach. He imagined the oxygen spreading to every corner of his body as he inhaled and flushing away the toxins as he exhaled. He saw his body as a galaxy of its own—the air, the breath, the wind that flows, making the planets spin, making the blood flow, delivering the nutrients and oxygen to the far reaches of space, his body, his cells.

There was a mantra he had memorized for occasions like this: *Breathing in, I know I am breathing in. Breathing out, I know I am breathing out.* He repeated this mantra several times, matching his breaths with the words. The panic stayed in his heart, but began to subside.

When he breathed in deeply, he changed the mantra: *Breathing in a long breath, I know I am breathing in a long breath. Breathing out a long breath, I know I am breathing out a long breath.* When his breath was short, he changed it accordingly. It was an old meditation he'd learned while doing tests with Dr. Wright, to prepare his mind to stay sharp and focused, and his body relaxed.

Ben's mouth began to open. He was going to tell Dr. Wulfric he was on the verge of having an aura migraine and needed a Sumatripan, but he didn't speak. He felt the blood in his head drain out like a stopper being pulled from a bathroom tub. The release of pressure felt amazing. The bright images consuming his vision began to subside, instead of growing and crystallizing into zigzag patterns.

It was passing.

The fresh air outside felt good. He could smell everything: the leaves on the ground, perfume from a woman who passed had moments earlier, the grime on the streets rank with that sweet-rotten smell. His senses were sharp. He dodged the bullet, but it wasn't over. He would have to close his eyes on the ride back to the airport.

***

As the cab pulled up to Charles de Gaulle Airport, Ben felt better—fine even. He was lucky—so lucky—that it had passed.

He stepped out of the cab and said goodbye to Paris. There was so much of the city he wanted to see, still so much he wanted to do. The first few nights he'd walked around a bit, sometimes with Dr. Wulfric. They took in the sights, the fountains and churches, but all the while that guilty feeling was present—*he shouldn't be there*—if he couldn't be in Paris with Emily, then he shouldn't be in Paris at all.

Dr. Wulfric had led him to Notre Dame, and he stared up at the horned and birdlike gargoyles through binoculars while Dr. Wulfric snapped countless pictures and pointed out the nuances of Gothic architecture. The guilt, along with a dull headache from hours of intense focus at the Louvre, overshadowed the fun he should have been having. A voice inside his head told him he should go back to the hotel and be alone, get a bottle of whiskey, and let the warmth of the liquid hold him tight. The voice told him he should feel guilty, that he should feel inadequate, that he didn't deserve to see such beautiful things; he wasn't good enough, smart enough—he didn't belong there.

Go home and have a drink. Stare at the painting of the cabin in the woods and lose your mind.

The rest of the trip he was just a man doing a job. He conceded to the voice in his head and looked forward to his little apartment, his small couch, and tiny kitchen. He wanted to be alone. He wanted to open a bottle of whiskey, light up a cigarette, and stare at that painting. *Ahh, the cabin in the woods ...* His mouth watered and he licked his lips. A night of anguish and pain was long overdue—a night of drunken torment, recollection and loss, rolling on the floor wet with tears, consumed by emotions, the chemicals in his brain swirling, releasing a constant flow of dopamine and serotonin to mix with the alcohol, creating seesaw-like patterns of pleasure and pain.

These thoughts and feelings swirled in his mind as he sat reading a book in the airport terminal. The flight from Paris to Philadelphia was boarding in less than thirty minutes. He read and reread each line, each page. His mind was elsewhere.

"Is it any good?"

Ben jumped. The voice came from his side. He snapped back to reality, and looked to the voice, not sure who or why anyone was talking to him. He locked eyes with a black-haired girl sitting in the chair beside him. His own voice was momentarily lost in an inward flutter of air.

"I ... I'm sorry, what's that?" How had he not noticed her? She was sitting right beside him. She was beautiful. His heart began racing.

"I'm sorry, did I scare you? The book, is it any good?" Her words came out in a light French accent. Her lips curled at the corner of her pale, flawless skin as she waited for a reply with one of her pencil-thin eyebrows raised. Ben looked at the book; he couldn't remember the last ten pages.

"Umm," he cleared his throat, "yeah ... yes, it's good." God, his face was reddening. His cheeks were so warm—hot even.

Am I sweating?

She smiled, showing him the cover of the book she was reading, holding it awkwardly so her thumb kept the place. They were reading the same book.

"I see you have good taste," she said, then chuckled.

"I see you do, too."

"It's so rare to see people reading books these days—real paper books. Everything is electronic. You know, those e-readers?"

"Sure, I, uh, thought about getting one, but I have so many books at home I still haven't read." Currently Ben was reading three books: the book he had with him at the airport, Nietzsche's *Beyond Good and Evil* at home—for the mornings and late afternoons—and a book by Thich Nhat Hahn about mediating in the moment—also for the mornings and late afternoons.

Books were everywhere in Ben's apartment: in the boxes in his dining room, hidden in drawers, stacked on his coffee table, and on his dresser and bedside table. He tried to keep his books in neat piles and not scattered about. He did not want to be mistaken as a hoarder. However, the reason he didn't get an e-reader wasn't because of all the books he still had at home or because he simply liked paperbound books, it was because he couldn't get himself to buy something he really didn't need.

Maybe if Emily had wanted one, he would have bought one for himself as well. Maybe he would have liked it. Maybe not. He would never know. It was hard enough talking himself into buying a new pair of jeans. In Ben's world, extra things weren't necessary, not when he spent the majority of his time alone staring at an old painting on the wall.

"I'm Sophia." She held out a hand.

He hesitated a moment, then took it. "I'm Ben. Nice to meet you." He hoped his hand wasn't clammy.

"You going to Philadelphia?"

"Yes, but I live in Baltimore. I'm going home. You?"

Her eyes widened, "I'm going to Baltimore, too! That's so strange! My sister moved to the U.S. a few years ago with her husband. They just had a baby. What brought you to Paris, business or pleasure?"

"Congratulations on being an aunt. I, um, guess you could say I was here on business. Only sort of … it's hard to explain." She was about to say something, but Ben quickly interjected. "Where in Baltimore does your sister live?"

"Oh, ah," she put the book down, looking through her bag, "I don't know the area; it's my first time going to see her since she moved from Annapolis."

"Annapolis is a nice town; I know it well. You don't have to get the address if you can't find it; it's all right."

She looked up at him. Her big soft eyes took Ben's breath away: her dark pupils floating in large pools of clear white pierced through him. She was stunning, her hair so straight and black, her features so delicate and small, yet perfectly proportionate. Her teeth were even whiter than her skin, if that was possible, and he tried to think of the whitest thing he had ever seen to compare them with, but he couldn't.

"Why, you don't want to talk to me anymore?"

"No, I ..." Ben felt words disintegrate on his tongue, and the air grew incredibly hot on his skin.

"Oh, I'm making you blush!" She laughed. "I'm only joking with you. It's no problem. Here, I have it." She reached out and put a hand on his knee—briefly, a touch. Ben's blood boiled.

He looked at the piece of paper.

"Oh sure, I work at a bar a few blocks away. That's close to the harbor."

Sitting across from Ben, Iain put down his cell phone and nudged Dr. Wulfric awake from a light snooze.

"Why, what—what's the matter?" He fumbled for his glasses, which were already on his face.

"Take a look."

Dr. Wulfric rubbed his eyes. A lovely girl was talking to Ben, leaning over the armrest. She was smiling and laughing, touching his arm.

"Well look at that," Dr. Wulfric said.

The loudspeaker rang out:

"Now seating business class only on Flight 815, Paris to Philadelphia."

It repeated itself in French, and then English again.

"That's me," Ben said, putting his book in his carry-on, and standing.

"Business class, my-my. You must be a very important bartender."

"Trust me, it's nothing like that. I assure you."

Sophia stood as well.

"Good thing I decided to upgrade. Where are you sitting?"

Ben looked at his ticket, and Sophia looked at hers. They were on opposite sides of the plane.

"That's a pity; I wanted to hear how you liked Paris. Do you have a pen?"

"I think so, in my bag." Ben fumbled inside his carry-on until he found one.

"Here," she took the pen from Ben's hand and scribbled something on the back cover of her book. "Trade you."

She took the book out of Ben's hand and gave him hers.

"Hope you remember what page you're on."

"I'll find it." Ben smiled. He'd stopped using bookmarks years ago. He enjoyed using his memory to remember the page number. It was much easier than people thought when he told them. All he had to do was look at the page number and tell himself: *I will remember.* That was it. Simple. He wondered why no one else did it, or at least tried. Ben believed the human brain could remember *anything*, down to the smallest of detail, if focused correctly.

"I'll be in Baltimore until Wednesday," Sophia said, putting Ben's book in her bag. "Give me a call; show me the city. I love my sister, but I'd like to get out of her house for a bit. Maybe see the harbor."

"I, umm …" Ben couldn't speak. His heart felt like it was going to explode.

"It's okay," Sophia said, putting her hand on his shoulder, smiling. "If you don't have time, that's fine. I won't be upset."

"No, no, of course not." Ben looked into her eyes. They reeled him in like a tractor-beam. He wanted to kiss her. He wanted to lean forward and kiss her, right then and there. So badly. Her lips were so soft, her skin … God … he hadn't felt an urge like this in years. He couldn't control himself. "I'll call you, definitely. I'll call."

She put out a hand to shake, "Well, it was nice meeting you, Ben …"

"Oh, Walker. Ben Walker."

"It's nice to meet you, Benjamin Walker. I'm Sophia Lorenz."

"It's nice to meet you too, Sophia Lorenz." He cocked his head, "That sounds so … I don't know … familiar."

Sophia rolled her eyes. "Yes, there's a famous actress named Sophia Loren. And yes, I look kind of like her when she was young. Not really, but that's what everybody says—been hearing it my whole life. My parents thought it would be cute to name me after her."

"I don't even know what she looks like. I'm sorry; I won't bring it up again." He remembered Emily liking Sophia Loren movies, but he wasn't sure if he'd ever seen one.

"It's all right." She smiled, "My name is Lorenz, with a 'z,' not Loren."

Dr. Wulfric and Iain stood behind Ben as they filed up the ramp and into the plane one by one. Ben stepped aside to let Sophia stand in front of him. He could feel Iain's and the doctor's eyes on the back of his head and thought he could hear them snickering like schoolboys.

"She's pretty," Dr. Wulfric whispered.

Ben half-turned. "Shut up."

Sophia smiled and stared ahead, giggling to herself.

***

There was a man sitting in the terminal far from Ben and his company, yet within eyesight. He had a Nikon camera with a telescopic lens resting on his thigh, connected to a laptop. He focused the camera using the screen on his computer, not wanting to draw any attention to himself.

Just another tourist, he knew people would think seeing him.

He snapped away until Ben and Sophia stood to get on line. After a moment he closed the monitor, put the lens cap on the camera, and packed his gear. He took out his phone and sent a text: *Boarding. See you on ground.*

The man adjusted the rim of his hat, grabbed his gear, and stepped up to the back of the line.

Chapter 9

Ben stared at the phone number scrawled on the inside page of the book, *her* book, remembering the feeling as Sophia spoke to him, touched his arm, and had that look in her eyes. Her smile burned in his mind, and he lost himself in a daydream thinking about her light-fragrant scent. Jasmine and vanilla. He found himself wanting to bury his face in her dark, black hair. He wanted to breathe in her intoxicating aroma. He wanted to squeeze her hair in his palms and feel the softness rebound between his fingers.

The flight from Paris to Philadelphia turned out to be an incredible eight hours. The seat beside Ben on the plane was empty. He waited for his neighbor to appear, stealing glances over his shoulder trying to see Sophia, but the backs of the seats were too high.

Then she appeared and sat beside him.

"I'll get up if someone comes."

No one came, and Sophia and Ben talked for the next eight hours. Ben told her about his trip to the Louvre, and the paintings he had seen, and the ones that he liked. They discussed the *Raft of the Medusa*, and Sophia could not believe how much detail Ben knew about the painting.

"It's one of my favorites," She told him. "Théodore Géricault was an amazing artist. His real passion was painting and drawing horses, which is ironic, because he died from injuries after falling off a horse. He was only in his thirties."

"Wow, that's young. I didn't know that."

Sophia, as it turned out, was taking night classes majoring in Art History. She taught English during the day to get by, but her real passion was art.

They discussed the life of Théodore Géricault for a while longer, and then began on Leonardo da Vince, when the movie came on. They quieted down to watch it together. *Forrest Gump.*

"Air France isn't very up-to-date," Ben said, and they laughed, and whispered over the movie.

The eight hours breezed by. Ben never thought he would want to spend more time in an airplane, but during the descent, he felt a pang of sadness that they would soon be parting ways. They said goodbye at the airport. Ben promised to call, then they both went their separate ways. Ben watched Sophia run to her waiting sister, and the two girls hugged as if they were still children.

He thought about this back in his apartment, alone.

Pangs of guilt overtook him at times, as if liking these thoughts were in direct violation of his now-nonexistent marriage. It was so long since a woman had paid any attention to him. He never tried to pursue any girls at the bar. He did not rebound the way many people did after losing a boyfriend or girlfriend or a spouse, by sleeping with anybody who could give them some comfort. It was wrong to replace the person he loved, still loved, with a substitute—even for just a night. It was not fair to anyone, especially the other person. The thought of sleeping with anyone other than Emily rarely crossed his mind, and when it did, he immediately suppressed it with intense feelings of guilt, as if he were cheating on her, and disrespecting her memory. All the regulars at the bar heard his story, felt his pain, and left him alone.

He liked it that way.

Now, just a full day after returning from Paris, Ben was staring at his phone. Dialing the numbers scrawled on the back page of his book would be the hardest thing he would ever do. He stared at each number, the numbers she'd written in the book—*her* book—with her own delicate fingers. The handwriting looked exotic, something mystical. He put the pages up to his nose, breathing them in. He thought he could smell faint wisps of jasmine mixed with the starchiness of the paper. He followed the gentle curves and crests of each number with his eyes, lost in a trance, as if deciphering some ancient and divine secret.

Old feelings crept up on him: panic, fear, … hope.

The previous day was lost in a fog.

Did I really talk to her on the plane?

His tongue did not seem capable of such things. Having a conversation was one thing, but asking her out on a date? What would he say when she picked up the phone?

He poured a drink, touched the rim of the glass to his lips, and drained it entirely.

Then he picked up the receiver and dialed the numbers. His hands moved unaware of themselves. It rang three times and someone picked up.

The phone was shaking in his hand.

It felt like a dream, as if he was watching himself do it. His stomach fluttered and warmed with the booze.

"Hello?"

It was Sophia. His throat became dry and his voice squeaky.

She spoke again.

"Um, *hello?*"

He had to speak.

"Uhh." Words were large and sticky, unable to pass his constricted throat. He swallowed. "Hi, Sophia?"

"Yes?"

"Hi, it's Ben."

"Yes, of course." Her voice was bright and cheerful. He knew she was smiling on the other end, her exquisite lips curled ever so slightly, forming small dimples in her cheeks. *My god*, he thought, *she's beautiful.*

Words escaped his mouth faster than he could process them. Was he really doing this? His heart beat against his ribs, louder than his voice, and each word turned into a blur as soon as it passed his lips.

She laughed when he said, "Well, I was just wondering, you know, if you want to grab dinner sometime? While you're in town?" His voice was so loud, too loud, squawking and piercing his ears. He felt lightheaded, and stupid. He must have been mistaken; a girl like Sophia would never go out on a date with him.

"*Maybe* while I'm in town?" She laughed. "When else would we grab dinner, when I'm back in Paris?" Her accent made every word crisp and clean, carefully contrived and constructed.

Ben laughed. Something about her voice and her laughter calmed his nerves.

He asked, "How's tomorrow?"

"How's tonight?" she answered.

So there it was. A date. They set up a time and place. Unfathomable. He was not ready for this, he never would be ready—but it was happening. Events were set in motion that could not be undone.

***

He waited for Sophia in front of a bar near her sister's house. He paced, wondering if he had really called her at all. Maybe it was just a dream.

Women don't like you, Ben. You had one once and now she's gone, and you're supposed to be alone for the rest of your—

Then he saw her far up the street, walking toward him. She wore a simple dress that showed her body exactly as it should. Not too much and not too little. Just a bit of cleavage, a little thigh, and the gentle curves of her hips.

When she got closer, he walked to meet her.

Should I shake her hand, give her a hug, a kiss on the cheek?

She reached out and hugged him, her palms like little doves on his back, and kissed his cheek with the corner of her mouth. His stomach turned on a spit, and a tingling sensation jolted from his brain and spread throughout his body.

"Sophia, you look great—I mean, beautiful. I love your dress."

"Oh, you're sweet."

He opened the door to The Metro, holding it open for her. The lights were low and the music was not so loud that they could not talk. The décor was swank and hip, with couches and polished concrete floors. The staff all looked like models and athletes, wearing form-fitting black outfits that looked tailored to their bodies.

They took a seat at the bar.

Ben ordered a Manhattan for himself and a glass of Shiraz for Sophia.

She touched the glass to her lips, "It's good."

"Oh god," he said. "I wasn't thinking. Why did I order you wine? You live in Paris, the wine capitol of the world. That was so stupid!"

"No really, it's good. Try it."

Ben looked at the light, red lipstick mark on the rim of the paper-thin glass. He wanted to break it off in his mouth and chew it. He took a sip.

"See?"

"Yeah, it's not bad."

Halfway through their drinks, Ben started to relax. By the time they were nearly done, he felt great, confident even.

"Our dinner reservations are in twenty minutes, want to get going?"

Sophia smiled. "I'm going to use the ladies room, I'll meet you outside."

Ben asked the bartender for the check and handed him some cash. "Keep the change."

"Thank you." The bartender stroked his neatly groomed hair off his forehead. "You don't want to finish your drinks?" He nodded toward the glasses. They were both nearly empty. Ben took a sip from the Manhattan. The bartender was closing the check at the register and looking at him in the mirror behind the bar, smirking.

Ben got up from the stool and waited for Sophia by the door.

What an asshole, Ben thought.

Ben worked with plenty of bartenders who would move in on a girl the moment her boyfriend went to the bathroom, or out for a smoke. Girls on a first date were particularly vulnerable with liquor in their system.

Sophia came out and they left.

They had dinner at Steaks & Capital, a fairly upscale restaurant. The lights were low and the table settings were polished and precise. The tablecloth hung over the table in a perfectly straight line without a single crease. Ironed most likely. The silverware and glasses twinkled like stars in the sky, and there were different utensils for each course, to the left, right, and above the plates.

Ben knew that a server polished each piece of silverware and glassware before placing them down on the table, probably holding each piece up to steam and scrubbing them so the slightest imperfection vanished. Everything was exactly in the right place, set perfectly—perhaps a bit obsessive compulsive and pretentious, he thought.

What a pain in the ass for the staff, he thought. Even so, it was nice.

The waiter was immaculately dressed and freshly shaved, except for a well-groomed mustache. He carried himself with a demeanor that Ben found infuriating. He made eye contact with Ben alone, not even acknowledging Sophia. Jealous, like the bartender at The Metro, that a regular guy like Ben was on a date with such a beautiful woman. And most likely, the server was exasperated with all of the demanding customers he had to put up with on a regular basis. Ben wanted to tell the guy, "Relax, I'm in the business. I feel your pain."

When the waiter saw the menus folded on the table, he hustled over.

"We'll start with the crab cakes." Ben ordered.

The man nodded, scribbling on a dup-pad with a short pencil. Ben waited until he finished.

"She would like the Miso Salmon, and I'll have the fillet. Medium rare please."

"Of course, sir." He picked up the menus. "And how are we doing on drinks?"

Their glasses were full.

"Fine, we're fine."

"And the lady?" He was looking down at Sophia, perhaps at her breasts, Ben couldn't tell.

"She's fine."

"Very well." He turned and left.

"You know," Sophia said, "when I first saw you at the airport, do you know why I talked to you?"

"No, actually, I don't."

"It's because when you sat down next to me, we made eye contact, just for a moment, but then you looked the other way. It was not because you were intimidated, or nervous. You were indifferent. You didn't stare at me."

"So you talked to me because I was indifferent toward you?"

She laughed, "Kind of. Men are fools; they try so hard to get my attention. They make conversation when it's not needed. They have to prove that they're big shots, that they're big and strong and important. They think that talking about themselves—inflating their egos—is a turn-on for women, when all they have to do is *not* talk about themselves as much, and *listen*.

"Men, especially in bars, make me uncomfortable. They stare at my body, like they're molesting my soul. I feel eyes on me everywhere I go. You work at a bar; you must see it all the time: the guys who talk to every woman, trying to take anyone home. It's so desperate.

"Of course, the girls are usually no better. They may not be willing to go home with just any man, but they are more than happy to take every free drink that comes their way. In fact, some of my girlfriends go out drinking all night and don't spend a dime. They expect it. I'm not that type of girl."

"That's admirable, really, it is."

"Not only did I talk to you because you were indifferent to me, but I saw a deepness in your eyes during the brief period we made eye contact. You're intriguing. Not to mention handsome." She smiled.

Ben felt his cheeks turn red. "I think you're intriguing yourself, but I don't know about any deepness in my eyes."

"There is. I can tell."

They took a sip of their drinks.

"So," Sophia said, "what were you *really* doing in Paris? I know you went to the Louvre—but you said you were there on business?"

"Well … It's kind of difficult to explain …"

I can't explain. I signed those papers.

Just then, the waiter appeared carrying the appetizer on a small bone-white rectangular plate, thin and fragile. Ben let out a sigh of relief. The waiter placed it down with such grace that the plate seemed to float to the table. Two small crab cakes the size of half dollars sat off center atop paper-thin slices of cucumber in a circular arrangement. Ben could smell the smokiness and heat from the chipotle in the red cream sauce that was drizzled in lines crossways on the plate. His mouth watered.

The crab cakes were just as good as or better than any found in all of Maryland, and the sliced cucumber was slightly pickled and tasted of ginger and sesame. They finished the plate faster than what might be appropriate for a fine dining establishment, along with their drinks, and ordered a second round before the entree arrived.

"Have you been here before?" Sophia asked.

"No, I haven't. I've passed by a million times, and everyone at the bar raves about it. I don't know why I've never come."

"Probably because you didn't have me to bring with you." She smiled. An openly flirtatious smile, her eyelids fluttering, and they both laughed.

"I think you're right." He knew she was right. Not only had he never had Sophia to bring with him, he never had anyone.

Not a moment after they finished the appetizer, the waiter arrived carrying two circular plates on the tips of his fingers.

"The miso salmon, and the fillet." He placed them down with the same fluid grace and disappeared on spring-like steps.

The portions were small, but beautiful. Sophia's salmon filet was more of a thin strip than a filet, lightly browned, and served opposite a soy lentil concoction mixed with spinach and kale. Ben's fillet was the size of a fist, crisp about the edges and glistening with the seared juices. A few pieces of steamed baby carrots were on the side, shining with the butter and honey mixture they were sautéed in, and tied about the middle in a bow that could have been the string off a piece of celery.

A mixture of porcini and shitake mushrooms was spooned beside the steak, in a thick red wine and shallot sauce that smelled earthy—like sage and thyme, and deeply of garlic. They sat smelling the rising vapors before picking up their forks and knives. Sophia cut a small piece of the salmon, and held it up, blowing away the steam. Ben could not help staring at her; even the way she ate was sexy.

After a moment of respective silence she said, "Oh my god."

"Good?"

"You have to try this."

It did not take long for them to eat, and when they finished, they leaned back and talked about the meal. Ben was waiting for Sophia to bring up his work again. He hoped she would understand that he could not talk about it. However, she did not say anything. Maybe she already understood, and he would not have to explain himself. Maybe.

The waiter appeared a moment later. "Are we finished?"

"Yes, thank you."

"Would you like anything wrapped?"

Ben looked at Sophia's plate. It was nearly empty, just a small piece left. Sophia shook her head.

"No, thank you," Ben said.

"Very well." The waiter took the plates and walked away.

Ben felt his body tense, and Sophia put a hand on his forearm.

"These places," Sophia said, "they're so pretentious. They think that just because they serve good food, it gives them the right to treat people like idiots. It's the same in Paris; the restaurant people consider themselves artists, and artists can be very sensitive. Don't let him bother you; I'm having fun. Why don't we get the check and go for a walk, maybe find something for dessert?"

"You're right. That sounds good."

***

Ben walked Sophia home—insisting—so she would not wind up in a bad part of town. She reached out as they walked and held his hand in hers. Her hand radiated warmth, like a kitten.

"This is it," Sophia said, stopping before a brownstone. "My sister's house."

She turned to face him; the weight of her gaze made him look away.

"This is the part of the date when you kiss me."

"Sophia, I …"

"Ben, look at me."

Ben looked up, her gaze crushing the thoughts going through his mind. His attention was enraptured, causing that moment to become locked in time.

"I don't know who she was … but I'm sorry, and I understand—"

Ben leaned in and kissed her. His lip hit her tooth, and for a moment he was mortified, but she kissed him back. A good kiss—not too long, but hardly a peck on the cheek. Long enough for it to mean something. They split apart. That moment would be forever stuck in time, for all of eternity—yet it was over in a flash.

"Thank you for tonight, Benjamin. I had a great time."

He felt tears coming, but fought them back.

"I'm leaving Baltimore tomorrow to visit a friend in New York before I go home. Will I see you again?"

"I'm traveling to Rome in a month or two, but I don't know the date. Maybe you can meet me there?"

"You're going to Rome? Lucky bartender." She smirked. Perhaps his silence on the topic was becoming evident. She continued, "It's a long drive to Rome. I would have to take off from work. I don't know if I can; I used my vacation days for this trip." She looked at him inquisitively. "Why are you flying to Rome?"

"It's a long story. Fly then, don't drive. I'll take care of the ticket. I'll even book it for you."

"You're full of long stories." She lifted an eyebrow. "I think there's more to you than meets the eye."

"How about I tell you more about myself when we're both in the Vatican."

"The Vatican? I thought you said Rome? I didn't take you for a religious man."

Ben smiled. They kissed again, and slowly pulled away.

"Call me," she said. "Let me know when you're going to Italy. I'll try to take off from work. I'll take care of the ticket; you don't have to pay for it."

"No, I insist. If you have to take off from work, let me at least pay for the ticket. Seriously, it would be my pleasure."

"We'll see. Goodnight, Benjamin Walker."

"Goodnight, Sophia Lorenz."

She walked to the doorway, stopping to turn and smile, and then vanished. The door closed behind her.

Ben stood on the sidewalk, watching the light emanate from the curtained windows of the old townhouse. He wanted desperately to be inside with her, in the warmth of the house, seeing her beauty in the light. He did not want her to go. Was the night really over? It felt like it had just begun. He stood there in the silence, enjoying the faint sound of the wind. The street was dark and quiet in the late hour, save for the streetlights overhead, buzzing like flies in a jar. He turned and walked down the deserted sidewalk.

***

As Ben walked home, he thought about something else that happened *earlier*, that same day. It was sometime in the afternoon when Ben was mustering up the courage to call Sophia. He was sitting on the couch looking over the numbers scribbled on the back page of his book and contemplating having a drink to calm his nerves. His cell phone was in the palm of his hand, the number pad beckoning him to dial the ten-digits that would connect him with Sophia. Suddenly, the phone lit up, vibrating in his hand. The screen said '*Doc Wolf.*' Ben picked up.

"Hello, Doctor."

"Ben, my boy. How are you?"

"Good. You're sounding rather chipper."

"Ah, well, yes. There is a lot to be chipper about."

Dr. Wulfric began to explain to Ben about their new assignment in the Vatican, and then Ben said, "Oh crap. That's a ton of work."

"Don't be glum. Our work in Paris is turning out to be extraordinary; we won't need to spend nearly as much time on each piece of art as we did at the Louvre. I think it's safe to say we can cut our focusing time in half."

"Well, that's something. Still—the Vatican? The Sistine Chapel?" Ben had only ever seen pictures of the church, never having gone there himself, but he knew the scale of the art in the building to be extraordinary. "What's with all the art?"

"Excuse me?"

"I'm just wondering—why do we keep studying art? Not that I'm complaining about going to Paris, or Rome."

"It's Mr. Kalispell's decision regarding where we conduct our experiments."

"It just seems odd that Mr. Kalispell is sending us all over the world. Couldn't we study something else, like a tree outside? Again, I'm not complaining. I'm just wondering."

"He's a, well … an interesting man. I don't think the cost of sending us overseas bothers him in the least, not as long as we continue to get results."

"Right. Okay, I guess it's best to not ask questions." *Because they're not going to give me answers.*

"Mr. Kalispell would like for me to inform you that there will be no shortage of work for a long time to come. That is essentially why I'm calling you, as well as to tell you that the results we processed from Paris are extraordinarily good. I wasn't supposed to mention anything about the Vatican, but it is such exciting news. When Iain calls, act surprised."

"I will."

"We're going to Italy, Ben! And who knows where to after! Spain, Belgium, Austria, Germany …"

Ben smiled. He was excited, even though he was still jet lagged from Paris. They had only just returned.

"You're right, Doc. This is great news."

"We also have a few smaller jobs for you, closer to home, before we go. The Met in New York, the Philadelphia Museum of Art, and we're looking at a few in Baltimore."

Ben agreed to do any job that came up. He felt it was his duty. Over the years, he had never turned down an assignment with Dr. Wright, and the money Mr. Kalispell was paying made it possible to work fewer shifts at the bar. It was not like years ago when he was working side by side with his wife. Putting the bar business behind him would be relieving, but he could not quit just yet. He needed to stay on payroll. The money coming in from Lucy was all in cash—illegal but essential. With a pay stub from the bar, he could deposit small amounts of the cash at a time.

In Ben's bedroom, in a shoebox under a loose floorboard, he kept stacks of hundred-dollar bills wrapped tightly in plastic wrap. If everything stayed the way it was going, he could survive that way for a long, long time.

Chapter 10

The flight to Rome was long, but Ben barely noticed. He was flying in business class again, a luxury he could get used too. The flight would have gone much faster, though, if Ben had Sophia on the seat beside him. Instead, he had Dr. Wulfric as a neighbor, and the doctor had no problem sleeping the entire duration of the flight.

The hotel was only a half-mile outside of Vatican City. The architecture of the building was not quite as inspiring as the hotel in Paris. As they checked in at the front desk, Iain Marcus informed Ben and Dr. Wulfric that the hotel had a rooftop lounge with incredible views of the city and an open-air bar at night. They agreed to meet in the lounge in two hours, after they freshened up.

"*Grazie*," Iain said to the receptionist.

"Of course you speak Italian," Ben laughed.

Iain passed out their room keys. Ben's room was next to Iain's, and Dr. Wulfric's was across the hall. The view from Ben's room window overlooked an alley, but the interior was bright, vibrant, and incredibly modern.

Ben put his luggage on the carousel, removed the toiletries, and stood before the bathroom mirror to brush his teeth. It was a marvelous bathroom, with large white marble tiles accented by smaller black tiles lining the edge of the floor. There was a bidet, a heated towel rack, and a large marble bathtub with a mirror spanning the wall behind it. This large mirror reflected the vanity mirror, creating multiple images that appeared to stretch to infinity. Next to the bathtub was a separate standing shower with a glass door. Mr. Kalispell had spared no expense in their lodgings. Ben opened the balcony doors and stepped outside into the open air. The sun was warm on his face, and the breeze felt dry and cool.

There was plenty of work to do the next nine days. The thought of craning his head and staring up at the high ceiling for hours on end, in a poorly lit chapel, sent Ben's mind in a tizzy.

He already had a slight headache from the last three weeks when he, Dr. Wulfric, and Iain visited several local museums in the New York and Baltimore areas. Three days before departing for Rome, they spent hours in the Met.

The day before departure, Dr. Wulfric asked Ben to come to the lab to discuss what to expect in Rome. When Ben walked into the lab, Dr. Wulfric was in the process of laying out large, square photographs on a cleared work desk, like a puzzle. When he finished, a panorama of the cathedral ceiling and walls lay before them. Dr. Wulfric divided the room into a grid, one through nine, each representing a day of work. They went over the art and compositions so they would not waste time when they arrived.

After preparing for over an hour, Iain Marcus joined them and took Ben to a different desk.

"Mr. Kalispell is offering you six thousand dollars for your work in Italy, and, of course, all of your meals and lodging will be taken care of."

It would take Ben over a month to make that kind of money at the bar. Ben knew he should not bargain, but he thought, *what the hell, I have something to bargain with—they need me.*

"Ten thousand. Let's make it ten thousand dollars, one thousand dollars a day. I'm not looking forward to craning my neck at the ceiling for hours on end; it's not going to be easy, not by any means."

Iain didn't flinch. He picked up his leather briefcase and removed a black binder. He flipped it open, trailing his eyes over a page. "Eight thousand," he said.

Ben remained silent. It was an old trick Emily had taught him years ago when they were buying a new car. *'Don't say anything when he makes us an offer,'* she would say. *'Stay quiet, like you're thinking, even when it gets uncomfortable.'*

The trick worked. After a few tense minutes of silence, the car salesman had cleared his throat and came back with a better offer. Iain, however, did not wait until the silence became uncomfortable. He flipped a page in the ledger.

"You received a thousand dollars each night for the first three tests. You received five thousand for your work in Paris, and then one thousand dollars for your work at the Met; one thousand dollars at the Philadelphia Museum of Art, and one thousand dollars at the Walters Art Museum. That gives us a total of eleven thousand dollars. Let's meet at nine thousand for Italy, giving you a total of twenty thousand dollars for your work with us so far. I think that's adequate, don't you? We're going up three thousand dollars from our original offer, and you're going down one thousand from your counter offer."

Ben had the feeling Mr. Kalispell would not care if it cost him fifty thousand—the man had bottomless pockets, but it was Iain's job to set boundaries.

"Okay, Iain. That's fair."

"Excellent."

Iain Marcus took out a stack of money from his briefcase, counted out four-and-a-half-thousand dollars, and placed the money in a blue zippered bank bag.

"That's half of the sum we agreed upon. When we return from Rome, you'll receive the rest."

Ben's original idea was to include a tape of his dreams into the bargaining. Perhaps they thought he no longer wanted to see it since he stopped bringing it up, but he did. Not only that, but Ben also wanted to know what was going on in the room next to the lab, behind that door in the center of the room. He'd spent six nights in the same bedroom on the second floor, and each morning subsequent each night, he heard the noises behind the wall: ticking, like that of a cab meter, with various mechanical bumps and grinds. Sometimes the sounds were very loud—like an auto garage with power tools and compressors.

The noise did not bother him, but whenever he asked Dr. Wulfric or Dr. Egan, they stuttered some excuse, changing the subject. Moreover, there were always cars and trucks parked along the side of the lab that seemed to belong to no one; but they had to belong to someone, because they came and went without Ben ever seeing anyone. What Ben really wanted was knowledge, but in the end, after some thought and consideration, he felt it was better not to bargain and leave the subject for another day. Maybe it was better to be kept in the dark. Why should he care? As long as they were paying him, and paying him well, he would quell his pursuit of knowledge, at least for the time being. Later, maybe, after Rome, he would rethink his strategy.

Ben left the balcony, closing the double doors behind him. He laid on the bed and flipped through the various channels on the television. Italian soap operas and foreign news reports flashed on the screen. One channel was showing American sitcoms—currently an episode of *Friends* was playing. Another channel showed world news anchored by a heavily accented newscaster speaking English. He should be concentrating on the work ahead, but his mind kept wandering to his last day in Italy, the day when Sophia Lorenz was flying to meet him. She could not spend the night in Rome; taking two days off from work was impossible. Somehow, Ben persuaded her to fly in for just one day, returning to Paris that very same night. It was silly, impractical, stupid, exhausting, and a waste of both time and money, but that was all the more reason Sophia agreed to do it. The fact that Ben would pay a round-trip ticket just to see her for only a few hours made her swoon. It was something people did in the movies, not in real life, and that made it even more exciting.

***

The men stood inside the Sistine Chapel, in complete and utter awe. The art in the building was all encompassing, everywhere to be seen, impossible to take in all at once. For nearly an hour, they didn't say a word, but wandered around in astonishment. Dr. Wulfric broke the silence.

"Breathtaking. Absolutely beautiful."

"We have our work cut out for us, don't we, Doc?"

"It's Peter, Ben. Peter."

Dr. Wulfric locked eyes with Ben, and the intense feeling of being in over their heads, drowning in a sea with no horizon in sight, made them break out in laughter. Iain Marcus snapped out of his hypnotic wandering and began elbowing past the crowd of people to get back beside them.

"My god," Iain said. "This is amazing."

Dr. Wulfric nodded, "Let's get to work, Ben. We have a long day ahead of us."

They began in Zone One: The Last Judgment. An enormous fresco spanning the entire wall behind the alter. Dr. Wulfric swung his satchel bag in front of him, removed two small binoculars, handing a pair to Ben. He rummaged through the bag for his sketchpad and charcoals.

"All right, Doc—Peter—where do we begin?"

"Let's just take it in for a few minutes."

Three hours later, they were still standing before the enormous painting. The image of Saint Bartholomew, with his face contorted in contempt, his hand holding out his own flayed skin, was etched in Ben's mind.

"It is believed that the face of Bartholomew is a self-portrait of Michelangelo himself," Dr. Wulfric informed Ben, squinting through the binoculars.

"Why does he look so mad?"

"Well, because he was flayed alive."

"No, I don't mean Saint Bartholomew. Why did Michelangelo depict himself angry?"

"Because Michelangelo never wanted to do this—to paint the ceiling, paint the Sistine Chapel. He told the Pope he would prefer *not* to be commissioned, if possible. But the Pope commissioned him anyway."

"That's crazy. I wouldn't think an artist of his caliber would turn down an offer to compose something of this magnitude. Arguably, the greatest artistic achievement ever created—in the world. Something to live on long after his death."

"At that stage in Michelangelo's life, he thought of himself as more of a sculptor and was frustrated that he would have to spend years of his life painting the Chapel instead of doing what he felt was his calling. But who knows, it's just a theory."

***

On the third day of the trip, Iain Marcus made an appointment at a local spa for Ben and Dr. Wulfric after seeing how fatigued they were becoming. They had both spent hours staring straight up at the ceiling, squinting through binoculars, developing headaches that aspirin couldn't cure, and painful cricks in their necks that became unbearable at times. Dr. Wulfric often joked that it would be easier for them to lie on the floor while studying the ceiling. It would be so much easier. The spa was enjoyable, and when they left they felt recharged, but the pain came back the moment they reentered the cathedral.

The fifth night, Ben retreated to his room so completely drained and mentally fatigued that his knees were wobbly the last few steps in the hallway. He opened the door to his room and collapsed on the bed. An hour later, he was still in bed, his hands and feet tingling with exhaustion, and his stomach growling audibly with hunger. However, he didn't feel he had the strength to leave the bed to get food. He sat propped up with pillows and swaddled with blankets, aware that he had to use the bathroom, but unwilling to get up to do so.

A news anchor on TV was covering a story about a small earthquake that had hit a rural area in southern Italy. The olive-skinned, clean-cut man explained the level of devastation in a coarse accent that matched the rugged and earthy terrain of the small town he was describing. A clip of an old woman in a black shawl played along with his commentary, crying and howling outside the rubble of what was only minutes ago her family's home.

The scene changed to an interview with a dusty-looking, sunbaked man speaking in rushed Italian. An English translation followed: *"I don't know where we'll sleep tonight. It happened so fast. I felt the earth rumble and didn't know what was happening, and then the buildings around me started to shake, and I started hearing loud crashes. Everything was coming down. My house is destroyed; it's gone. I don't know what we'll do, but I am so thankful that my wife and children are safe. I praise the Lord for saving them. So many were not as fortunate."* Behind the man, people stood in a group beside the rubble of his home, staring into the camera with drawn faces. Everyone looked grey, as if they belonged to the rubble that was all around. A group of sheep appeared in the distance, followed by a Shepherd, and even their white fleeces were grey with dust.

Ben blinked his eyes away from the television. He saw the bright outline of the screen on the blank wall, etched in his vision. He blinked again—the image stayed, burned in his retinas. He closed his eyes for several seconds, taking deep breaths in and out. The colors became brighter in the darkness, twinkling like lights on a Christmas tree.

"Oh hell," he said. "Oh shit."

He kept his eyes shut.

In the darkness, the crisp lines of the screen blurred around the edges, branching out in crystalized colors, zigzagging in thunderbolt arrays both colorful and blinding. Bright white patches and black spots grew and changed form.

He turned off the TV and picked up the phone next to the bed, dialing Dr. Wulfric's room. The numbers on the keypad were hard to make out, and he had to use his memory.

"Hello?"

"Doc, it's Ben." There was a waver in his voice and his hand was trembling on the receiver.

"Ben, what's the matter?"

"I'm getting a migraine. The aura is starting."

"I'll be right there."

Ben hung up, and not a moment later there was a knock at his door. Ben let Dr. Wulfric in.

"How bad is it? Are you in any pain?"

"No pain. It's dull."

"Lie on the bed."

Dr. Wulfric turned off all the lights in the room except for one small reading lamp. He gave Ben two Triptans, popping the pills out from their protective shells. The pills instantly dissolved on Ben's tongue like snowflakes.

"How bad is the aura? Can you see?"

It was impossible to focus on any one area of the aura; it grew along the edge of his vision, along the border, like how a camera flash might leave an impression in the corner of the eye. It had grown now to the point where it encompassed his complete field of vision, and Ben could only see the outline of Dr. Wulfric through patches of pitch-black and bright, colorful lights. If he had to count how many fingers the doctor held up, it would be difficult.

"It's bad, Doc."

"Follow this pen with your eyes. Don't move your head, just your eyes."

Dr. Wulfric moved a pen back and forth before Ben's face.

"I think we've been overworking ourselves. We're on break, as of right now."

"Can we do that? I mean, we have to finish on schedule, right?"

"We're ahead of schedule, and judging from our results so far, we can start spending less time in each zone. Rush things a bit. And we can always stay an extra day or two if need be. But that's not important right now. Right now, you don't worry about any of this. You have to relax."

"Do you think it's from the serum, the umm …"

"Nano. No," he shook his head, "I can't see that being possible."

The serum they used, the red liquid with the microscopic robots swimming around, had been altered slightly before the trip to Paris and again this time in Italy, to compensate for the different machinery they were using—Lucy III. It looked about the same, just a little darker. Ben would not have noticed at all if Dr. Wulfric had not told him.

The next big leap for Lucy was to run off the neuronal signals themselves, without the aid of the serum. Soon, Dr. Wulfric hoped, a serum would not be needed at all. When the project was ready to hit the market, a Nano pill would replace the serum and eliminate the need for an injection. That would be fine for hospitals as long as the FDA approved the pill—but if they intended to sell a model of Lucy to private consumers, they would have to do away with the serum altogether. That sort of thing— pills, injections, and medicines—would not sell to individuals. The next big step in Lucy's evolution was to work unaided.

"I'm doubtful the serum has anything to do with this, although I am not going to rule it out. If you were going to have a reaction to the formula, it would have happened immediately. I think the intense focusing and strain, along with having to use binoculars for hours on end, caused too much stress in your mind. You need to get plenty of sleep—not just tonight, but tomorrow as well."

Dr. Wulfric left the room and returned a minute later holding his leather medical bag. He opened it and removed a bag of IV solution and a length of thin tubing. He held Ben's arm tightly to stop it from trembling as he drew a blood sample and connected an IV drip.

"Here, Ben, take these." He held something in his hand and offered a glass of water.

"What's this?"

"Aspirin. You need to drink plenty of water and rest for a long time."

***

When Ben woke the next morning, the aura was gone. It was replaced by a dull headache emanating from different parts of his head like little balloons inflating between his skull and brain, ready to burst, and then quickly subsiding.

He was surprised to see Dr. Wulfric waking up on the chair beside him.

"You didn't have to stay the night."

"Nonsense. Besides … I fell asleep by accident. How are you feeling?"

Ben said he did not know, and the stress of trying to figure out how he felt added to the anguish in his mind. His hands and feet were out of rhythm with his body, and he was so incredibly weak that just standing to go to the bathroom was difficult. He was tired. So tired. Unbelievably tired.

Dr. Wulfric gave him more aspirin and stayed next to his bed. He did not ask any more questions.

Later that afternoon, Ben felt better. Dr. Wulfric went to get some soup and bread. The food made him feel both better and worse. His mind straightened out a bit, and some of his strength returned, but his stomach wrenched.

He went back to sleep.

When he awoke late in the night, a tingling sensation issued from deep within his forehead, behind his eyes, sending pleasurable sensations out from the frontal lobe of his brain like a tolling bell. It was the feeling of stress leaving his body. The numb pain and confusion was melting and washing away, replaced by an odd sense of pleasure. Ben thought he could feel the congested blood in his brain begin to ebb away. The migraine was passing.

The next morning, the migraine had passed entirely. His strength returned and his mind was sharp. The previous day and a half was a complete blur—it did not seem to have happened at all. His dreams during that time were intense and deep. Tidbits came back to him while he stood in the shower under a steady stream of hot water:

He was on a dark road, the headlights of his car passing up and down over hilly terrain, illuminating thickets of dark trees on either side. He was alone wherever he was, and it was late at night—pitch black, bitterly cold— and surrounded by pure wilderness. He had a sense of dread and isolation of the outside—the wilderness—but also a feeling of warmth and security being in a car that was driving fast. Warm air was blowing on his face from the vents, and pockets of fog glided over the windshield of the car in droves.

The dream skipped, the timing of events irrelevant, and he was suddenly walking along a sidewalk in a town. The street was barren; the only sound came from something rattling in the wind that Ben could not see—a store sign, perhaps. The wind was damp and cold, and a fine mist fell over his face and over the black trench coat he was wearing. Droplets formed that ran down his cheeks, and over his coat. He hugged his arms to his sides, his hands tight in the jacket pockets. He could see the rim of a hat before his eyes, a men's old-fashioned hat, the type he'd seen in gangster movies from the twenties. He also knew, although he could not see himself, that he was wearing a suit under his trench coat; the fabric felt light and silky on his legs and chest.

He was aware of his surroundings, looking around the upturned collar of his coat at the shadows in the doorways, but nothing stirred. His adrenaline was pumping, and he felt excitement mixed with fear. He slipped into a doorway quick and quiet, like a dark object melding into shadow.

Again, the dream skipped like a reel of video with whole scenes spliced out. There was a person in a room sitting before him. The room was dark and smelled thick with sleep. The man was naked down to his underwear, and he was looking up, his blurry face framed by his sleep-matted hair. Ben knew this man, at least in the dream he knew him. He felt a sense of relief, fear, anxiety, and adrenaline all at once. He was helping the man; somehow, in that late hour of night, he was helping him. A dark circle was forming around him as beads of water dripped off his trench coat to the carpet underfoot. His hand came out of his pocket with the tight feeling of a leather glove pulling against his skin. There was something in his hand; he was giving something to the man. The man held his hands out for it, on his knees, sitting upon the heels of his feet. The look on the man's face was wonder and astonishment, and maybe something else. There was nothing sinister, nothing even strange about the transaction. A feeling of relief swept through him, as if he had done the naked man a great favor.

The dream skipped again and he was walking outside. The air was just as cold and damp as before, but the rain had picked up. Droplets of water fell off the rim of his hat, falling before his eyes. Behind him came a gust of warm air, ripping through the cold of the night.

That was all Ben could remember—a feverish dream. Very intense, and emphatically real, yet, it felt distant. Another world. It was like watching a movie and acting in it all at the same time; he may have been playing the part, but he had no control of his movements or emotions.

That man kneeling on the ground, that face … he puzzled over it as he moved from the bed to the bathroom. He tried his hardest to recall details out of the darkness—the eyes and mouth—but as he stepped into the shower, the face continued to blur, and by the time he was brushing his teeth, it was blurred beyond recognition, like a greasy thumb rubbed over the wet ink of a photograph.

Chapter 11

Ben waited in the terminal at Leonardo da Vinci-Fiumicino airport.

His work at The Sistine Chapel was complete: hours upon hours of focus and concentration, the most interesting and exhausting nine days of Ben's life. The next morning he would leave Rome from this airport, seeing very little of the many sights and eating at none of the city's great restaurants. This was the same airport where Ben currently stood waiting for flight 806 out of Paris, carrying on board Sophia Lorenz.

He paced by the baggage claim, unable to stand still, the long metal belt just rumbling to life moments earlier. The crowd flowed by in a steady stream from various gates, and Ben scanned each face for Sophia's soft features and long black hair.

Five minutes felt like an eternity, and after ten minutes, he grew restless. He shifted his weight from one foot to the other. Perhaps she had not come; maybe something came up at work and she was still in Paris. Maybe he was in the wrong area in the airport, or maybe he scribbled down the wrong flight number. He checked the sign above the baggage claim.

Flight 806
Paris France CDG to Rome Italy FCO

This must be the right place.

Bags came sliding down the chute and swiftly got picked up from the metal conveyer belt. Ben looked up from the carousel and immediately recognized the facial features he was searching for. Sophia pushed through the crowd in the baggage claim. She did not spot him right away, her gaze sweeping from person to person as she wound her way toward the conveyor. His breath was momentarily lost in an influx. His blood warmed, and he feared he would stammer and stutter when they spoke. Words seemed impossible, lost and troublesome, and he wasn't sure what he should say or do—was he supposed to give her a kiss when she walked up, or just a hug? Maybe it was best to follow her lead … or did women not like that? Maybe it was best for him to be aggressive and give her a kiss …

Damn it Ben, be a man!

She saw him and smiled, then walked up to him. They hugged.

"I can't believe I'm doing this!" She was glowing. "How are you, Benjamin?"

Ben found his voice, and it was strong. "I'm good. How was your flight?"

"It was fine. I've never done anything like this before, I'm so excited!"

"Neither have I. This is crazy! I'm so glad you could make it, even if we only have a day. Do you have any luggage?"

"I'm leaving tonight. Just this carry-on."

Words loosened on Ben's tongue, melting away like ice chips. "You look … you look beautiful. I'm so happy to see you." He spoke with abandon, not purposefully choosing his words; his heart spoke and formed the words into sentences. "I'm so, so, happy to see you."

Her smile was wide, and her cheeks blushed bright crimson, set alight on the pure white canvas of her skin. "Oh Ben, I'm so happy to see you, too. I haven't been able to get you out of my head."

"Sophia," he chuckled, "you have no idea."

They hugged again and kissed, holding each other longer. The crowd around the carousel grew heavier, and a middle-aged man fighting his way to the conveyor belt nudged Ben with his shoulder, looking back to give him a dirty look.

He took her hand and led her toward the exit. "Let's get out of here."

The cab dropped them off in front of Ben's hotel, where Sophia wanted to freshen up before going out. When she came out of the bathroom she said, "I look better now."

"I thought you looked beautiful before."

"You're such a romantic." It was fun watching her blush and look at her feet like a little girl.

She took his hand and they left the hotel. He took her to the Vatican, and they walked in the large open area of Saint Peter's Square, taking in the basilica and obelisk, Bernini's matching fountains, and the massive colonnade circling the grounds. Over a hundred sculptures of saints, chiseled in dramatic gestures and dressed in flowing robes and shawls, crowned the colonnade. There was so much to see; even the cobbled ground was an extravagance of beauty.

Sophia smiled. "I feel lightheaded, there's so much to see. I could never leave Paris, but if I had to, I think I could live here." She walked in a circle, absorbing the encompassing grandeur. "I was here once, when I was a child. It has been too long."

Ben wished he could tell her about the work he had done in the cathedral, but he couldn't. Not yet. Perhaps one day. Where would he begin? He barely knew what he was doing himself. How could he explain it to someone without sounding like a complete lunatic?

I, uh, get injected with this Nano-serum stuff that I don't understand at all, then go stare at paintings all day, and then later, my mind gets read by a machine while I'm sleeping. Oh, and none of this is FDA or government approved.

Moreover, he could not risk angering Mr. Kalispell by breaking the nondisclosure agreements that he had signed. The risk of losing such a well-paying job—one that brought him to Rome and Paris, where he met Sophia Lorenz—was not worth taking. If it were not for the job, at this very moment he would be back at home rolling on the ground in a drunken stupor, instead of walking hand in hand with the most beautiful woman in all of France—all the while strolling the cobbled streets in one of the most stunning cities in the entire world. Life was good. The feeling of change, of sobriety and hope, was like cool water washing over his head, seeping into his brain, and coursing through his veins. Calm and clean.

Ben had spent an hour at the Internet bar at the hotel combing the web for the perfect restaurant to take Sophia for a romantic dinner. The numbers and choices were staggering. He read dozens of user reviews and scribbled down a few names before leaving for the airport. But now it didn't matter, because after a few glasses of wine along their walk, they settled on a rather nondescript place that hadn't come up at all on the Internet search.

A few small tables with flimsy wooden chairs lined the front of the fading and cracked stucco building. They sat outside enjoying a bottle of wine as the sun descended in the colorful evening sky. A waiter lit a candle on the table, and the small flame played tricks with the shadows, bouncing light about on the red-and-white checkered tablecloth. They both ordered pasta, and the food was presented on thick white plates. The pasta was fresh and doughy, slightly yellow from the semolina flour, tossed with olive oil, roasted garlic, and cracked black pepper. Shavings of salty Parmesan cheese and some rough-chopped parsley finished it off.

It was the best pasta Ben had ever tasted.

Sophia slowly twirled the pasta around her fork, using a spoon as a guide. "So," she said, "you promised to tell me more about yourself if I came to Rome. And here I am."

Ben's cheeks flushed. He had been waiting for this. It was not right stringing her along, but at the same time, he had to be very careful about what he told her.

"It's … hard to explain," he said.

"I gathered that much."

He took a deep breath. "Basically, I get paid to look at art. When it comes down to it, that's what I do."

"What, for like school or something?"

"Not exactly. I really can't give any details without getting in trouble. What I can tell you is this: I'm testing something, an invention of sorts.

The man who's funding the project sent me to Paris, and now here, to Rome."

"Sounds interesting." There was hesitancy in her voice. Anxiety? Fear? Ben thought he could read her mind: *Sounds illegal,* she was probably thinking; or, *Sounds dangerous.*

"To tell you the truth …" he did not want to say this, and should not say this, but he did, "I don't really know what I'm doing."

An emotion escaped. It was unplanned, and three seconds earlier, the feeling was not there at all. It was evident in the wavering tone of his voice; it was not just the topic of his recent work that made the anguish inside him bubble to the surface. Suddenly, the clarity of his recent life flashed before his eyes: the drunken nights, his life alone, his years of taking experimental medications for money, the depression he never allowed himself to admit, and Emily … his Emily.

Being with Sophia, knowing that there was still hope in his life—someone he looked forward to seeing, and more importantly, having someone who looked forward to seeing him—was causing Ben to understand how melancholy his life had become. How near rock bottom he was.

He suddenly felt very close to tears.

"Ben." Sophia reached across the table and touched his hand. "Are you okay?"

"I'm fine, I'm fine," he choked.

Come on Ben, this isn't the time. Get yourself together. Stay in the moment. You're with a beautiful girl in a beautiful city—don't fall apart now.

"I'm fine." He looked up, smiling. Her face showed concern and her eyes were large. "Seriously, I'm fine. My life has had some … complications, but not anymore. Not since meeting you. I feel a surge of happiness when I'm around you that I haven't felt in years. Things are getting better."

"Oh, Benjamin." She was close to tears herself.

End the topic, Ben. For Christ sakes, end the topic.

"Look, I really can't tell you much about what I'm working on. We can discuss the specific pieces of artwork that I was sent to study, but that's about it. I'm under contract and not allowed to disclose anything about it. I promise to tell you more about my life, my past, everything—just not now. Look around; we're in Rome, eating pasta. Let's have some more wine, and save the sad stuff for another time. Okay?"

Sophia nodded, but she looked upset. "Just tell me … you're okay, right? You're not in any danger, are you?"

"No, Sophia I'm not in any danger. And, yes, I am okay. I've never been better in all of my life. I promise you that."

He squeezed her hand and she smiled.

"All right," she said. "No sad stuff during dinner."

They finished their plates, along with a bottle of wine, and Ben asked Sophia if she wanted dessert.

"I do." She smiled like an excited little girl, with her fingers to her lips, her brown eyes mischievous. "I saw a pâtisserie down the street."

Ben paid and they left. He let Sophia pick the desserts from the many trays of decadent little pastries—each bite-sized, and each just as much of a work of art as the city itself. The shop smelled deeply of chocolate, powdered sugar, and warm sweets right out of the oven.

"Do you want to go to a park to eat them?"

"No," Sophia said. "Let's go back to your room."

Along the walk, Ben told Sophia about Emily. He did not elaborate on his years of sorrow after Emily's death. He did not have to explain. She got it. She understood. When they got close to the hotel Sophia said, "Thank you for telling me about her."

She squeezed Ben's hand.

They stopped for a quick glass of wine to change the subject and brighten the mood, and walked into the hotel entrance.

Ben felt slightly drunk as he shuffled down the hallway, and saw Iain Marcus standing wearily before the door to his room removing the electronic card-key from his wallet. He knew Iain had a long conference call with Mr. Kalispell that day, and his eyes looked deep in their sockets, and red.

"Hello, Ben," Iain said.

"Iain, you remember Sophia, right? We met at the airport."

"Um, yes, I think I do. You were talking to someone, I remember."

"Hello, Iain," Sophia said from under Ben's arm.

Iain opened his door and stood as if waiting for something in the silence. "Goodnight, Ben." He closed the door behind him.

Ben unlocked his door and hurried inside.

"What a strange man," Sophia said. "He's rude."

"He's all business, not the chatty type."

They were happy to be in the air-conditioning. The dry-heat outside was pleasant, but being in a cool environment for a change was nice. They had been in the room for only a few minutes, opening a bottle of wine and pouring it into water glasses, when they started kissing on the bed. The lights were low and the mood was calm, but still, the pangs of sorrow and guilt were popping in Ben's heart like bubbles on water—some bubbles held pleasure, others held despair, and others held guilt. Yet he was overcome with desire, and his body moved despite his trepidation. His hands and legs were shaky, but if Sophia noticed, she didn't say anything.

After a few minutes of kissing, Ben's hands realized they worked—and touching, kissing, smelling, absorbing this girl, Sophia, in every physical sense, was all he desired. His arms gripped her tight and pulled her close as if their bodies would become one, meld together, and he felt her eagerly reciprocate.

His shirt came off, and she pushed him back on the bed with a soft touch. She slipped the shoulder bands of her dress off each shoulder, slowly, and the dress slid to the floor like a silk cloth falling in a breeze, gracing her curves as it fell. He stared upward, looking at her body framed in shadow, licking his lips, wanting to take a huge gulp from the glass of wine on the bedside table—but not daring to move.

She stood before him wearing nothing more than dark lacy lingerie, nearly transparent. Her stomach was flat and smooth, and he desperately wanted to touch her soft pale skin with his hands and feel the heat of her body against his. He realized she wore this lingerie for him—*just* for him. She must have put it on before she left Paris, or earlier when she freshened up. The thought made his heart race. He wanted to speak but couldn't. Slowly, she crawled on her knees over the mattress until she hovered above him, her long black hair circling his face and smelling so sweet, so incredibly sweet. He grabbed handfuls of it in his palms and squeezed it lightly.

***

They lay naked on the bed, a thin sheet barely covering their bodies. They sipped wine from the water glasses and picked from the box of desserts, feeding each other bites of the tiny pastries.

A great stress had lifted from Ben's chest. His body tingled: his head, his hands, his feet, and his mind. His whole body absorbed each breath that he breathed, bringing new life to the far regions of his mind and body, as if a million tiny galaxies inside him had just felt a warm breeze after decades of frozen nights.

"Are you okay?" She rubbed his hand, resting her head on his shoulder.

"Yes, Sophia," he looked at her. "I'm the best that I've been in a very, very, long time."

She smiled and he smiled, and they started kissing again. They made love a second time, moving with a degree of fierceness, wanting to see and experience each other's bodies in entirety. She was breathing deep and fast, in and out, exhaling warm breath on his neck as she squeezed him close to her, making the little hairs on his neck stand on end.

He felt like a teenager. He could do this all night.

God, how I've missed this. How I've missed having a person to hold, to feel their warmth against my skin.

***

All the days of planning, of scheduling, and booking the flight and waiting day after day—it all ended in a flash. Ben took Sophia to the airport, and they walked hand in hand to the gate, waiting for her flight to be announced. Sophia motioned toward a bench and they sat, just like when they had first met, only this time she rested her head on his shoulder, and their hands folded together at the fingers. Her eyes were closed. Ben sat in comfortable silence, tired and wishing desperately they were still in bed, fooling around under the sheets and sleeping together under the same warm blanket, body against body.

When the flight began boarding, he nudged her awake and they stood, yawning and stretching.

Her eyes were puffy with sleep and wine, and she was holding back tears.

"I don't want to go," she said.

"I don't want you to go."

"Call me when you get back to the States."

"Call me tonight when you land in Paris."

She smiled. "I will."

They kissed. Ben wanted to roll around on the floor with her right then and there, but she stepped away and joined the line. He waited and watched, and right before she disappeared down the long corridor, she turned and waved. He smiled and waved back.

Chapter 12

Ben woke with a start.

The mattress was wet beneath him, and the sheets were plastered to his body like plastic wrap.

Since returning from Italy the week before, his dreams had been strange, intense, and uncontrollable. Not all of them, but many. In these mesmerizing dreams, the scenery and people all around him were disjointed and random.

One dream in particular stuck in his memory. Castles appeared on a street full of regular houses in a fairly suburban American town—real medieval castles—towering into the air at unrealistic heights, into the clouds. The walls were covered with carved statues and engraved with the writings of an indecipherable script, the likes of which belonged in a Tolkien fantasy.

These castles sprouted from the ground like weeds. A flock of enormous birds the size of dinosaurs blackened the sky, their wings the length of Mac Trucks. Battles erupted, raging down every street. Men wearing chainmail with axes and swords clashed with one another alongside modern soldiers in olive drab uniforms holding M16's and AK47's. Helicopters flew with the giant birds, and tanks rumbled over the streets. Castle walls exploded out and toppled over, raining down piles of rock and debris. Houses caught fire, blazing and spreading flames from one to the other. Ben stood in the dream, watching the events unfold, fearful for his life as explosions rang out and large men crushed each other with massive maces and war hammers.

And this was just one dream in many.

What bothered Ben—not just in this dream but in all of them—were the people he encountered. His imaginary society was full of random people and faces he came across at some time or another: a man on a bus ten years ago, a girl on a busy street playing on the sidewalk last month, an elderly gentleman driving a taxicab last week. Every face in every dream was one already seen in real life—a hypothesis Dr. Stuart Wright had shared with Ben many years ago.

A few of the people in these dreams reacted to his presence with fear and hostility. They shrieked and ran, cowered and hid. An old man came out of nowhere, running to attack Ben, then punching and kicking him, all the while wailing as if he had seen a ghost. His eyes were crazed, looking beyond Ben, focused on something far away. The pain from the attack was just as real and vivid as if it were happening in real life, and when Ben woke with a start, the places on his body where the man had struck him in the dream felt momentarily numb and throbbed with his pulse.

These people were out of his control, and their faces were not as blurry and forgettable as the countless other random characters in a normal dream. Their faces were crisp, features recognizable. Ben could have sworn that the old grey-haired man who attacked him was his downstairs neighbor, Mr. Levy. The dream was so real, so vivid, that when he passed Mr. Levy in the hall the next day he felt uncomfortable, as if Mr. Levy shared the same dream—their minds meeting in some astral field, and that Mr. Levy was again going to scream and attack him—but the old man smiled his normal full-denture grin. Ben felt relieved.

That night, before waking in his sweat-soaked bed, Ben had another dream involving his grandmother. It was just like the first dream, only this time they were in his apartment, not her house. The boxed wine sat on the counter, flooding the floor with the red liquid—gallon upon gallon flowing from the open tap. Ben tried his best to close the spout, but it was impossible. The box stuck to the counter as if cemented there. His grandmother stood in the center of the room, not moving, yet she followed him with her eyes wherever he went. She shook her head in disappointment all the while, saying things like, "He would never approve, your father. He would never approve," and, "This is all your fault. I did my best, I tried my hardest."

It was nonsense, pure nonsense.

Ben peeled back the wet sheets. The clock on the side of the bed said 9:37. In two hours, Sophia would be home from work, and if he timed things right, he might get a chance to call her before leaving for the lab.

***

The driver opened Ben's door and he stepped out onto the gravel driveway. The tinted-windows in the back mislead what a beautiful day it was outside. He thanked the driver and started walking toward the lab.

This was the day Ben was going to demand some answers. It was time to see some of the test results and learn what was going on; if not for himself, then for Sophia—he owed her an explanation. He promised her that he was safe, and if he planned to stay on the project, he needed to be kept better informed.

The door to the lab suddenly opened, and Iain Marcus stepped outside, meeting Ben in the parking lot.

"Ben, how are you?" He extended his hand to shake.

"Good, Iain. Yourself?"

"Very good. Here, come with me. We're not going to the lab just yet."

Iain started to walk, waving him forward, while going up the driveway in the direction that Dr. Wulfric told Ben was the main house.

"Are we going to the house?"

"Just follow me."

The driveway curved through rolling hills and sandy soil covered with tall grasses, trees, and scraggly brush normally found near a beach. After a few twists, the path straightened, and the ground flattened to expose Stone Hollow Estate in all of its glory. The property was massive—acres of land, slightly wooded on either side of the sandy soil. Off in the distance, the ocean glimmered in the sunlight, stretching along the horizon straight as an arrow, and as far as the eye could see.

Directly before Ben was the house itself, similar to the lab in that the shingles were light blue and a portion of the facade used the same round stone veneer. The houses were similar in style and color; however, the proportion and size were nowhere in comparison. Five labs could fit in the main house, with room to spare.

Far to the left of the property, away from the house, Ben saw something bright yellow through the trees and bushes. Heavy machinery, maybe a dozen excavators, backhoes and tractors, sitting in rows with their engines idle. The land, almost twice as large as a football field, was stripped bare of trees and brush. The metal skeleton of a very large tent jutted out of the ground in a domed arch in the exact center of the clearing. Ben had seen similar tents when he drove past forts and army bases, typically hangers to house small aircraft. A bright white tarp would later be stretched over the metal frame, tight, like skin on bones.

"What's going on over there?" Ben asked.

"Mr. Kalispell is doing some work. This way."

Iain led Ben to the side of the house, to a small door hidden from the front. They entered a mudroom, quite similar to the one in the lab. A Persian rug ran the length of the room with glimmering old hardwood floors visible along the sides. They brushed their feet on a mat, and Iain opened the next door. A long hallway lay before them, lit along the way by colorful sconces, larger and casting more yellow than those in the lab. Ben followed Iain down the hallway, and they stopped before a great intricately carved wooden door—quite old, and held up by massive bronze hinges. The door would be fitting in an old Greek church, Ben thought. Iain put a key in the lock and turned the handle.

"After you, Ben." He opened the doors and stepped back.

Ben stepped inside a long and narrow room; the ceiling had to be two stories high and was vaulted in the center.

"My god," he said.

The room was an art gallery. The walls were lined on either side with paintings—*his* paintings—the very same paintings Ben had studied and spent countless hours focusing on with Dr. Wulfric. They were all there—

St. John the Baptist, Salvator Mundi, Evening Landscape with an Aqueduct, Baptism of Christ, the Raft of the Medusa—all of them; the list went on.

The room was dim and cool, with the lingering presence of oil paint and varnish in the air. Small overhead lights illuminated each painting individually, casting shadows over the dark hardwood floor and the plank benches in the center of the room.

A man stood at the far end of the gallery, his hands clasped behind his back as he studied the work of artist Martin Schongauer, a sketch of a man wearing a hat and gazing upward, which also happened to be the title of the piece: *Man in a Hat Gazing Upwards*. The man broke his concentration and began strolling toward Ben. He was older than Ben, in his fifties maybe, stocky and a little chubby around the waist, with graying blonde hair combed neatly to the side, cut as meticulously as Iain's. He wore a light-tan suit and a white button-down shirt open at the collar. A baby-blue silk handkerchief stuck out from the breast pocket. He stopped before Ben, smiling, and extended a hand.

"Mr. Walker, it is a pleasure to finally meet you. I'm Timothy Kalispell. I'm a huge fan of your work."

Ben followed Mr. Kalispell down the gallery, contemplating the art on the walls.

"I must apologize, Ben. You've been an employee of mine for some time now, and I haven't had the opportunity to formally introduce myself. I am truly sorry for that. I only just arrived in town today. I assure you, I've been following your progress with the greatest of interest and admiration. I could not be more enthusiastic with the results we are seeing. Dr. Wulfric and Mr. Marcus have kept me abreast of all developments."

"Thank you. It's a pleasure to finally meet you as well. I understand that you're a very busy man. Are these paintings … are they, I mean, where did they come from?"

"All of these paintings, these masterpieces …" He looked up, his hands wide, gesturing at the room as a whole. "These paintings—they came from you, Ben. I'll explain, but please, let me show you my gallery. I understand that this is all very strange, and I am sure you have a myriad of questions, but trust me, before the day is done you will have a clear understanding as to why I've had you examine all of these masterpieces, and why you were selected to do it. Now, there's a lot to see, so come. Follow me, and please, take your time. Enjoy these wonderful pieces of art. They wouldn't be here if not for you."

Ben was desperate to cast a volley of questions at Mr. Kalispell—like, how was this possible? Why are you doing this? But he just nodded, remained silent, and followed Mr. Kalispell, whose eyes trailed each piece of art adoringly in turn, his hands clasped behind his back again.

"As you've probably guessed, I'm a bit of an art enthusiast," he chuckled. "For years I've been collecting the rarest pieces of art that I could get my hands on, no matter the cost. However, the majority of art in the world can not be bought, no matter how much money you are willing to spend. They belong to galleries; they belong to the public, and will never be available for sale. Never.

I could easily find another artist to reproduce these paintings, and in the end I would have a collection of amazing reproductions—near exact copies. But that is all they would ever be—reproductions and nothing more. Forgeries.

"I assure you, the work you've done is not merely replicating a few pieces of art; *it is creating the originals a second time*—as close to the originals as humanly possible. Your mind, your dreams—you're capable of memorizing these paintings in such unbelievable detail that every shade is correct; each brush stroke is exact, as though from the hands of the masters themselves. With the help of Lucy, we can transfer copies of the images in your mind to a digital format. Yes, in the end they are only reproductions, but they are extraordinary reproductions. This gallery has been a way for me to fulfill my love of the arts, all the while further testing Lucy. This might be considered overkill for most, but not for me. As you've probably been told, I am a bit of an eccentric. However, human advancement cannot further progress if not for eccentrics like me. And Lucy is just that: an advancement for all of mankind."

"Is this …" Ben leaned in close to *The Baptism of Christ*. "This is real paint."

"Yes, and each and every brush stroke matches the original down to the smallest of detail."

"How—"

"I'll get to that later. This machine, Lucy, has such amazing potential that the applications are nearly limitless. Every psychologist in the world will get a glimpse into the mind of their patients, get an accurate depiction of their suffering—sufferings the patients themselves may not be fully aware of. The inner depths of a serial killer's mind will be analyzed in ways never before thought possible. Being able to explore a person's dreams—their deepest and most intimate and coveted thoughts—is on the verge of becoming a reality. Completely new fields of science will be introduced and their mysteries unlocked. Secrets of the human mind will play out before our very eyes, and answers to questions we never thought possible will be assembled like jigsaw puzzles. This, Ben—all of this art—is research. Amazing research. And it's all thanks to you."

"It's-it's incredible. I don't understand how it's possible."

"Follow me."

They stopped before the *Raft of the Medusa*, the painting Ben was quite fond when he stood before it in the Louvre. After hours studying every inch, every detail, he thought he would never again be able to enjoy it like he once had; but now he could see it in a new light. Ben remembered every inch by heart—every crest of paint, jagged edge, swirl of shadow, and clean brush stroke. This reproduction was a flawless copy of the original.

"Come with me, Ben." Mr. Kalispell led Ben to the far end of the room, to a second set of double doors. "As you can see, most of the walls are still blank." He waved his hand in the air. "There's a lot of work still to be done." Mr. Kalispell opened the doors and let Ben walk through. Iain Marcus stayed a few steps behind, locking the first set of doors behind him.

Ben stood in the room. "I'll be damned," he said.

"It's a work in progress, but you can see where it's going." Mr. Kalispell's face beamed. "This room used to be a greenhouse. The glass walls have been replaced, and the measurements done to exacting proportions."

Large floodlights filled the room, tilting upward to the walls and ceiling. Canvas sheets covered the floor and scaffolding ran along the far wall, extending from floor to ceiling. The room was barren, but it was clear to Ben what was being constructed: the room was an exact duplicate of the Sistine Chapel. Behind the scaffolding, small sections of the altarpiece were already in place. Ben could see a portion of the image of Christ high in the air. He walked closer. At the base sat a dozen ceramic tiles, neatly arranged, each maybe a half-inch thick and three-feet square. Each tile was painted with a different section of the altarpiece, so that they would fit together like a puzzle once mortared to the wall. He looked at the already finished portion high above him. It was flawless, beautiful—each tile fitting seamlessly with the others, so that it was impossible to tell that it had been assembled in sections. The bright floodlights illuminated the blues, whites, and flesh tones. The robes and clothes of the various saints, angels, and people were crisp greens, blues, and reds. The creased flayed skin of Saint Bartholomew hung from his clenched hand, his hair and hollow eye sockets dark against the brightly colored flesh.

My God, Ben thought. *To think that all I was going to ask was to see a portion of one of my dreams. This is so much more.*

"It's going to be a present for my wife. We'll be married for thirty years next November. We went to Rome on our honeymoon, and the Sistine Chapel was—and still is—a favorite of hers. I want to see her face light up like it did the first time she saw it."

"I can't … I don't have words. How?"

"I'm going to show you, Ben. I'm going to show you everything."

***

Dr. Wulfric joined Ben and Mr. Kalispell outside the lab, meeting them as they walked down the gravel driveway, stopping to shake hands. A moment later, Dr. Egan stepped outside with an unlit cigarette in his mouth.

"I didn't know you smoked," Ben said.

"I don't smoke. Don't tell my wife." He lit the cigarette and walked with the group as Mr. Kalispell led them to a door on the opposite side of the lab, in the rear. Iain Marcus opened the door for everyone to pass. The mudroom was the same as in the lab, only a row of smocks hung from hooks on the wall instead of lab coats. Mr. Kalispell opened the second door.

"After you."

Ben entered the large room. There was no second floor here, just one massive space from ground to ceiling. The concrete floor was soaked deeply with dark patches of motor oil and different colored splatters of paint. A noxious vapor cut through the air like gasoline and grease—both stinging Ben's nostrils and making his nose itch.

Dozens of various-sized tool chests, in fire engine red and dark grey, lined the sides of the room. Some had been wheeled out to stand beside thick worktables or alongside various unidentifiable pieces of machinery—motors with wires and tubes connected to metallic and greasy components that Ben could not begin to understand. Worktables were set in a 'U' shape around the room, with various gears and cogwheels piled in a haphazard, yet, somehow orderly manner. Stacks of sheet metal lay off to the left, some cut and some in the process of being welded, so that they yielded strange and jagged looking shapes. And in the rear of the room, on the far wall, Ben saw the large door, which connected to the lab. Dozens of time he'd stared at the opposite side of that door, guessing at what could possibly be on the other side—and now he was there, standing in the room.

In the far corner, tucked in an exposed alcove to the side, was a small kitchenette, where several men wearing stained jumpsuits sat around circular tables, holding cups of coffee and looking their way.

The main focus of the room wasn't any of this: it was the gigantic machine sitting in the very center of the U-shaped worktables.

"Ben, I would like to personally introduce you to one of our recent inventions." Mr. Kalispell led him to the machine. "I know you've been curious about what goes on in this room, and I'm happy to finally show you." He patted the slick, stainless steel side of the machine like the adoring owner of a pedigree horse. "We call this the Vitruvian Machine. Something the guys came up with. You know, like the *Vitruvian Man?*"

"Yeah, I got it."

The machine was constructed of two large metal blocks, one on top of the other. The top block was about the size of a Smart car, the bottom about double the size. Bolted to the front was a sizeable stainless steel table. A long robotic arm emerged from near the top, coiled slightly like a snake, yet leaning out precisely over the exact center of the table. The arm was thick and hefty, with different sized plastic tubes running the length. Ben counted five separate joints along the length of the arm, causing it to look fluid in its coiled pose. Attached to the end of the arm was a rectangular metal contraption, about the size of a shoebox—like those Emily used to store her boots.

Another long arm came straight out from the very top of the machine, arching to overlook the table. This arm was skinny and ridged, without any joints or gears. Additionally, two identical ridged arms jutted out from either side, arching slightly upward, so that they encompassed the table like a claw. The machine had various doors and openings in rectangular and square patterns, with blinking green and red LED lights indicating activity. Thick electrical cables and clear tubing ran from one area of the machine to another. Several high-speed cables trailed off from the back like a tail, connecting to various computer stations.

A man stood from the table in the kitchenette and put his coffee down. The other men stayed where they were. The man wore a stained black plastic apron from neck to knees over his jumpsuit—the type Ben remembered wearing in his high school chemistry class. The front of the man's apron was flecked with paint and patches of dark oil.

"Ben, let me introduce you to Bernard Richter."

The man extended a calloused hand, stained deeply with grease and paint. His grip was tight.

"Ahh, you must be Benjamin." Bernard spoke in a French accent, his words smooth like the purr of a cat. "It is a pleasure to finally meet you. It's as if we've been working together for some time now." The right side of

Bernard's lips moved as he spoke, and the left remained motionless, making his voice sound deep and slightly slurred. Ben wondered if Bernard had recovered from a stroke sometime in the past.

"It's nice to meet you," Ben said.

"I'm sure you would like to see the Vitruvian Machine in action." He gestured to the machine, his hand waving overhead like a symphony conductor.

"I … yes, I mean … sure. I'd love to see it, of course."

Bernard smiled, pushed his dark framed glasses up the bridge of his nose, and turned to the group of men around the table. "Jack, Stephen." He looked back to Ben with a finger raised as if to say 'one minute please.'

Two men rose from the kitchenette table, one going to a tall cabinet in the wall where he removed a rectangular blank canvas. The man nodded to Ben, smiling as he approached the stainless steel table in front of the machine. "Hello," he said. He secured the canvas with a set of custom-made vises. The other man took a seat at a desk behind the great machine, hidden from view. Ben peered around to see the man sitting before two computer monitors, rattling on a keyboard with such speed that there was no break in the sound of keys being struck. Taped to the back of the machine, about eye-level, was a paper copy of the *Vitruvian Man* by Leonardo da Vinci—the iconic sketch of a man standing inside a perfect circle with four legs and four arms. The paper was tattered and smudged, and a buildup of Scotch tape at the top showed how many times the paper had fallen and been reattached.

Then Ben heard the noise—the deep noises he had heard so many times from behind the wall of his bedroom in the lab: the hum of various motors, gears grinding, the rhythmic ticking of a cab-like timer, and random clicking and popping sounds. Only this time the sounds were much louder, much deeper, vibrating the soles of his feet through the ground.

The hairs on his arms stood on end.

The master robotic arm and hand came to life. It first went rigid, and then began to move in a circular fashion, slow and deliberate, each of the joints turning with a certain life-like grace. Then, quickly, it moved to the center of the canvas. The box-like hand held an array of natural bristle brushes—large, small, flat, fantailed, skinny, and thick—in a drum-like device hidden inside. Ben bent over the table and strained his eyes to watch closely. The heads of the brushes darted in and out from the bottom of the hand, at times moving with a slow grace, and other times in short, rapid mechanical jolts.

Bernard Richter fished a rubber band from his breast pocket, holding it in the corner of his lips as he pulled his long dark hair from his eyes.

"The machine is quite simple," he murmured, barely audible over the rumble of the machine.

Dr. Wulfric shot Bernard a look. "Please, Bernard."

"Well," Bernard cleared his throat, "maybe not simple, but it's easy to understand the basic principles. Whatever you want painted is transmitted to the machine by the computers, over there. The first Lucy was hardwired into the system, but the newer models rely on memory cards, or the data can be transferred via a USB cable from a laptop. We are not wireless yet, but that is something simple to add.

"These three skinny arms you see are sensors. They determine the exact shape and depth of the canvas, how the paint should be applied, and so-on-and-so-forth. There are many small sensors on the bottom of the master arm as well—the arm doing the actual painting. The sensors guide the arm to paint exactly what the computer has programmed. This machine will make an exact replica of the original. Not like a photocopier, but a complete three-dimensional replica with real paint and exacting brush strokes. It can mix colors precisely as it should—the exact shades and colors of the original—better than a human could ever replicate, and follow each brush stroke and crest in complete and accurate detail. It will never create a flawed painting. In fact, if the original in question already has flaws, damage done over the years, the machine can be programmed to either make the copy with the flaws and damage, or paint it how the original looked when it was first created. Imagine that—a copy of history's lost art, displayed how the artist first created it, how their hands moved over the blank canvas or sheet of paper to bring it to life. Can you imagine that?"

Ben's mouth opened but Bernard went on. "On the very top of the machine there is a door that opens to many small wells. We use a funnel to fill each well, or bladder, with different paints. There are over eighty wells as of today to incorporate the many different colors and paint mediums—oils, watercolors, acrylic, and even latex. Once the machine is programmed, it determines the various colors and shades that are needed and mixes the paint accordingly with the correct brushes to match. Many of the paints are mixed using the original pigments used by the masters hundreds of years ago. A process that is very labor intensive. Many artists mixed their paints from scratch, prior to the nineteenth century, and each brush stroke could be as unique as a thumbprint. Egg yolks were a common ingredient, as well as dried herbs, clays, ground minerals, and even insect shells. Lead was used as an additive—before people realized it was dangerous—as well as linseed oil."

Ben was leaning over, his face close to the table, watching the many brushes dart in and out of the robotic hand, painting with both the fluidity of a human hand and the precise rapid and rigid movements of a machine. It produced a whistling sound, like a songbird, from deep within its interior, in contrast to the harsh sounds Ben had grown familiar with. And then suddenly … it stopped.

A beeping noise came from the computer. The arm raised, circled like before, and contracted back to the coiled position. Ben looked up. It was over so quick that he never saw what the machine was painting on the canvas—not that he could see much behind the large master arm. Bernard stepped before him, blocking his view.

"We wanted to make you something to show our gratitude for all you have done. I don't know the significance of this, but according to Dr. Wulfric, it is something you hold very dear. I hope you like it." Bernard leaned over the table, releasing the canvas from the vises. Ben strained his neck trying to look over his shoulder.

"It's done?"

"Yes, it's done."

Bernard turned, holding the corners gingerly in his palms. "Be careful. It needs time to dry."

The painting was that of a cabin in the woods.

Ben knew it well.

***

Mr. Kalispell took Ben and Iain Marcus back toward the main house. A new path led them away from the gravel driveway in the direction of the excavation and the incomplete metal-framed tent. They walked in single file, as the path was nothing more than matted down tire tracks from the heavy excavators and equipment. Mr. Kalispell stopped at the end, opening his arms to present the open space.

"What do you think?"

"I'm not sure what I'm looking at."

The field was stripped down to bare earth and leveled off. If it were a football field, they would be standing in the end zone, right around the goal post. But the size of the leveled area was much larger than a singular football field. The metal frame in the center covered only a small fraction of the excavated space. The end of the field opened up to the sandy beaches and ocean beyond. Even from his distance, Ben could see the waves glimmering in the sun as they broke on the shore.

"I'll explain as we walk. I know this area is rough, so try to visualize what I tell you. Use your imagination."

They stepped out on the muddy soil.

"This, Ben, will be my garden, my greatest artistic achievement to date. We've taken the Vitruvian Machine to the next level. Well, maybe not the next level, but the next step of its evolution. What good is it to reproduce art if you are limited to one media? Once the walls of that tent are constructed, it will house a machine so advanced and gigantic in scale that even I have a hard time visualizing what it will look like once complete. It will be a machine capable of carving stone—pure stone—on a scale never before seen. It will cut and mold granite and marble boulders like butter, with the exact precision you witnessed the Vitruvian Machine painting oil masterpieces. These sculptures will be so large and exact that it would take an army of men *years* to reproduce them.

"I'm sure you're wondering, why build these machines? Why not use a 3-D printer? The answer is simple: these machines create the artwork just as the artists themselves first created them. They are not entirely unlike 3-D printers; only these machines use the same brushes, chisels, hammers, and paints, as the master artists had at their disposal centuries ago. These machines don't put the art together in layers, or cut the stone using lasers and modern tools; these machine will create the art the same way as the originals."

"Right, that makes sense." Ben had little idea what he was talking about, and had an even smaller idea what a 3-D printer was or how it worked.

"This, Ben, *this*, will be the most beautiful garden you will ever lay your eyes on … and it's going to require a massive amount of work. I'm presenting you, Ben, with a very large assignment: years of work—full time employment. A salary."

Ben stared, transfixed at the massive clearing. "Damn, I wasn't expecting this. I wasn't expecting any of this today. I need time to think."

"Of course. I know this is a lot to take in all at once, but stay with me. It's important that you become a full-time employee, a member of the team. Your job—the work you've done so far—is invaluable. That's why I felt it was time to show you everything. I want you to understand that you are part of something bigger, not just working a mindless job. Now, let me explain my plans for the garden." Mr. Kalispell stopped a quarter-ways into the massive field.

"I'm listening."

"Picture this area: a perfect rectangle, perfect angles, the length running from here to the water. It will be divided into three separate lanes, from one end to the other. The two strips of land dividing the plot into three will be impeccably gardened with trees, rocks, and all sorts of plants—you get the idea. The middle path will be the widest of the three, so that the paths on either side will be about the width of a single-lane road."

"I can see it."

"Of course, you would be able to cross back and forth between the three lanes. There will be pathways cut across, and arched bridges going over koi-fish ponds. Now, on the far walls to the left and right, there will be nearly hidden passageways cut out from the tall hedges. There will be circular trails in the woods leading to hidden alcoves, round clearings with stone benches around sculptures and fountains. The great fountains from Rome and Paris, the strange, umm ..." he cleared his throat, pronouncing the word precisely, "*Kin-dlif-resser-brunnen*, a statue in Bern, for example. These little fountains and statues will be hidden in niches, tucked into the trees. The small path will wind around until you are face to face with the art. Now, all along the main straight side paths will be some of the most famous pieces of sculpture in the entire world. The Caryatid Porch from the Acropolis, for example, will be displayed in all of its grandeur. The six columns, each chiseled to display a female form draped in loose tunic, will be life sized and as exact as the original."

Ben nodded. He knew what it looked like.

"*The Fontaine de Medicis*, from the Luxembourg Gardens; the *Horses of Saint Mark* and the *Tetrarchs* from Saint Mark's Basilica in Venice; the famous *David* in Florence—they will all be here, mixed in with the colorful flowers and trees and shrubs of the immaculate landscaping. These sculptures will be arranged along the paths, with benches and gazebos provided along the way to study and admire the art in leisure. Academics and artists from all over the world will pay good money to spend time on these grounds."

Ben looked from left to right. It was difficult imagining the layout with the ground so rough in its current state, but Ben could visualize it.

"Now, for the *piece de resistance*. Picture it as you stand here, Ben, with the ocean off in the horizon. In the center lane, you will see the famous obelisk from Paris's *Place de la Concorde* jutting out from the exact middle, pointing to the heavens above. Far behind the obelisk, visible from where we're standing, will be the *Arc de Triomphe*, in all of its grandeur. Now, in the far back, framing this entire garden will be the *Trevi Fountain* from

Rome. Have you ever seen the *Trevi Fountain*, Ben? Do you know what it looks like?"

"Um, yes. I mean, I think I do. I've never seen it in person, but I think I know what it looks like. It's the one with the horses, right?"

"The fountain is set before the *Palazzo Poli*, a palace—that is now a museum—that serves as a backdrop to the fountain. The wall of the palace will be created here, with its marvelous columns and window facades. And yes, there are horses in the fountain, along with the magnificent form of Oceanus with his long beard, standing on the oyster-like coral, and the two Tritons grappling with their horses in the very center. Aquamarine water will cascade down from the rock fountain to the large center bowl, bigger than many swimming pools, large enough to sail a small boat in. All of this will be illuminated at night, just as the original one is today, and framed by the ever-moving ocean in the background. There will be nothing to rival this garden anywhere, in the entire world. You would have to spend months—years—traveling around the globe to see all of these sculptures, and I'll have them all in one place. In one magnificent garden."

There was silence for a moment, just the squawking of seagulls overhead and the light sound of water far in the distance.

The words, '*You would have to spend months—years—traveling around the globe to see all of these sculptures,*' bounced around in Ben's brain. *Months of work. Years. At the rate they're paying me, that's what, like …* He couldn't do the math in his head. *A lot of money.*

"Ben, perhaps I am a bit crazy. Maybe I am as eccentric as everyone thinks." He seemed to be speaking to himself, facing the water. "But when art comes from a mind, a *human* mind, and in every way as exact as the original, it remains *human*, despite the fact that machines are producing it. The work still originates from a person's mind, a living and breathing human being. You, Ben, happen to be that person."

Mr. Kalispell turned back toward the house and Ben followed, the tilled soil underfoot was soft and spongy.

"So," he continued, "you might ask: what is the end result of all of this?"

"I, umm …" Ben faltered on the uneven ground and caught himself. "I don't have a clue."

"The end result isn't the garden at all, or my gallery. These are just hobbies, a byproduct of research. Profit is the goal. I would be a liar if I said it wasn't. Lucy is the product. We will sell the machine to nearly every hospital in the world. One day Lucy will be for sale in stores, for anyone to buy. As for the Vitruvian Machine, when Lucy goes public, we will let people produce renderings of their dreams … for a price of course. Whole pieces of art—masterpieces—will be created and contrived in an instant, and we will have the technology available to produce them.

"For centuries, artists have attributed their masterpieces to dreams, yet so much of our dreams remain shrouded in mystery, forgotten. Now, both artists and ordinary people will be able to record their compositions in full detail. We could have their art created, painted, framed, and delivered. Just think about it, Ben. Not only are we creating whole new fields of science, but also an entirely new genre of art will emerge. *Sleep art,* or something of that nature. Whole galleries will open, and best of all, the artists can be ordinary people, just like you and me. No professional experience required. And you, Ben, are our first artist."

Ben shook his head, trying to process the full extent of what Mr. Kalispell just told him.

"Hot damn," he said.

Chapter 13

Iain and Ben sat at a desk in the lab going over a contract page by page, with Iain explaining the finer points.

"For obvious reasons, the work we have done up to now will remain undisclosed." Iain kept his eyes on the papers before him. "Before today, you have never been an employee of Mr. Kalispell, Kalispell Industries, or any of its subsidiary enterprises, including but not limited to: Advanced Tomorrow LLC, East Coast Applications LLC, Kalispell Sporting Goods Inc., and Kalispell Property Management LLC. Involvement on this project begins upon completion of this contract, signed by both you and Mr. Timothy Kalispell's legal representative, which in this case is me. That is to say," Iain looked up at Ben from the papers, "none of the work you've previously done exists. It never happened."

"Right," Ben said, looking over a fairly standard liability sheet, picking out the words he understood. "I thought you said you weren't a lawyer?"

"I'm not." Iain tapped the edge of the papers together on the desk. "I'm a little bit of everything."

Iain offered Ben a salary of eighty thousand dollars a year with a guarantee of two years employment. The salary could be renegotiated at that point.

"How about a hundred thousand a year?"

"How about seventy?"

Ben smiled. "All right, how about eighty-five, and I'm thinking a share in Lucy. Ten percent of sales."

Iain left the room, dialing his phone. He returned a moment later.

"Your proposition has been turned down. A piece of the business is not negotiable. He offers you the same eighty thousand a year—however, he will offer you considerable stock options when Lucy goes public. You will be given ample notice to invest however much of your own money as you see fit. I will personally handle your account, keeping you informed of the market's conditions. My service is free of charge."

There was a silence as Ben deployed his 'staying quiet' technique, but after only a minute, he got the feeling Iain wouldn't crack.

I can quit the bar. I can tell Sophia that I work exclusively for Mr. Kalispell, and even if I can't tell her about Lucy, I can at least tell her that I'm making a salary.

"You got yourself a deal."

They shook hands and finished the paperwork, signing and initialing various pages.

Ben left Iain at the desk to organize his things and gave his attention to Dr. Wulfric and Dr. Egan, who were patiently waiting to perform a routine checkup of his vitals and take a blood sample. Over time, Ben had acclimated to the injections: they no longer bothered him, and that surprised him. After the first dozen or so times they drew blood or injected the serum into his veins, he no longer became lightheaded or sick. Not like before.

"So, how have you been feeling?" Dr. Wulfric asked while peering into Ben's eyes with his ophthalmoscope. "Any migraines, headaches, nausea?"

"No, not since Rome."

"How have you been sleeping? Any insomnia?"

"I've been sleeping fine—but there is one thing, actually. It's kind of strange."

"What is it?" Dr. Wulfric placed a stethoscope over Ben's chest. "Take a deep breath, in and out."

Ben inhaled deeply and exhaled. "It's my dreams," he said, and explained as best he could through several rounds of deep breaths. He explained the fearful people and the odd events that were out of his control and completely out of context with the dream itself. Dr. Wulfric listened, taking the stethoscope out of his ears and resting the earpieces around his neck. He leaned back stroking his beard.

"When you wake up, are you in any pain? Do you have any headaches, even dull ones?"

"No, nothing like that. It's strange, I feel like … I feel like I'm not in control."

"Have you been drinking?"

"Well, that's the thing. I really cut back. I haven't had more than a drink or two, tops, since before we went to Rome." As the words came out of his mouth, he seemed to register their meaning for the first time, feeling a mix of uncertainty and surprise.

Is that true?' he thought. *I had more than two drinks with Sophia, but I wasn't drunk. When was the last time …*

"That could very well be it, Ben. We don't discuss it often, but the fact that you remember your dreams at all with the amount of alcohol you consume is astonishing in its own right. Especially since you work nights and drink late. Alcohol blocks serotonin production and shortens the REM cycle. Once you begin abstaining from alcohol, after long periods of heavy drinking, it's not uncommon to begin experiencing certain degrees of delirium, hallucinations, an overproduction of serotonin, a rise in the body's core temperature, and an increase of cortisol—a hormone released by the adrenal gland. Having these intense dreams is not strange, nor uncommon; your body is leveling out, getting back in shape. Also, it could very well be the stress of work recently: the constant traveling, all the jobs. In addition, you did just experience a severe migraine. Your body and mind need some rest. We'll run some tests, but I don't think it's anything to be worried about. It is important, however, to be sure that your ability to dream lucidly hasn't been compromised."

Ben nodded. "I had this one dream in particular, twice now. The first time I dreamt it was the same night I had the migraine, in Italy, and then again on the flight home. I'm driving down a road late at night, somewhere with trees—lots of trees—like in the middle of a forest, and it's very dark.

The road is curvy and the weather is bad. The second time I had the dream, on the plane, I saw an old wooden town sign on the side of the road, nearly covered in weeds and vines. It was weathered, splintered, with the white paint peeling off. The headlights only hit it for a moment, but I saw Drapery Falls—"

"What's that?" Dr. Wulfric stammered, his posture straightening. "What was the name of the town?"

"Drapery Falls. Do you know it?"

"No, no, not that I'm aware. Go on, please."

"I meant to look it up, see if I've been there and don't remember. Anyway, the dream bounces around a bit. I'm walking through the town, Drapery Falls, the weather is misty and raining, and there isn't a person in sight. The town is like a ghost town. The next thing I know, I'm in some guy's room. He's looking up at me from the floor, wearing only his underwear, like I just woke him up. All the lights are out in his house, and I give him something I'm holding in my pocket. I know it sounds strange. It feels like I'm doing him a favor. My adrenaline's pumping, my heart is racing, and I feel nervous and jittery. My senses are very intense. I don't know how else to explain it."

"What do you give him?"

"I don't know. The dream cuts out before I take my hand out of my pocket, but I know it's for him, and I know it's important. I'm helping him in some way, I think. I don't know."

"Interesting. Is there anything else?"

"It cuts to me walking down the street again in the rain. Oh yeah, and I'm wearing a suit and an old-fashioned hat, like a gangster. It's strange. The dream, the details—they're just as real and vivid as any of my lucid dreams, and I was fully aware that I was sleeping as they played out, but I had no control. It was like I was watching it happen from someplace else."

"Do you remember anything else, anything at all?"

Ben shook his head. "No." He thought for a second. "No, that's it."

"Run it by me again in as much detail as possible. The way the streets look, any houses you see, any businesses—everything."

Ben did as he was asked, giving every last detail he could remember.

"Do you think there's something to it?"

"No," Dr. Wulfric shook his head. "No, not at all."

"Do you think these dreams are going to affect my work? Because, and I'm serious, I had no control during them."

"I don't, and I don't think it will do you any good stressing out over it. The best thing you can do is to forget all about it."

Just then, Ben heard a chair scrape on the floor behind him.

"Iain. I thought you left?"

"Just finishing the paperwork." He picked up his briefcase and walking toward the door.

"I want to run a few tests, Ben," Dr. Wulfric said. "Let's take a blood sample."

***

An hour later, Ben left the lab.

Iain watched Ben get into the idling limo waiting to drive him home. Iain sat in the driver seat of his own car, parked on the far side of the lab. The limo started moving, and Iain watched until the red taillights disappeared around a bend in the road. Once he was certain Ben was gone, he left his car and hurried back to the lab.

"Peter!" he shouted at Dr. Wulfric. "Was Lucy running the night he had the migraine, in Rome?"

Dr. Wulfric stood hunched over a computer screen. "Yes, it was running the entire trip. It was never turned off."

"Get it on the scree—"

"I'm doing it, Iain. That's what I'm doing."

The men hovered over a monitor at the control center behind the lumbering Lucy I.

"Where's Charles?" Iain looked about the room.

"He's upstairs eating dinner. All right, here we go. This is the night." He slowed the fast progression of images on the screen using a swivel-knob like that on a stereo system, called a jog and shuffle; only instead of adjusting volume, the shuttle knob controlled the rewind and fast forward speed. A blur of artwork from the Sistine Chapel along with various faces, people, and the all-too-familiar cabin in the woods, flashed before their eyes. Then came the image of headlights making sharp turns on a dark road.

"There, right there. Stop." Iain commanded.

Dr. Wulfric slowed the image to real time, and the video played out just as Ben explained it. They were looking out the front windshield of a moving car. Leather-gloved hands held the steering wheel, and the instrument panel radiated light in contrast to the darkness. The headlights illuminated pockets of mist that rolled over the car in thick waves. After a few minutes, a white sign became visible on the side of the road.

"Drapery Falls," Iain said.

"Is this … is this it?"

Iain didn't answer. They watched the video play out until the person on screen got to the front door of a building.

"Pause it, Peter."

The doctor did just that.

"I think you should leave the room."

Dr. Wulfric stood from his chair and moved across the room from the monitor. Iain sat, his eyes glued to the screen. Several minutes passed … then almost a half-hour. Iain stood, the legs of his chair scraping the floor beneath him

"Is this the only copy?"

"Yes," Dr. Wulfric answered from the far corner of the room.

"Did Charles see it?"

"No, I don't think so. We usually fast-forwarded through the nonsense to get to the artwork during the REM phase, about an hour in. It's like clockwork with Ben. The counter on the screen shows this dream began thirty minutes into his sleep. He must have entered REM early that night—there's no other way he could remember the dream as vividly as he does. I didn't watch any of the recordings from that night because he was having the migraine and wasn't focusing on the artwork, and I don't think

Charles watched it either. There wasn't a reason to watch it. I only saved this recording so that it could be studied later, since data during a migraine could be quite fascinating, especially—"

"How did he enter REM early, is that even possible?" Iain cut him off.

Dr. Wulfric went on to explain that a typical person enters REM an hour and a half into sleep, after the brain goes into the theta wave stages and enters the delta. "That's when people typically remember their dreams. In Ben's case, on an average night, he enters REM a full half an hour earlier than the average person."

Iain looked dubious, "So, how do we know he won't remember more?"

"We don't," Dr. Wulfric said. "Ben typically remembers only the REM portion of a dream, about an hour into his sleep. However, in Ben's case, he can enter REM almost immediately after falling asleep. He did a test once with Dr. Wright, years ago, when Ben trained his brain to reach REM quicker by changing his sleep cycle. In the first phase, he slept six hours during the night and took a single twenty-minute nap during the afternoon. During the second phase, he slept four-and-a-half hours during the night and then napped twice during the day, each nap twenty-minutes long. This continued over a month, until he was only taking six twenty-minute naps, and not sleeping longer during the night. Dr. Wright monitored him for several full days. The findings showed his brain went into REM only minutes after he shut his eyes, nearly bypassing the theta cycle completely.

"Strangely, he reported that he felt great the entire time, not tired and miserable as Dr. Wright expected, and performed quite well on cognitive functioning tests. Ben and I discussed this particular experiment a few times—he learned how to trick his brain into entering REM immediately after going to sleep. He does it often, when he wants to take a short nap. When his brain knows—or thinks it knows—it won't be sleeping for a long period, it enters REM much faster, as a defense mechanism. That way a twenty minute nap is actually a deep sleep."

"So … what are you saying?"

"We don't know what he will remember, because we don't know when he entered REM. The computer was not set up to measure brain wave frequencies and patterns."

"Great. That's fucking great. You let your personal feelings get in the way of your job once again, Peter. His brainwaves should have been monitored the entire time; *especially* since he was having a migraine."

Dr. Wulfric flushed. "Ben told us everything he remembers. As long as he doesn't have another dream, he shouldn't recall anything further."

"Find out for sure what Ben remembers, and tell me immediately if Charles saw anything." Iain ejected the memory card, sliding it into the inside pocket of his suit. "Wipe the hard copies from the computers. I have to make a phone call."

"Iain, this could be noth—"

"Damn it, Peter!" Iain could feel the heat from his face turning crimson as the words spit through clenched teeth. The veins around his neck pulsed in anger against the collar of his starched shirt. He turned away from Dr. Wulfric, dialing his phone.

Chapter 14

Ben persuaded Sophia to travel to Baltimore again, only this time she stayed at his apartment rather than at her sister's place. Not that she needed much persuasion. It was a long flight for a visit lasting only a few days, but there was excitement in these last minute arrangements, the kind of excitement only couples who have just started dating get to experience. Ben knew the day would come when these last minute trips—the long commutes—would become tiresome, inconvenient, and unfeasible; but until that day, the excitement they experienced when seeing each other, if only for a brief amount of time, was well worth the effort—not to mention the expense.

For now, Ben was in an oblivious state of contentment. So much so, that he did not notice the black Lincoln Town Car follow him from his apartment to the airport. He did not see the car park near him in the airport parking lot, or notice it when it tailed him back home. Later, neither Ben nor Sophia detected the car parked across the street from The Metro while they were having drinks, or witness the man behind the wheel snapping pictures of them with a large telephoto camera lens.

Mr. Kalispell liked to protect his interests. He protected them so well that he assembled a surveillance team to observe Ben, months earlier. A van was parked outside Ben's apartment day and night, monitoring not only Ben's movements and phone conversations, but everything: his past work with Dr. Wright, his internet browsing history, his bills and spending, even the stores where he bought groceries. The team assessed Ben's every move and concluded that Ben was not only a prime candidate for the job based on his abilities to control his dreams and his past, but because there was no indication of him ever becoming a threat. He lived a sullen life with no friends and no family, a part-time job that held little interest to him, and had a minor alcohol problem—a fairly boring individual living a fairly boring life. His phone never rang, he seldom made phone calls, and nobody ever came to his door.

He was a prime candidate, and after a few months of employment without consequence, the surveillance team was thinned out to a skeleton crew. There was not much to do anymore—no additional data to compile, no new phone lines to tap, or bank records to hack. The fun stuff was over.

That was until they received the call—the dark Lincoln was on its way, and all hands were on deck. The team was back to work, full time.

***

The days flew by, and Benjamin Walker was back at the airport, walking Sophia to the international gate, and watching as she walked down the quiet corridor. He smiled and waved. She waved back, and then she was gone. He drove home, passing through "Maryland's Inner Death Circle," and found a parking spot less than a block from his front door. He walked past a dark van with no windows. A magnetic sign on the side said:

Mrs. Rose's Roses
New York, NY
Delivery 7 Days a Week

The black Lincoln drove past Ben and the van, going around the block and back toward the "Inner Death Circle." The driver, a middle-aged man in a tweed suit, spoke to the computer on the dashboard.

"Call Iain Marcus."

A robotic female voice repeated his commands; *"Dialing Iain Marcus. Is this correct?"*

"Yes."

"Just a moment please."

After a pause, a dial tone rang out from the car speakers.

"Hello?"

"Iain, it's me."

"Where are you? How's everything going?"

"Not good, I'm on my way back. Call a meeting."

***

Iain Marcus walked down the barren hallway on the second floor of Mr. Kalispell's estate in Stone Hollow to a door at the far end. He walked with urgency, the handle of his briefcase slippery with perspiration. He stopped before the solid mahogany door, closed his eyes, and took a deep breath.

He knocked.

"Come in, Iain," came a voice.

Iain opened the door, blinking away the darkness of the room, letting his eyes adjust. The middle-aged man wearing the tweed suit sat on a plush, brown leather sofa to the right of the room. The man looked neat and tidy, as he always presented himself. His suit jacket parted around the midsection, and Iain noticed the man's stomach resting over his belt, stretching the buttons of his white shirt.

He's getting soft with age, Iain thought. *And he's aged significantly the last several years.*

He nodded to the man.

"Hello, Michael," Iain said.

"Hello, Iain."

"Iain, take a seat," came a voice from behind the desk in the far rear of the room. The chair swiveled, revealing a man wearing a suit nearly as dark as Iain's. It had been a while since Iain last saw him, and the man had barely aged. His black hair was slicked back, as always, yet the sides of his head were now winged with grey streaks. That was new. He looked even more distinguished than he already was—if that were at all possible.

"Yes, sir, Mr. Kalispell." Iain took a seat in a matching brown leather sofa across from Michael. "Sorry to keep you waiting."

"Not at all." Mr. Kalispell leaned back in his chair, hands clasped at his midsection. "Your partner and I had a few things to discuss."

Iain nodded to Michael Bennet, the man in the light tweed suit, and then looked back at Mr. Kalispell. "We won't keep you waiting any longer."

Iain and his partner, Michael Bennet, put their briefcases on the coffee table between them and removed file folders, all carefully organized and labeled with multicolored tabs.

"I've been informed," Mr. Kalispell announced, "that we have a situation on our hands."

He paused, and Iain felt the words sink in. Iain and Michael stopped what they were doing and looked up.

"Yes, sir," Iain said.

"If this is anything like Drapery Falls …" Mr. Kalispell shook his head. "It better not be anything liked Drapery Falls." He was staring at Michael.

Michael swallowed. "Mr. Kalispell, we're assessing—"

"Start at the beginning. Let's start with Ben. What's going on with him?"

Michael removed a crisp black and white photograph from a manila envelope and stood to hand it to Mr. Kalispell across his desk. "This, sir, is Sophia Lorenz." Mr. Kalispell studied the photograph that Michael had taken at the Charles de Gaulle Airport. It clearly showed a lovely young woman sitting beside Benjamin Walker in the airport terminal, her head turned to him in conversation. A few long strands of her straight black hair had fallen over her face, and she wore a genuine smile of happiness. Michael handed Mr. Kalispell several additional images and files, explaining each in turn.

"These, sir, were taken in Rome. This whole file is from Baltimore, and this file is from Paris, before Ben met Sophia at the airport." He put the stack of photos on the desk before Mr. Kalispell. "And this," he cleared his throat, "was taken yesterday."

"This is troubling." Mr. Kalispell said.

Michael nodded. "We have full audio from Ben's phone conversations on the dates he called her—"

"Play them."

Michael went to the media center at the side of the room. A stereo, TV, speakers, and other various communication devices were carefully arranged on built-in mahogany shelving. He inserted a disk in the CD player and hit play. Mr. Kalispell inspected the numerous photographs and files before him as he listened to the recording, not issuing a word until the recording ran through.

"Has any of this—the recordings, the photographs—has any of it been altered in any way?"

"No sir."

"Michael, did Ben believe that you were me when you showed him the house?"

"Yes, sir."

"Good. Let's keep it that way. It's best if he doesn't know my identity."

No one knows your identity, Iain thought. *You never leave your offices, or even open a window.*

Mr. Kalispell arranged the photographs, and put them back in the envelope. "Iain, play the tape. Drapery Falls."

There was a moment of hesitation. Then, Iain went to the media center with a thumb drive in the palm of his hand. He inserted the drive in a USB port, and after a moment, the television screen came to life. He stepped aside, holding his palms behind his back, and the three men watched the silent images on the screen come to life in the dark room. From inside the office, with the fabric curtains drawn, it was impossible to know the temperature outside was nearly eighty-five degrees with sunny skies. Iain felt he stepped into some vortex whenever he was in Mr. Kalispell's office, where the outside world, time, and nature, did not exist. The office was cold, dark, and sterile—always—and nothing moved or flourished.

The video ran its length, and Iain removed the drive.

"Is this accurate Iain?" Mr. Kalispell asked.

"Yes, sir. Extremely accurate."

"Is there anyone else—and I mean *anyone*—who could possibly know what happened in Drapery Falls, other than yourselves and Peter Wulfric?"

Iain was taken aback. "No sir, of course not. Not a soul."

"Good." Mr. Kalispell sighed. "Get ahold of Peter right away, and figure out how the hell this happened." He swiveled in his chair, facing a large window on the wall behind him that would normally display the ocean in spectacular grandeur, only dark curtains kept the view at bay.

"Is this the only copy?"

"Yes, sir."

"Destroy it. Better yet, put it on my desk. I'll destroy it. Keep things normal with Ben until you talk to Peter. When are you going back to MoMA? Next week?"

"In three days."

Mr. Kalispell rested his chin on a palm, keeping his back to the men. After a moment of silence, during which Michael and Iain exchanged nervous glances, Mr. Kalispell began to speak.

"This project hit a major snag in Drapery Falls. Things did *not* go as expected, or as instructed. I believe that I specified there were not to be any, and I meant *any,* problems this time around. We have to take care of this with swift resolution. Do I make myself clear?"

Iain and Michael's eyes focused on their boss. "Yes, sir," they said in unison.

"Michael. Am I crystal clear?"

"Yes, sir. Crystal clear." Michael was starting to sweat. Iain glance at him and then look away.

Mr. Kalispell sighed, still facing the curtained window as he began speaking:

"I would like to share a few things with you, since we're all friends here. Are we not friends, Michael?"

Iain and Michael exchanged hurried glances, and then turned back to Mr. Kalispell. "Yes, sir." Michael swallowed a lump in this throat. "We're friends, sir."

"Good. That's good, Michael. Now … let's chat. When my father began Kalispell Industries, before I was even born, he longed for the day when his children would grow up and work for the company, to one day succeed him. It was his recipe for immortality. The way he could live forever was through this company. He would become a portrait on the wall for the following generations to admire, and never forget. Naturally, he became understandably agitated when I, his oldest son, declared that I wanted to go to art school rather than follow in the family business. Typical teenage angst, maybe; at least, that is what I was told at the time. The idea was unfathomable to my parents. 'Hippie bullshit,' I believe my father said.

"Not having much in the way of artistic ability, and learning quickly that art school can only teach you so much if you are not already blessed with inherent talent, I longed to become a gallery director, or an art historian, something of that nature. I fantasized in my youth about one day running a major art gallery, a task I knew would never become a reality, but the fantasy gave me much pleasure back then. I was young and full of unrealistic ideals. My imagination was great and my resolve even greater.

"I held on to those unrealistic ideals for quite some time. It was only after seeing my parents' grief at my decisions that I relented and took business management classes at Stanford University. Not to mention that my brother's willingness to participate in the family business only fueled my competitive nature and made me quickly climb to the head of my class at Stanford, and later rise in the family business.

"All the while I yearned for the peace, the tranquility, and the unbelievable joy of spending hours—days, even—immersed in the world's greatest works of art and sculpture. I wanted to live in paintings and portraits, saturate myself, not spend a moment doing anything else. I made it my life's ambition to visit the world's most spectacular museums and artistic sights. I spent years studying abroad, from Cairo, to Britain, to Taipei, examining every brush stroke and chisel mark, in every museum I could find. There is such a depth in art that it seems incomprehensible to many people that such things can be devised by the hands of men. And yet, we humans *do* create such wonders.

"However, just visiting these places and seeing these masterpieces were not enough. My happiness waned considerably the farther I distanced myself from museums and galleries. So naturally, I began collecting. It has been a great source of pleasure and relief for me. Walking in one of my galleries is like taking my daily medication—it *is* my medication. And where Lucy is concerned, I'm currently blending my newest business venture with my own private interest, as you both already know—creating a sort of bridge between the two.

"So here we are now, at a crossroad along that bridge—and what is there to do? Losing my newfound capability to reproduce art is not something I take lightly. I would be losing my supply of medication, and believe me … I'm a much nicer man when I'm on my medicine."

There was a pause. In the silence, Iain thought Mr. Kalispell had finished speaking, but he did not dare speak himself.

Mr. Kalispell continued. "Losing Lucy, losing the Vitruvian Machine, well, that would be disastrous. Unthinkable. Unfathomable. Impossible. After all this time, all this time and money spent researching, exploring the boundaries of human law and nature, and going well beyond those limits … well, that is something we can't simply walk away from.

"I hope you two understand the importance of the task I gave you. Kalispell Industries must produce Lucy. The company's name is at stake. The company my father began, and which my brother and I now run, it is my father's name; it is his legacy. It is my own name, and it will be my legacy. I will not see it tainted by failure. Lucy is the future of Kalispell Industries; it is what will live on long after all of us are dead.

"You are part of this, Iain, Michael. You helped create Lucy, and now you must help protect it. You must work very carefully; there is no room for doubt or error. Your decisions must be carefully thought-out and absolute. Iain, I give you and your men complete authority to do whatever is necessary to resolve this situation, no matter how it dirties your hands. I will wash them clean. We cannot afford to let this project come crashing down on us. All of our livelihoods are at stake. The production of Lucy is going to be a huge monetary gain not just for myself, but for you two as well. I assure you."

He paused and the air grew still.

"That will be all."

Iain and Michael stacked the papers and folders, and snapped the clasps of their briefcases shut. They left Mr. Kalispell's office without uttering a word or making a sound, closing the door behind them. Halfway down the hallway, Michael let out a sigh and Iain put a finger between his neck and collar.

"You look pale," Iain said. *Not to mention fat. Soft.*

"I wasn't expecting this—another incident, another setback. Everything was going great this time."

Iain forced a nervous laugh. "We'll figure it out, Mike. We did before. We always do. Things could be worse."

"Yeah, we could be back in Afghanistan."

"Come on now, this is nothing like Afghanistan, Michael. This may be worse."

Chapter 15

"Why do you have two of the same painting?" Sophia held the unframed painting of the cabin in the woods, raising it up to the identical copy that hung from the wall.

Ben didn't feel like explaining.

"They look identical."

Ben was in the kitchen, opening a bottle of wine and unwrapping a piece of incredibly soft Camembert cheese that Sophia had snuck in her baggage. Sophia knew Emily's story as well as Ben could tell it, and occasionally Ben was open to discussing it further. Today was not one of those days. Sophia knew the subject was painful, so she never pushed the conversation.

"It's, a … Emily painted it. Many years ago."

He came out of the kitchen holding two glasses of wine.

Sophia stood next to the painting, her hair tied high in the back, and for a moment it was not black but brown and curly. Her long thin body turned curvy around the hips. He saw Emily standing there with her back to him, looking at the painting, holding it up by the edges of the frame. They were back in the studio, his old house and life. She stood from her stool, the painting complete, and Ben at the doorway. She didn't hear him, she didn't see him, and he stood there watching her as she gazed upon her finished painting, holding it up to the light. Then he shifted, leaned his body against the doorframe, and made a noise. Her paint-freckled face turned, startled …

"*Emily ...*" Wine circled in the glasses, jumping out over rims.

"What?" Sophia turned and her face was hers, Sophia Lorenz. Her hair was straight and black, her body thin and delicate, and they were in his apartment in Fells Point, Maryland. Ben shook his head. He put the glasses on the coffee table and went to get a napkin.

"What? Nothing. I'm sorry. Emily painted that years ago."

Sophia looked at the painting on the wall, then at the other in her hands.

"They are so identical," Sophia whispered to herself. "Why—*how*—did she paint it twice?"

She put the copy down.

"It's very good," she said.

Despite their plans to travel while Sophia was visiting—go to Manhattan, or see the shore at Ocean City—they spent most of their time in Ben's apartment, drinking wine and talking and laughing.

The days flew by, and before Ben knew it, he was back at the airport. He stood at the terminal, watching her off, waving as she disappeared toward her gate. He was grateful at having just spent a few days with her, but felt deep reluctance to see her go.

***

He parallel parked on his street, again not noticing that the dark Lincoln Town Car, which had tailed him the entire time Sophia visited, was now passing him as he walked toward his door. The delivery van he'd seen parked on the block dozens of times, for months now, was parked right before his apartment. Rose's Roses, or something. Catchy. He didn't give it a second thought.

He climbed the stairs to his apartment and opened a bottle of whiskey once inside. That feeling arose in him, the numb pleasure that could only be achieved through alcohol and dwelling on the past. That feeling of both pleasure and pain that felt so damn good. Ben sipped the whiskey and his body flushed, sending warmth coursing through his veins, pulsating pleasure from his stomach to the corners of his body.

No matter how detrimental this sort of behavior was, drinking and dwelling on the past was Ben's way to relieve his immediate pain and suffering. He knew it was unhealthy and addictive, but it felt great to wallow and cry. It numbed the pain and made him feel both better and worse. Stopping the experience was unfathomable. No matter how many mornings he woke up hung-over, promising himself, *No more booze. From here on out, I'll never touch the stuff again. I'll stop dwelling on Emily,* he would only stay sober for a day, maybe two. He could not stop torturing himself with memories both real and imagined. It was a temporary cure for a long-term illness, and it prevented him from healing properly. It kept his wounds fresh and painful, and that was something Ben found hard to admit.

In one gulp he finished the glass and poured another.

After some time, he stood from the couch and walked to the painting. A light wind blew from the open window nearby, moving the thin curtains rhythmically. The breeze felt cool on his skin.

There it was. The cabin. Same as the day it was painted. It would stand the test of time. It would exist longer than he, and perhaps one day end up in a yard sale—or maybe a dumpster—but it would still be intact long after he was dead.

The breeze blew over Ben's face, over the swirls of paint in the sky, the blues and oranges and yellows, the whites … and …

Wait …

The paint … it moved with the wind … the colors swayed and swirled with the breeze. The smoke from the chimney, brown and grey, rose in the sky to dissipate with the oranges and blues. The bushes and trees swayed, and the grass moved like waves in an ocean.

The painting—it was different. *How is it …?* Ben looked away, blinking rapidly. His hand twitched and a significant wave of whiskey splashed over the rim of the glass, falling over his fingers to the floor.

He looked back at the painting. The oils on the canvas swirled much faster now. The clouds rolled in the sky, bright and incredibly vibrant, as if he were watching a time-lapse video. Whites and blues swirled with oranges and reds. A turbulent world, despite the sunny blue sky. Ben stared, entranced, his mind becoming numb with radiant pleasure. His thoughts lost. He fixated as the swirling paint entranced him in hypnotic rapture …

… and then …

he …

… touched the painting—the canvas—his face only inches away, his finger just gracing the swirling sky. It was cool along the surface, and soft. The top layer rebounded at his touch, resistant, like the skin on pudding. He pushed harder, and his finger penetrated the soft skin of the paint, popping through, sinking to the first knuckle and then to the second.

The paint was warm underneath, another world entirely, and it swirled rhythmically over his hand, now up to the wrist and inching higher the more he pushed into it. His forearm, lost forever in the flowing sea of paint, his flesh and bones melting, becoming the paint, swaying and churning.

His mind went blank, stopped processing basic thoughts—or any thoughts at all. He felt numb pleasure and nothing else. He wanted to be inside the painting, enveloped by the warmth. The paint moved outward from the wall like something alive, cupped over his shoulder in a warm embrace, and guided him in. His other hand grew weak, and the glass of whiskey fell to the ground, shattering silently in a circle around his feet.

There was no noise.

The room was a void of reality and time. The image of the cabin stayed on the painting all the while, enlarging, stretching and contorting to engulf his body. Sunlight and clouds swirled together against the canvas of blue sky: oranges, whites, blues—always swirling, always changing—as it enveloped him. The paint guided him in, gently, reassuringly. It crept over his shoulder blade, stretching toward the square of his back like something alive. His nose touched the cool outer layer, slightly resistant like the skin on pudding about to break …

Wait …

A voice spoke to him from somewhere else: *This isn't real, Ben. This isn't real. Look around you.*

He pulled his nose off the warm outer layer of the paint and looked over his shoulder. The apartment was his, but the kitchen—it was larger than it should be … and the couch and lamps, they were different. Everything was hazy, as if a layer of steam sat heavy in the air.

I'm dreaming.

He looked back to the painting, next to his enveloped arm, the swirls so vivid and bright. The door of the cabin began to open an inch before the pupil of his right eye, making a creaking sound that broke the stillness of the room. He looked back and forth between the painting and the room, and each time the room behind him changed ever so slightly—the kitchen counter a different color and the walls shifting in size and proportion.

Than all at once, everything changed. He felt like he was on a rollercoaster, his stomach fluttering, his head spinning, his body going a hundred miles an hour just standing there. Blurs of color streaked by in circular arrays. He clenched his eyes shut. He wanted to scream, but the only sound he made was a quiet, *Hhhmphhh.*

And just as suddenly as it began, the sensation stopped. His mind and body went back to being stationary. He blinked his eyes open. The room was not his apartment anymore; it was the studio in his old house—Emily's studio. He blinked several times, fluttering his eyelids. His eyes were wet. The room stayed physically the same, yet was becoming brighter, more vibrant, with each passing second. The film of haze over his vision cleared, the steam in the room dissipated, and he could see the room as it was—as it is. A drop-cloth spread over the floor like a carpet, with Emily's easel at the very center. It was dark outside the wall-size windows, and the glass was black and reflective.

The painting still embraced Ben's arm, up to his shoulder, his hand departed to some other dimension. And then the world began to spin again in endless loops. His eyes fluttered closed, and when he opened them, he was laying on his back, the drop-cloth beneath him, and warm tears streaking down his face.

A person sat on his chest, laughed a muffled laugh while pinning his arms to the ground. The face was blurred beyond recognition—blank, like a thumb smeared over wet ink. But he knew her voice, could hear Emily's squeaky laughter behind her obscured words. The smudge of paint on his nose felt warm—hot even. He wanted to scream, "Emily! Emily!" But he couldn't speak, couldn't move, couldn't breathe. He felt his face contort unnaturally, the muscles twitching and flexing. *My god,* he thought, *I'm having a stroke … am I having a stroke?*

The blurry face came down, smearing burning hot paint on his cheeks and chin, and laughing, and he felt warm lips touch his own. Fireworks went off in his body, and his blood thumped fierce in his veins. *Where is my body, my real body? Am I twisted on the bed, choking on my blankets? Am I dying?*

Ben heard flowing water, then felt warm liquid on his feet, and then his legs, soaking through his pants, making his skin tingle. The liquid spread fast, covering his ears, creeping up his face.

He couldn't move.

Emily was still on top of him, laughing, and talking, but the words were jumbled beyond recognition. Ben could not turn his head, but in the corner of his eye, he saw his grandmother looming large above him, shaking her head, standing shin deep in a tidal pool of red water. The warm liquid was over his neck, over his stomach, up to his chin. It was touching his lips, tickling his nose.

"G-g-grandma!"

The liquid covered his lips, and his breathing became fast, nearing panic levels. It splashed in his nostrils and he huffed it out in horror. It covered his eyes, red as blood, and then it covered his face entirely. All Ben could see through the red haze was the outline of Emily, still playing around on top of him, still laughing and mumbling words. And then he couldn't see or hear anything at all. He held his breath, with his heart thrashing against his ribcage.

It might have been an eternity that he was submerged, drowning, and he could only hold his breath a second more. His lungs and head felt ready to burst.

Then he opened his mouth and the fluid raced down his throat, shooting down his esophagus. It was like breathing in broken glass.

Ben began twitching his head like he taught himself to do, and immediately the room around him vanished to absolute darkness, as if sucked away by a vacuum. He was still deep down, lost somewhere inside himself, and he continued to twitch his head. The horizon quickly became brighter, like a train coming out of a tunnel.

His eyes darted open. He was staring up at the slow moving ceiling fan blades going around and around above his bed.

Holy hell.

He sat on the edge of the bed. It was still dark, but the appearance of blue out the window suggested morning was near. His mattress was soaked with sweat, and the air was thick with the pungent smell of sleep.

Ben shuffled to the bathroom, flipped on the light, and urinated for a long time. Thick waves of delta were still being produced in Ben's brain, and he felt wobbly, almost hallucinatory. He stood over the sink and splashed handfuls of cold water over his face. His mind throbbed.

Jesus … what a dream.

The best thing to do, he thought, would be to go back to sleep. His eyes were so heavy that he saw floaters in his vision—little blue spots, sometimes white, that suddenly appeared, moved around, and then fizzled into thin air. The sun was nearly up, and the sweet morning air came filtering in through the blinds. Instead of going back to sleep, he made coffee. He walked over to the painting. He was afraid to look at it, but he did anyway. And there it was: the cabin in the woods. Snow was on the ground, and the paint remained solid and dry on the canvas, cracked in spots. Just like it should.

Relief washed over him; obviously, the painting was not going to come to life before his very eyes as it had in his dream.

The painting looked the same as always … except, Ben squinted, moving his face closer. He knew every square inch of that painting by heart—by memory; he could read it with his fingers like brail. That little white spot should not be there.

"Sophia, you better not have smudged—"

Then there was another white spot and another, and they floated down the canvas. *It must be the floaters,* he thought, and closed his eyes. Occasionally—and especially when he was very tired—Ben got white floaters in his vision that streaked across his eyes, from the top going down, like bright shooting stars. Dr. Stuart Wright told him they were nothing to worry about, as long as they did not happen very often. It was not a torn retina or anything serious. This time, as he closed his eyes, they disappeared. But when he opened his eyes again, the white spots were still on the canvas.

It was snowing.

A wind blew. Ben could feel it against his face, but not from the window. It came from the painting. The air was frigid. His breath clouded as it neared the canvas, and little white flecks came trickling over the frame, blowing outward onto his face and skin, and melting away to little wet dots. The painting came fully to life before his eyes: the dry paints were now fluid and wet, swirling among each other to form a three-dimensional reality, just as in the dream.

I'm dreaming. It's happening again. Jesus, help me.

Ben twitched the back of his neck.

Nothing happened.

He did it again, harder, and it hurt. The painting still moved; the clouds passed in the sky, the smoke rose to the heavens from the chimney, grey and brown, with white and orange and blue and red and—

"Hello, Ben."

Ben startled, his nerves struck like lightning. The coffee spilled over the mug and burned his hand. The mug fell to the floor and shattered violently. He turned toward the voice. There was a person sitting comfortably on the couch with legs crossed high.

Chapter 16

Dr. Peter Wulfric sat at his desk until the evening turned to night. A small light illuminated the stacks of files piled in great heaps around him. He would soon put them all in cardboard boxes, and they would never be seen again.

However, at that moment, he did not feel like doing anything.

He needed some time to think.

His forehead throbbed as he massaged the bridge of his nose. This project—this experiment—that had consumed years of his life, was almost over. Soon Lucy would be complete, and he would reap the fame and wealth that accompanied a breakthrough of this magnitude.

He pictured himself several years younger, his beard just as long, but not quite as grey, working on this experiment that would grow to consume his entire life. It was then that Mr. Timothy Kalispell approached him, in his office at Johns Hopkins. The research Mr. Kalispell had done on him and his work was impressive. Mr. Kalispell knew all about Lucy, back when in it was still in its infancy, and the concept of tapping into a dream was just a hypothesis. He knew things very few people knew, and he understood the principles behind them well. The man was smart; there was no doubting that.

Not only did he know about the project, but he also knew that the university recently canceled its funding, deeming the project too risky. Johns Hopkins claimed that the serum, Nano in its early stages, was possibly hazardous and potentially lethal. Pure rubbish. They feared the project was crossing the line from science to fringe, and any misfortunes, injuries, or hazards, would affect the university's reputation. The official report stated that the project was canceled due to recent financial hardships, but everyone at the hospital, including Dr. Wulfric, knew the reasons were far different.

The board treated Dr. Wulfric as something of an eccentric. They viewed his ideas as far-fetched, dangerous, and perhaps immoral. Rumors spread through the university among the students, and Dr. Wulfric became known as the *reclusive mad scientist.* His long beard and ever-whitening hair only fed the stereotype, making him something of a legend on campus. Stories about him abounded. The most infamous, and ridiculous, rumor was that he lobotomized students while they were still alive and had a machine that could read the removed brain like a book.

The stories spread from student to student and class to class. The freshmen classes found the doctor particularly fascinating and could not wait to see the crazy scientist for themselves. To this day, a rumor remains that Dr. Wulfric still wanders the halls to carry out his cruel and fascinating experiments on randomly selected students in some forgotten wing of the school, unknown to the rest of the staff.

The university not only canceled the research, but also disassembled the Lucy team, reassigning everyone to various positions throughout the hospital and university. Dr. Wulfric was offered a lucrative, and as some would consider, an *agreeable,* position away from the laboratories. He was delegated the life of a professor, teaching Advanced Cognitive Sciences. It was at that very time, before he accepted this new job proposition, that Mr. Kalispell came into his life, offering him a way to continue research on Lucy, but this time with unrestricted support and nearly unlimited finances.

For many days, Dr. Wulfric contemplated the offer before making a decision. The board at Johns Hopkins left a rather unpleasant taste in his mouth. After years of developing a solid proposal, they finally accepted the project—only to shut it down when it was still in its infancy. Not only that, but Dr. Wulfric knew about the many rumors and the constant talk behind his back, not only by students but by the faculty as well. He left Johns Hopkins to disappear from the scientific community for good. The official record stated an *early retirement.*

Mr. Kalispell's first lab was much like the one Dr. Wulfric worked in now in the Hamptons, only the first lab was smaller. Now, years later, and in a different lab, he found himself in the same predicament he'd faced back then: sitting in front of a desk with piles of folders ready to be destroyed—countless hours of research and study, all to be thrown in the incinerator.

His personal anguish was beyond despair. There had to be another way. This could not have happened again. How could he fail? If only Mr. Kalispell would listen to reason. All he needed was another day, maybe two. He could fix this. At least, he thought he could, and if he couldn't, it was still worth a try. It was worth the risk, especially for Ben's sake.

There was no use arguing with Iain. When he came into the lab with orders to eradicate all research done over the last six months, Dr. Wulfric was devastated. He didn't speak, only nodded his head that he understood, and sat heavy in his chair. There was nothing he could do. Now, with all the piles of folders gathered on his desk there was only one thing left to do—burn it all.

Leave no trace ... just as before.

He failed. He had failed himself, and he had failed Ben.

The glow from the singular light on the desk cast shadows from the stacks of papers in long dark columns across the floor. He stared at the shadows for a while, working up the strength and courage to do what needed to be done. He rubbed the bridge of his nose as tears slowly fell from his eyes, one at a time, leaving dark splotches on the manila folder on the desk before him. The folder contained recent blood tests of Benjamin Walker, taken only a day ago. Dr. Wulfric wiped his eyes and found his reading glasses on his forehead. He opened the folder and looked over the pages. There was not much time before Iain, or even worse, Mr. Kalispell, would call to make sure the research was destroyed. No, there wasn't much time at all. But with the little time that he did have, Dr. Wulfric would have to focus, and look for something—anything—that would help him to dissuade these men from doing what they were about to do.

Chapter 17

Earlier that evening, Michael Bennet and Iain Marcus had rushed into the lab before leaving for Baltimore.

"Where's Charles Egan?" Iain asked Dr. Wulfric.

"He's not here. He's off today."

"Is there anyone else here, at the lab?"

"No, we're alone. Here, sit." Dr. Wulfric motioned to two chairs at the front of his desk and sat down himself. He rubbed the bridge of his nose with his thumb and pointer finger.

After a moment he said, "Let's get down to it."

Dr. Wulfric took a file from a stack of files on the edge of the desk and flipped it open.

He said, "We have a bit of a situation on our hands."

No shit, Iain thought.

"I've reanalyzed Ben's blood sample. I don't understand how the results I'm seeing are possible. The Nano, it can't work this way. It's just ... not possible."

"What is it Peter? Speak frankly." Iain's professionalism was wearing thin.

Dr. Wulfric paused a moment, closing his eyes to continue rubbing the bridge of his nose. "The nanoparticles, they're still alive in his blood. Rather, they are dying, but also replacing themselves. They are regenerating."

"Replacing themselves? How is that possible? He has not received an injection in over a week. The stuff lives for, what, twenty-four hours?"

"Twenty-four to thirty-six. It doesn't have a set parameter for its own demise, but rather dies off naturally. Some particles die before the others. However, it simply cannot survive for longer than thirty-six hours. It doesn't have the capability."

"So—"

"So … it has begun to replace itself. The Nano is reproducing in his body. It is adapting to its own, well, ecosystem, if you will. Ben's biological cells are coexisting with the nanoparticles, and they have formed a rather symbiotic relationship. It's reproducing much the same way as many single-celled organisms, a process called binary fission. Basically, each cell divides in two, grows, and then divides in two again. Even though the Nano is dying off, it is reproducing at a greater rate than its natural mortality; and although it is reproducing very slowly, slower than we would see with most bacteria, it is not dying off. The numbers are steadily increasing."

"Jeeesus," Michael let out.

"How is that possible?" Iain asked. "We designed it—*You*—designed it to leave the body, flush itself out completely, so no traces could ever be found. We learned our lesson with Etha—"

"I know, Iain."

Dr. Wulfric leaned across the desk. The saga of Ethan Moore was the saddest and most difficult chapter in Dr. Wulfric's entire career, the worst outcome that could ever happen as a byproduct of his scientific research. He screwed up badly, and the result wiped out an innocent man's existence. Ethan was a young man, only twenty-three. He was troubled, had no family or friends, was raised in foster care most of his life, and continually suffered with headaches and insomnia. It was Dr. Wulfric's fault that Iain and Michael visited Ethan's apartment all those years ago.

He screwed up the serum back then, and he did it again now.

But how—how did I make another mistake?

After the debacle with Ethan Moore, depression plagued Dr. Wulfric, and he announced his retirement—for real this time. Without any choice,

Mr. Kalispell scrapped the project. All that time and money wasted. The old lab was stripped, the documents burned, and his precious Nano serum poured down the drain.

Several years passed, and Dr. Wulfric was enjoying his retirement, alone, in a little house out in the woods, surrounded by nature. His dirt driveway never saw any visitors, until that one day, when Iain Marcus showed up unannounced. Dr. Wulfric heard the car bounce over the rolling potholes from where he was fishing at a shallow lake, only a stone's throw from his house. It was too early in the morning for the mail delivery truck. He felt a sense of dread.

Dr. Wulfric waited, staring out over the gentle lake's surface, shining back a million reflections of the sun, like the razor-sharp edges of a broken mirror. He turned to see a man in a dark suit walking toward him through the trees. "Iain. What are you doing here?"

"Peter, It's good to see you. How is everything? I see you're enjoying your retirement. It's pretty out here. Quiet."

Iain was smiling, but he stopped short of the lake by several feet. The hairs on Dr. Wulfric's body stood on end.

"Listen," Iain went on, "I'll get to the point. Mr. Kalispell sent me to talk to you. We're starting work on Lucy again and he wants you back on the team."

The doctor's eyes went wide. "After everything that happened? That's prepos—"

"He's not just asking, Peter."

"Iain … the work we did, all of the research. It's gone. We'd have to start from scratch. It would take a lifetime."

Iain shook his head. "Not exactly. Mr. Kalispell never destroyed the Lucy prototype, and I kept backups of many of your files. Lucy is safe and in working order. We're in the process of setting up a new lab."

"That was my work, Iain, years of my life!" Dr. Wulfric felt his blood boil. Lucy had been his obsession, his baby; it even cost him his career at Johns Hopkins. It changed him from a respected member of the scientific community, to someone the other professors—his colleagues—rolled their eyes at. His recent retirement gave him plenty of time to contemplate the choices he made, the mistakes with Lucy, and to accept the fact that he was now too old to change the outcome of his decisions.

"Mr. Kalispell ordered me to destroy all of the files and told me Lucy was going to be dismantled, melted down. He told me—"

"It's time you stop talking and start listening."

There was a moment of silence as Dr. Wulfric absorbed the gravity of Iain's words and demeanor. He looked at the ground.

"Lucy will resume with or without your help. The research is not yours—it belongs to Kalispell Industries. Lucy belongs to Mr. Kalispell, not you. If you come back, he is offering you all the time you need and unlimited finances. Your pay will be beyond adequate. There can be no mistakes this time around. You are being given the opportunity to finish the project you spent your life trying to perfect, and this time, we *will* finish Lucy."

"But Iain, what about Ethan?"

"What about him? That was the past, Peter; it's time to look to the future."

"I … don't think that I can."

"I advise you," Iain's voice lowered, stressing each word with emphasis, "to weigh your options … carefully. Mr. Kalispell not only has backups of the research, but enough paperwork tying you to Ethan Moore, and the Nano that you made back then—illegally."

"Iain … what are you saying?"

"What I'm saying," he took a step forward, shifting Dr. Wulfric closer to the water's edge, "is that you have an amazing job opportunity presented to you. And if you don't know exactly what I'm saying, then the best course of action would be to choose your next move wisely. You know what Mr. Kalispell is capable of."

Dr. Wulfric swallowed back words that were now lost to him. The gentle lapping of lake water against the bank cut through the silence as Dr. Wulfric weighed his options. There weren't many.

"Let's go inside," he finally muttered. "Let's go inside and figure this out."

Iain nodded, stepping aside. "After you."

After nearly an hour of negotiation, Dr. Wulfric agreed to once again lead the Lucy team. He was offered ample time to perfect his research, perfect the Nano. Nothing would be rushed. He would have time to correct any mistakes. He would be in complete control of the lab. His word was God.

After months tinkering with the serum with the help of his new assistant, Dr. Charles Egan—a genius he hand-picked—the Nano was finally perfected. With all the positive results, the doctor felt confident to restart human experimentation.

Now here he was, with Iain Marcus looming before him, just like that time in the woods.

Dr. Wulfric spoke, swallowing down the lump in his throat. "No one was as affected by what happened to Ethan Moore as much as me. No one."

Iain sighed, "Just tell us what's going on, Doctor."

Dr. Wulfric sighed. "The Nano is working with the neurons in his brain, interacting with the electrical output and signal they emit, especially in the pons and frontal lobe—"

"In English, Doctor. Please."

"The Nano in his system has infiltrated the circuitry of his brain, using it almost how we use a computer. It must have begun in Paris when the serum was slightly altered, but it was reproducing in such low numbers that it was easy to overlook. I reanalyzed a blood sample taken in Paris, one in Rome, and one from two days ago. The Nano transmitters from the injections in Rome recognized the Nano transmitters left in his body from Paris; it adjusted to the weaknesses of its outdated self and began growing stronger. The Nano in his body now is not the same as the Nano we've been injecting him with. It's mutated." He took a sip from a glass of water. "The Nano is programed to learn, to remember particular nuances in the circuitry of a subject's body and brain. But never was it programmed to learn from itself. The Nano is doing its job, and doing it well. Too well. It's evolving."

The color drained from Iain's face. "Is it contagious?"

"I … don't know. No, I don't think so. I have to further test it to be sure; introduce it to new hosts and different blood samples."

"There's no time for that." Iain looked like he was about to scream; the veins in his temples were throbbing with his pulse. "All right," he said, "so the serum is still in his body. How does he know what happened in Drapery Falls? His dream, it played as if through my eyes, what I saw, exactly how it went down. It's not possible."

Dr. Wulfric sighed. "Do you dream about that night often?"

"I … don't know." Iain felt his cheeks redden. "I guess I do. Occasionally."

"Occasionally, or often?"

"I guess often. Often enough."

"You must have dreamt about it that night in Rome, the night he got the migraine, and again on the return flight home. Do you remember dreaming about Drapery Falls either of those times?"

Iain shook his head. "No. I don't remember my dreams at all those nights."

"Well, I believe you must have. I believe that Ben's migraine in Italy was triggered by the quick reproduction and the changing nature of the Nano in his body. The mutated serum was able to achieve what we have been striving for—it picked up on the neurological activity of a person who had *not* been injected with the Nano. Your room in Rome was next to Ben's, and your seat on the return flight was right beside him. He received *your* dreams like a radio receiver picks up a signal within a certain range. It took itself to the next stage of it's own evolution."

"Jeeesus," Michael let out again.

Dr. Wulfric asked, "Did you sleep on the plane ride home?"

"Yes, I did." The color drained from Iain's face.

"The worst part," Dr. Wulfric sighed, "is that the Nano is not only picking up on Ben's neurological activity—it's becoming a part of it. He's beginning to experience dementia and mental instability because of it, and it may only get worse as the Nano continues to reproduce and evolve. The troubling part is that Ben's immune system should have flushed away the Nano from the very start. The Nano is designed to be recognized by the body as a low-level bacterium—a threat, like a common cold. Any Nano lingering twenty-four to thirty-six hours after injection is flushed out of the body by its natural defenses. For some reason, in Ben's case, his body is not fighting the Nano the way that it should. There's a block—something's blocking his immune system from working properly."

"Is it curable then? Can you cure it?" Michael asked.

"I … I don't know. I have to run more tests. I need to get Ben back in the lab. In time, maybe, yes. Almost certainly. All I have to do is find out why his immune system is failing." He paused. "I think we can all take a guess at what's causing that."

Iain dismissed Dr. Wulfric. "And while you're taking time to figure this out, he'll not only be experiencing severe mental instability from our experiments—illegal experiments, might I remind you—but could possibly be contagious with a blood-borne parasite, the Nano, or whatever it is now. He could also start remembering more about Drapery Falls at any given moment."

"Iain—"

"It's already there, in his brain. We saw it play back from his dream, all of it, not just what he told us. It could come to him at any time. Perhaps he'll remember that *you* were the one who filled the syringe with the toxic dose of heroin, along with whatever else you mixed in that concoction."

"I had to do it, Iain, and it will haunt me until the day—"

Iain put his hand up, waving Dr. Wulfric to be quiet as he took out his cell phone and dialed a number. He left it on speaker as it rang.

Dr. Wulfric went back to rubbing the bridge of his nose, very much wanting a large glass of scotch from the bottle he kept in the desk drawer, only a few inches from his knee.

A deep voice echoed out from the phone.

"Iain, what's going on?"

"Yes, Mr. Kalispell …" He did not know where to begin.

Chapter 18

Iain Marcus and Michael Bennet were close to the intersection of 295 and 40 at the Delaware Memorial Bridge. Iain called the surveillance team stationed outside Ben's apartment, leaving the call on speaker.

"Good evening. Rose's Roses."

"It's me. Have you heard anything?"

"No sir, Mr. Marcus, not since this afternoon."

"Has he left the apartment?"

"No sir, not that we're aware of. He's been silent all day. We're parked around the block with a clear line of sight to his car, and it hasn't moved. We heard some mumbling this morning, something about having a headache and wanting to lie down. There hasn't been any activity since. We presume he's sleeping."

Iain looked at Michael. He knew Michael could read the anger radiating from his eyes. He was furious at the incompetence of his surveillance team.

Presume ... Presume!

Someone should be watching the door at all times, and they should never answer 'not that we're aware of.' A simple *yes* or *no* is the only acceptable reply. But Iain bit his tongue. He would have to tolerate the unprofessionalism of his men, for now. He had no other choice; it was too late in the game to change the team.

"Did he talk to someone earlier? Was he on the phone, or was someone in his apartment with him?"

"No, sir; neither. He was mumbling. It was hard to make out. The shower turned on and off, a few doors opened and closed, and then he was mumbling, talking to himself. We could make out the comment about the headache, but that was it. Oh, and he dropped a glass of something hot, maybe coffee. We heard him shout like he was burned, and there was a crash. The audio from the microphone outside his window has deteriorated significantly since we were fully operational. We need to get in his apartment to run diagnostics. We could break a window again."

Iain rubbed his temples. "We were lucky that worked the first time. If he calls his landlord we'll be found out." Months earlier, the team had thrown a brick through Ben's window while he was at work. They showed up at his door early the next morning, wearing uniforms and carrying toolboxes, telling a very hung-over Ben that his landlord sent them to fix the window. The team did fix the window, as they said they would, but also installed a microphone in the high corner of the shade. "Besides," Iain continued, "do you even know how to repair a glass window? Mark Stevenson was on the team back then, and he did the actual repair work."

"I ... no sir."

Christ, he was lucky he wasn't paying these guys to think. "Don't do a fucking thing. Who's stationed outside the door?"

"No one sir, we haven't been given the order—"

"I gave you the order when I said we're back at fucking Status One. Do you not understand—" He stopped short and took a deep breath. "Station someone outside his door. Now. Call me immediately if you hear or see anything. When I give the order for the team to break down, do it at once. The truck has to be stripped and dismantled, and the team is to disperse. Understood?"

"Yes, sir."

Iain hung up without saying another word.

Michael sighed from the passenger seat and closed his eyes. Iain's old partner had really let himself go over the years. He had a tire around his belly, and his face was becoming wide at the neck. He was not the same soldier Iain had parachuted into Fallujah with in the dead of night, behind enemy lines and before the war had technically begun. Michael was old now—hell, Michael was old back when they were in Iraq—but he had really started showing his age the last few years.

The worst part, Iain thought, wasn't that Michael was gaining weight or showing his age; it was that he was beginning to form his own thoughts and ideas. That was something that could *not* be tolerated. In the services, orders were never questioned, and emotions were never displayed. They were like stones back then, rocks—silent and hard, emotionless and strong. They did what was asked, no questions, no complaints, no regrets.

He's becoming soft, Iain thought. *Not the hard man he used to be, and certainly not the same person he was two years ago.*

Drapery Falls changed him—that much was for sure. Drapery Falls made Michael question his actions. It made him feel regret and sympathy, feelings not allowed in his line of work. He'd seen Michael kill grown men over a dozen times. Iain himself had a tally of seventeen direct kills; many more indirect, from orders he'd given to his men. He once saw Michael slice the neck of a Taliban informant tied to a chair without the slightest hesitation or show of remorse. The informant was screaming, "I family, I father! I America!" His words echoed off the rock walls in that small cave. Michael walked to the man, grabbed the little hair left on his head, and slid the blade of his knife across the man's throat. Blood sprayed like water from a hose with a thumb pressed over it. They watched as the informant convulsed in the chair, gurgling and choking on his own blood, trying desperately to free his bound hands to grasp at the laceration that was quickly draining his life down the front of his chest.

Iain's experiences at war taught him that death was unfathomable to most, even to the hopelessly dying. Their eyes show their desperation—that look of shock, bewilderment, horror, and dread. Iain and Michael watched the man until he stopped twitching, and his eyes hazed over. Then they turned away as Michael cleaned his knife with a cloth torn off the man's filthy robes.

Michael killed that man because he had to do it. The interrogation was over, and they were at the point when the informant had to die—despite any promises made to the contrary. There was no other way, and Michael knew it. He carried out his job with unflinching resolve. There was no room for sympathy or remorse.

So why now? Why the sympathy? It didn't make sense.

When Iain watched the playback of Ben's dream, it struck such a personal chord that he felt lightheaded and nauseous. If Ben remembered the entire dream, and not just the small fragments he currently recalled, he would see Michael in the passenger seat of the car as it drove through the heavily wooded area outside of Drapery Falls, New York.

Iain remembered the events of that night as if they happened only yesterday, and they played out in Ben's dream exactly as Iain remembered.

Iain could see it all now: the headlights swerving along the dark road, illuminating the hazy rain, and the signpost on the side of the road reading Drapery Falls. Iain remembered parking behind Spaulding Grocers, the only grocery store in that shithole, one-gas-station town. The only thing in Drapery Falls that piqued any interest, the only reason Iain Marcus and Michael Bennet would ever visit such a piece-of-crap town, was because of Ethan Moore.

***

A younger Iain Marcus and Michael Bennet approached Drapery Falls in the dead of night.

He parked behind Spaulding Grocers and killed the engine. They would go the rest of the way on foot.

He asked Michael, "You ready?"

Michael nodded and stepped out of the car, clenching a black duffel bag in his hand. They tightened their jackets against the cold and the wind, as the light rain covered them from head to toe in a fine layer of mist.

It was almost three in the morning, late enough for the one pub in Drapery Falls to be long closed, and the patrons and staff home and in bed. Nothing stirred. No lights glowed behind shuttered windows. The only sound besides the wind was the rhythmic creaking of a wooden sign, shaped to resemble a giant tooth, swaying in a breeze outside Dr. Woodrow's Dental Practice.

Iain moved quickly toward the residential section of town, to the side street where Ethan Moore lived. He felt vulnerable out in the open, but driving any closer could have caused a stir in the peaceful community.

His hat protected his face from the rain, with the water building up to form small droplets on the rim that fell before his eyes. Michael stayed a few steps behind, both men silent and swift as dark ghosts as they entered the landing to Ethan's apartment building.

The door to the ground level was unlocked. Ethan lived on the second floor of the four-room complex, and the men crossed the entryway to the staircase in the back, trailing droplets of rainwater behind. They stopped before apartment 19C. Michael put his thumb over the peephole of the apartment opposite—19D—and Iain went to work picking the lock to Ethan's door. After no time at all, the small tools found the right pins and the handle turned free. Iain put the tools in his pocket and removed the pistol from the holster under his arm.

He carried a Sig Sauer Mosquito because of its small size and hoped he would not have to use it. Guns were messy. He removed the silencer from the inside pocket of his coat and twisted it onto the barrel.

Iain slid into the room, followed by Michael. They shut the door, locking it behind them, and moved quickly, scoping out the dark room. The living room and kitchenette were empty, and the bathroom was cold and silent. Michael positioned himself next to the windows in the living room, watching the street below for movement as Iain slipped into the bedroom.

Ethan must have heard a noise, or maybe he was awake before they entered, because when Iain stepped into the doorway, Ethan was watching. The room smelled of sweat and sleep, and the air was stagnant.

"Iain." Ethan threw the blankets off his body. The boy was quick, not trying to bypass Iain at the door, but rather leaped for the window on the far side of the room. But Iain was a trained soldier. He darted with one large step and grabbed Ethan's arm with his left hand and yanked him backward, hard. Ethan collapsed over his own feet and sat kneeling on the ground, naked except for his underwear, and at the mercy of Iain Marcus.

"Iain, listen … I made a mistake." Iain loomed over Ethan, black as night in the shadowy room. Droplets of rain fell from his jacket to form a dark circle around him on the carpeted floor. Iain noticed Ethan's gaze jump from his eyes to the silhouette of the pistol in his gloved hand.

Ethan looked back to Iain's face. Fear, sleep, and uncertainty, emanated from deep within Ethan's eyes. He was sweating all over, and Iain could smell the ripe smell of fear and adrenaline wafting in the air.

Before Ethan had a chance to speak again, Iain leaned forward and pressed the palm of his left hand over Ethan's face, covering his mouth and pushing him backward against the floor.

Ethan was making sounds like, *"Hmmmpphh,"* and as Iain predicted, Ethan's hands came up to grab at his wrist, trying to pry his palm away from his airway. Iain slipped the pistol into his pocket, and when he took his hand back out, he was holding a thin syringe. He removed the plastic cap with a flick of his thumb and pointer finger and injected the needle into Ethan's left arm, right below his bicep. He pushed the fluid into Ethan's vein before the boy realized what was happening.

The entire motion was flawless. Ethan's eyes went wide, and his muscles twitched and slackened. His grip on Iain's wrist loosened, and Iain watched as the boy's eyes fluttered upward and his eyelids shut. Ethan's underwear darkened as he wet himself.

Iain dragged Ethan back to the bed and covered his body before he soiled himself further.

"Michael," Iain hissed, looking into the living room where Michael remained at the window, gripping his own silenced pistol—a Sig Sauer just like Iain's—in one hand and the duffel bag in the other. When Iain whispered, "Clear," Michael holstered his pistol, and they both waited patiently in complete silence, listening for movement in the neighboring apartments, but there was no noise to be heard.

Then Michael opened the duffel bag, and they went to work. Iain made additional puncture wounds in Ethan's arm, in the veins in the hollow of his elbow, and several in the webbing between his toes. They planted syringes throughout the apartment, and stuffed empty baggies laced with heroin in the coffee table drawers, and in the garbage next to his bed. One bag, half-full, was left open on the bedside table along with a twisted and burnt spoon and a used syringe.

All of this was just in case the fire did not erase things properly.

They located the shoebox Ethan kept hidden under a loose floorboard—the box stuffed to the brim with thousands of dollars in cash, paid to him by Mr. Kalispell for his work with Lucy. They emptied the cash into the duffel bag. That amount of cash would certainly raise eyebrows at the precinct if found, and Ethan's death might be further investigated.

They used plastic spray-bottles, used for houseplants, to spray the drapes, the floor, the bedding, the cabinets, the kitchen counter, and the walls, with a thin mist of gasoline. Iain removed the batteries from the smoke detector, replacing them with duds. Michael went to the kitchen, put a frying pan on the stove, and cracked an egg inside. He lit the stove as Iain placed an empty pizza box only inches from the flame, and stacked several newspapers from Ethan's recycling bin precariously close to the pizza box and all along the kitchen counter. They made a sort of trail of flammable materials, from the counter to the furniture, to the drapes, to Ethan's bed, where they sprayed the carpet and mattress with gasoline, and stacked books from Ethan's bookshelf under the bed. They were sure to only use a fine mist of gasoline, to lessen the risk of the fire being determined as arson.

The last thing Iain saw as they left the apartment was a dark trail of smoke emanating from the edge of the cardboard pizza box.

Walking fast down the street, Iain turned only once at the end of the block to see the faint orange glow of fire illuminating the otherwise dark windows of Ethan's living room. He thought he could vaguely hear a fire alarm going off in one of the neighboring apartments. The fire was spreading faster than anticipated. Iain even thought he felt a rush of warm air, but that was most likely just a figment of his imagination.

The entire complex would be ablaze before the fire department in that shithole town could scramble together a truck. Still, though, the neighbors should be waking up soon and calling the police.

They quickened their pace.

Iain and Michael got back to the car just as a foghorn blared, so deep that it seemed to vibrate the thick fog in the air. They would be out of Drapery Falls before a fire truck left the station.

The story made local papers, but did not spread much further. All four apartments in the complex were destroyed. A couple on the first floor woke up when their own fire alarms began beeping and called the police once their children were outside. The husband received minor wounds attempting to rescue the elderly man who lived in the apartment across the hall. The old man died several hours later at the neighboring Twin Falls Hospital due to smoke inhalation. The fourth apartment, the one across from Ethan's—19D—was vacant.

The police found, among the wreckage in Ethan's apartment, two charred and half-melted spoons with their long ends twisted back, crusted with heroin residue. Two melted hypodermic needles were also found. The headlines in the papers read:

Drugs Involved in Deadly Apartment Blaze

A black and white photo underneath showed the burnt shell of the apartment building as emergency crews packed up their gear. Smoke still lingered in the air and the ground was still wet with the water that doused the flames.

Guilt never aroused in Iain. Ethan had an opportunity to make a lot of money, just like Ben. The Nano serum was still in its infancy, and Ethan began to experience serious side effects to his health after only three months of trials. Instead of working with the team to alleviate his distress, Ethan got greedy. He threatened to go public if certain demands were not met. He wanted money—a lot of money. Mr. Kalispell paid. He gave Ethan tens of thousands of dollars, but that wasn't enough. Ethan wanted more. He wanted every penny he could squeeze out of Mr. Kalispell and Kalispell Industries—he wanted everything.

The day after Ethan received his bribe—and promised to remain silent—he made a phone call to a lawyer. When the phone-tap on Ethan's phone registered the number as belonging to a law firm, the call was redirected to a team member who answered, 'Law office of Marshal and Byrne. How can I help you?' The call was then transferred to Michael Bennett, who did a fantastic job of impersonating a lawyer. Michael listened and talked to Ethan as he rambled on about the tests, the serum, the Nano, the lab, names and places—everything. He was going to expose it all, with no regret.

He had to be stopped.

Ethan made that call at 2:52 in the afternoon, and at three o'clock the following morning, Iain and Michael arrived in Drapery Falls in the fog and the rain.

Iain felt that the old man who died of smoke inhalation was just part of the risk, an unfortunate collateral death. Iain could live with himself. Innocent casualties were an unfortunate part of the job—serving the greater good.

However, Iain noticed upon reading the headlines the next day that Michael was very quiet, and as the days progressed, Michael's demeanor grew grim.

Chapter 19

"Hello Bennie."

"Jesus!" Ben shouted. Shards of shattered ceramic and steaming-hot coffee encircled his feet.

He closed his eyes and jerked his head, harder and harder, the blood in his veins pumping so fast he saw red around the periphery of his vision.

Wake up Ben. Wake up!

"Stop that, Ben. You look silly. You're not sleeping. Come, sit." She patted the seat beside her.

"Emma ... Emily?" His mouth fell open. "No, no, no ... what's going on?"

"Come, Ben. Sit down."

She was wearing that black dress with the red fabric belt in the middle that tied in the back. That dress fit her body like a glove, so snug, showing her curves just right. It rode above her knees when she sat with her legs crossed, showing just a glimpse of her cream-white thighs, and those stilettos on her feet that made her look so classy.

"Emma ..." A shiver went down his spine.

He walked in a trance to the couch and sat. The air around her was fragrant of Dolce and Gabbana, *Pour Femme Eau de Parfum*. He found an empty bottle of that same perfume mixed in with a box of his toiletries when he moved to Baltimore. He spent countless nights removing the red rectangular cap and placing his nose to the spray nozzle, breathing in the last traces of that sweet perfume. He shattered the bottle in a fit of drunken rage one night many nights ago, and wished to God he had never done so. This was the first time he smelled the perfume since that night, and the fragrance flooded him with memories.

"Emily …"

He started to cry. She touched his hand, and a jolt, like electricity, went straight to his heart. He spent entire days, weeks, dreaming of her touch, hundreds of lucid dreams embraced in her arms, but this was different, this was real. He could feel the warmth coming off her body, feel the softness of her hands—those amazing hands of hers—those hands that created whole worlds on canvas with nothing more than a few brushes and a dozen or so different colored paints.

"I missed you, Bennie."

"Emily, I miss you so much. Oh my god, how I've missed you! My Emma." He hugged her and their embrace was long and warm. He cried a stream of tears into her shoulder as she stroked back his hair. "Now, now, Ben. Now, now."

She straightened up, and they parted, holding hands, their legs touching at the thigh.

"We have to talk."

"This can't be real. I'm dreaming—I must be dreaming." Ben closed his eyes, lowering his face into his palm, letting the tears fall through the cracks of his fingers. "This isn't fair! This isn't fair!"

"Ben, look at me."

He didn't look up.

"Look at me, Bennie. Feel my hand. Can you hear my voice?"

Ben looked at her, squinting through his tears into her clear eyes. He nodded.

"You're not dreaming. You know you're awake, Ben. You know this isn't a dream. Am I wrong?"

Ben shook his head. This wasn't a dream.

"I'm as real as you need me to be, and right now you need me to be real. I'm going to help you."

"I don't understand. Help me with what? Everything is finally going good for me, for the first time … since … I'm making money, Emma, good money. I'm out of the restaurant business, maybe for good. I have a … umm …"

"It's okay, Bennie. You can tell me."

Words wouldn't come.

"I'm serious; you can tell me about her. I won't be mad."

Ben looked into her face. She was smiling, her big eyes framed by those gently bouncing curls of hair resting on her shoulders. She looked even more beautiful than he remembered, if that was at all possible. He looked at the ground.

"I … met somebody."

"I know, Ben, and I'm happy for you."

"Her name is Sophia. Sophia Lorenz."

"Who is Sophia Lorenz?"

"I met her at the airport in Paris, and we've met up a few times. I'm so sorry. If I thought for a second that I might ever see you again—*ever*—I never would have—"

"I'm not mad, Ben. This isn't a confession. Like I said, I'm here to help you. Now, who is Sophia Lorenz?"

"She's … I met her in Paris, when she was flying out here, to Baltimore. I'm going to, well, I *was* going to fly to Paris next week. I don't know what you mean?"

"She doesn't ask you why you travel so much, what you do for a living, or who your travel companions are?"

"Well—no, she's asked a little. We've talked about it. I can't tell her much."

"Tell me, Ben, who else has met Sophia Lorenz? You're not thinking clearly, you're not focusing. Your mind is clouded. Think, Ben. Clear your mind. Who is Sophia Lorenz?"

"I …" He strained to understand what Emily was getting at. Who was Sophia? Did he know her in the past? Did she work for Mr. Kalispell? Should he be wary of her—could she be dangerous? He pictured them together in Rome, the two of them at dinner, and their date in Baltimore at Steaks & Capital. He saw her face, her smile, the glass of wine touch her lips. He saw it all clear as day. What was she getting at?

Emily reached out and brushed his sleep-matted hair from off his forehead.

And that was all it took.

Her touch sent a spark to his mind. A flash of white light went off in his brain and he saw it all—saw the bartender at Metro give him strange looks, and the waiter at Steaks & Capital sneer mockingly, asking if he wanted a doggie bag. He saw her glass of wine actually full at the bar, her plate not touched as they left the restaurant. He saw his arm around her as they walked drunkenly down the hallway in Rome, back to his room, passing Iain, who stared at him. He saw himself ordering every drink, every meal, paying for everything himself. He saw her empty barstool at Metro, and saw himself talking to an empty chair at Steaks & Capital. He saw his arm over nothing but air, stumbling through the hallway, drunk and alone, with Iain looking at him with tired and confused eyes. He saw himself sleeping on the plane ride back from Paris, an empty seat beside him.

"No, no, no, no, no." Ben shook his head back and forth. "It can't be! No, it can't!"

Emily whispered in his ear, "Sophia Lorenz does not exist. She's just a girl you met in an airport."

"This can't be possible. How, why?" Ben saw himself sitting on that very couch several weeks prior, contemplating whether to call her; and in a dreamlike state, he did. But he heard it now, the other end of the line. The flat tone of the phone receiver ringing in his ear as he talked to no one, and after a while the stale voice of the recorded operator, *"If you would like to make a call, please hang up and try again."*

But it was so real, he thought. *I heard her voice, felt her skin. Christ … we had sex. I felt her, I … thought I … felt her. Jesus Christ, what is going on in my head!*

Ben started weeping in his palms. His forehead was throbbing. Emily pulled him in, embracing his body.

"Shhh; it's okay, baby. I'm here now. I'm going to help you. Everything is going to be okay."

"Emma …"

"Now, stop crying."

"What's happening to me? This is … I mean, how are you here? How do you exist? How do I know that Sophia doesn't exist, if you don't either?"

"I exist because you need me to exist. Look, there's a lot going on in that head of yours, and I know you're confused, but you have to trust me. I am real—at least to you I am, and that's what's important. I'm sitting here right now talking to you."

"But … I'm talking to no one right now. I'm on the couch, talking to thin air. Oh my god—I've gone crazy. I *am* crazy! I have to call someone … I have to go to a hospital … I have to call Dr. Wul—"

"You can't call him. You can't trust him, or Iain Marcus, or any of them."

"I can trust Dr. Wulfric. He's a good man … he's my friend."

"No, Ben. He's not."

Ben looked at his hand. It was shaking, trembling, and his vision seemed to be getting bright.

"Emma, I don't know what to do. You're not real—"

Her face sharpened and she slapped him. His head twisted to the side and his cheek stung.

"Was that real enough?"

He rubbed his cheek, felt it throb in his palm, and thought he could taste a faint coppery tang of blood.

"I don't want you telling me that I don't exist! Is that what you want, Ben? Do you want me not to exist? Do you want me to leave? Would you rather have Sophia? Your imaginary girlfriend?"

"Emma, I …"

For just a second, just a fraction of a second, Ben wasn't talking to Emily. He was talking to no one, alone on the couch, staring at the cushion. "Emily!"

He blinked and she was back. "If you can see me, hear me, feel me and touch me, what else do you need? Your mind created me for a purpose, Ben. You're sick, and I can help you get better."

The pain in his cheek *was* real enough. He looked into her eyes, saw the lines of anger fade to sympathy. "I'm sorry, Emma. I didn't mean to upset you. Please don't go; don't leave me again. I can't lose you. Please, God, don't go …."

"Now, now, Bennie." She put his head on her lap, stroking the hair around his ear, as he curled up in a ball.

"I don't get it, I just don't understand. Why … why did I imagine Sophia? What's wrong with me? Why … am I crazy? Have I lost my mind?"

"You made her up because you've been poisoned. You've been poisoned for a long time, and have been hallucinating all the while. Dr. Wulfric poisoned you. That serum—the Nano—it will kill you, and nobody will care. Sophia—she will kill you. She is the poison working inside your mind. You're lucky you haven't been locked away in a psychiatric hospital already. You've been going out on dates with an imaginary girlfriend, sitting down to dinner talking to an empty chair, ordering full plates of food for no one."

"Oh God."

"It's okay now, Ben. It's okay. I'm here to help you. I *will* help you, but you have to trust me. You have to do what I tell you. Your mind brought me here. It brought me here to save you, to get the poison out of your system. I know how much you missed me, Bennie. I know how much pain you're in. I know it wasn't fair that I died, that I was taken from your life when we were young and needed each other the most. I know you need me. I'm back now, Ben, if you want me to be. If you trust me, I'll stay by your side. I'll never leave you again, we can be together for all eternity; we can stay in each other's arms forever. Do you trust me, Bennie?"

Ben looked into her eyes. His mind was tingling and numb. Bizarre rushes of pleasure swept through his body, similar to what he felt during his freakish dream of the cabin, when his fingers were slipping into the paint.

Like his mind was a blank slate, incapable of basic thought or reasoning, just floating along on a sea of pleasure.

He stared into her eyes and the rest of the world disappeared. They were alone in a galaxy floating somewhere far, far away. A few seconds went by, or maybe it was hours. Time was irrelevant—just a thing that passed like water in a stream, always moving, yet impossible to see in individual parts. It just drifted by.

Whatever part of Ben's mind that allowed him to see Emily, hear her voice, touch her skin, feel the heat coming off of her body—and see these things as real—was warping the rest of his mind to entertain the fact that she *was* real, that she *was* sitting on the couch beside him.

He was locked eye to eye with the love of his life, and they were together forever, mixing souls like swirls of paint on a canvas, blending to form different colors and shades.

"Yes …" The words passed through his lips in a breeze. "I trust you. I'll do whatever you say."

Tears still rolled down his cheeks, slower now. She wiped them away with her hand and stroked the hair around his ear.

"I'm … so … tired … I think I need to sleep. Just for a minute. I have a headache."

"Rest now, Ben; rest. We have a long journey ahead of us."

Chapter 20

Michael saw the sign for Fells Point.

They were close.

Michael closed his eyes. *What's brought us to this? Iain and I, we used to be the perfect team. I know that I've changed, but ... why hasn't he?*

For years, Iain and Michael operated like a well-oiled machine. It was hard to pinpoint exactly when Michael began to ponder the consequences of his actions, but thinking back on it now, he guessed that it all began around the time Kabul fell to the U.S. and NATO forces along with the Northern Alliance.

Iain Marcus and Michael Bennet had recently been transferred to U.S. Task Force 373, stationed in Kunduz, Northern Afghanistan. The task force's main objectives were to find and neutralize, or occasionally capture, high-profile opposition forces. They were assassins for the United States Military.

For years, the task force stayed out of the limelight, operating in secrecy and proving to be an effective and proficient unit. When an order came in and the target was given the green-light on the JPEL list—Joint Prioritized Effects List, the list of individuals chosen to be assassinated or captured— the team moved out, typically in the dead of night, transported by plane, Humvee, helicopter, or on foot.

Task Force 373 included soldiers from every spectrum of the armed forces, and the men were typically aged about ten years younger than

Michael and Iain. Boys, really—just kids. By 2007, Iain Marcus and Michael Bennet were safely the two oldest soldiers in all of Task Force 373.

Talks of discharge were already in the works, when one fateful night in June, an order came through to eradicate a commanding officer of the Taliban spotted just outside of Jalalabad.

The events that followed remain in Michael's thoughts as clear as day:

The team had made their way to the perimeter of the objective, in a desert valley outside of Jalalabad. All at once, the team stopped cold in their tracks. Someone had spotted them. A bright spotlight swept their position, and Michael could hear people shouting in Arabic. The team ducked for cover.

Michael didn't know which side made the first shot, but within moments, both sides were engaged in a firefight. Michael crouched behind a crude rock wall, which surrounded the ancient ruins of a farmhouse in that isolated valley. Without hesitation, he aimed his rifle and fired in the direction of the enemy soldiers. Bullet rounds kicked up dirt and shattered the rock wall around him to dust.

Air support was called in, and an AC-130 Spectra gunship strafed the enemy position, raining fire from the sky, obliterating the ground in huge plumes of sand, smoke, and rock that rose ten feet in the air before plummeting back down to the earth. When the air cleared, the team moved in. Most of the enemy soldiers were strewn about, dead in the valley or still dying. A few escaped with their lives, and some badly injured were unable to rise. The injured rolled in the dusty soil, yelling, crying, holding their wounds, and shouting in their native tongue. Blood was everywhere, sucked down into that unforgiving, greedy desert sand. The blood of whole armies would never be enough.

Michael quickly discovered that the men they fought were part of the Afghan police force. They were the good guys, and a terrible mistake had been made.

Iain and Michael were given leave of Task Force 373 as diplomats and generals tried in vain to suppress any information leaking to the public.

Iain and Michael were then employed by Blackwater—paid to do mercenary work in Iraq as the main U.S. forces secured the cities and towns. They guarded oil tanks and supply lines from insurgents. In the end, they were stationed at a small makeshift airport. Jet planes and personal aircraft carrying men wearing suits with large briefcases and satchel bags came and went at random intervals, day and night.

It was then that they first met Mr. Timothy Kalispell.

Mr. Kalispell arrived on a jet. He walked out on the tarmac wearing a full suit and tie, carrying only a briefcase and a small bag of luggage. The dusty air covered his dark suit the moment he stepped out on that sandy soil. Iain and Michael were ordered to escort Mr. Kalispell to Baghdad, along with a third Blackwater operative named Frederick Marshal, and a driver whose name Michael could not remember.

They met and shook hands. Mr. Kalispell asked Iain, "Are you in charge?"

"I'll be heading the team, sir."

Mr. Kalispell nodded, and they left.

Thirty miles outside Baghdad, Iain yelled, "Stop!"

The armored SUV skidded to a halt, kicking up a plume of sand and dust that wafted into the interior. Iain looked out the passenger window with a set of binoculars. After a moment, he said in a casual tone, "Hostiles, two o'clock."

The driver put the car in reverse and pressed down hard on the gas, billowing smoke and sand in the opposite direction. Seconds later, gunfire erupted from behind a small mound far out in the desert. The hostiles were nothing more than tiny specks of reflected light floating in a sea of rolling sand.

"Jesus Christ!" Mr. Kalispell shouted, clutching his briefcase to his chest.

"Stop the car! Stop! Stop!" Michael yelled, squatting in the trunk of the SUV, facing the rear. "Two hostiles, seven o'clock."

The driver hit the brakes and grabbed the microphone on the radio, speaking quickly to Command. Iain opened the car door and dropped to the ground, his chest against the sand. He leveled his rifle, squinting through the scope. Michael flipped open the rear window, propping his gun on the ledge of the door. Frederick Marshal grabbed Mr. Kalispell's shoulder in his calloused grip and pushed him down to the floor of the car, where he curled up in a ball.

Bullet fire from the enemy was now intense. Rounds hit the side of the armored SUV, making noises like, *'Plunk, Plunk,'* and leaving behind silver flower-pattern dents in the dark metal.

Iain and Michael kept their breathing steady and deep—in and out, in and out—and began squeezing off rounds. They breathed, focused, and pulled the trigger, firing one shot for every five shots that the enemy fired. They saw their targets drop or retreat behind desert mounds.

The gunfire ceased. The air was so silent that time itself seemed to stop. Iain remained on the ground, a cloud of dust engulfing his body, turning his hair a reddish-grey. Then he stood and got back in the SUV.

"We're ordered back by Command," the driver exclaimed, holding the squawking microphone. Iain nodded, and the driver put the car in gear.

"Wait, wait!" Mr. Kalispell gathered himself from the floor of the car. He patted down his disheveled hair and straightened his wrinkled suit jacket. "We're fifty miles out. Are there more soldiers out there? More terrorists? Are they gone?"

Iain looked at Michael who shrugged. "I don't know, sir. I dropped two, and a third ran off. There could be more. We have orders to return to base." He wanted to mention that the men who fired on them were most likely not terrorists, or even remainders of the Republican Guard. From their sporadic firing, they were most likely local civilians, untrained, and poorly armed.

"I'm not ..." Mr. Kalispell was breathing hard, gathering his words. "I have to go to Baghdad. Now. Not later. I have to attend a meeting that won't wait for me." The man looked Iain in the eyes. "Take me to Baghdad. Continue forward. We're more than halfway there; turning back won't be a safer option."

There was silence in the truck. Frederick shook his head. "Iain, I don't—"

"Continue to Baghdad." Iain turned to face forward.

"Sir?" the driver asked. "We have orders from—"

"You heard me. Move out. That's an order from me."

"Yes, sir."

They met with no additional violence that day. They arrived in Baghdad as planned and returned to the airport without any further problems.

Iain Marcus was in serious trouble for disobeying a direct order from Command. As soon as they returned to the airport, Iain was ordered to the debriefing room by his commanding officers.

As Iain was thoroughly debriefed in a small room that resembled a jail cell, Mr. Kalispell made some phone calls and was faxed over detailed reports on Iain Marcus, Michael Bennet, Frederick Marshal, and the driver. He studied the reports outside the debriefing room until the door opened and Iain came out.

"Sir." Iain nodded.

"Are you in trouble?"

Iain held back a nervous laugh. "I'm sure I am."

"I have to thank you for saving my life back there."

"No, sir, you don't."

"Yes, I do. And I need to thank you for doing what you did back there, for listening to me. You broke your superior officer's orders and took a risk, only because I asked you to do it."

Iain looked down. Mr. Kalispell could see the words written on Iain's face, clear as day. He was battered and tired, sick of orders, sick of the desert. He was done with warfare.

"I've read your file and I have to say, you've had a very interesting career with the United States Military. You started out in the 10th Mountain Division, is that correct? You and Michael Bennet have worked together since boot camp."

"I believe my file is confidential, sir."

"It is. And it's very impressive." He thought he saw a smile on Iain's face. "How would you like to get out of here? Out of Iraq, out of this godforsaken desert. I'm in need of some people back at home, sort of like … bodyguards, you could say. People in your line of work, with your expertise."

"I'm under contract, I—"

"Let's talk in private." Mr. Kalispell looked over his shoulders, making sure no one was around. "If you can spare a few minutes."

Iain nodded, and the men walked to an empty office.

Two hours later Mr. Kalispell made a number of calls, and Iain Marcus and Michael Bennet were boarding a Hawker 850XP, bound for New York.

Years had passed since then, and Iain and Michael were still working for Mr. Kalispell.

Michael opened his eyes.

Iain was parking the car, a block from Benjamin Walker's front door.

Chapter 21

Iain walked up the flight of stairs to Ben's apartment. It was eerily similar to Ethan's apartment back in Drapery Falls, only the interior and hallway in Ben's building was much brighter and newly renovated. It was not the dark, upstate New York piece-of-shit apartment where Ethan lived. Iain recalled the splintering hardwood floors and the single exposed light bulb in Ethan's hallway. The hallway leading to Ben's apartment was well-lit twenty-four hours, and streetlights illuminated the sidewalk outside. Yet, both Ethan's and Ben's apartments were in four-unit complexes, with two apartment downstairs and two apartments upstairs.

This time things would be different. Iain could not afford a single mistake. He was in the middle of Baltimore, not some small town like Drapery Falls, where no one in the world would hear about a small house fire and a few deaths. In Baltimore, the news would spread all throughout the city, possibly even to New York and New Jersey if the fire was large enough. A criminal probe would be extensive.

As head of the team, Iain would enter the apartment alone. He ordered Michael Bennet to take up position across the street, where he stood in a dark corner next to a doorway pretending to be doing something on his smartphone.

From where Michael stood, he could see the darkness emanate from the windows of Ben's living room and bedroom, and he sighed deeply, knowing that inside that apartment, an innocent man lay sleeping in bed without a clue as to what was about to happen. It was Drapery Falls all over again.

Iain adjusted the radio-transmitter in his ear, blowing into the microphone to test it. Michael blew into his, and Iain adjusted the volume accordingly.

Iain stepped through the doorway of Ben's complex and into the shared lobby, moving like a ghost to the staircase, and slipped up the stairs through the shadows. When he was one step from the top, he peeled off two small strips of electrical tape he'd pre-cut and stuck to his gloved hand, placing one over the peephole to Ben's door, and the other over his neighbor's door across the landing.

He placed the duffel bag on the ground and unzipped it, removing a shower cap for his head and two smaller ones for his shoes, stretching the elastic band over his ankles. He went to work picking the lock, and in just a matter of seconds, the handle turned freely. Iain removed his silenced Beretta M9 from the duffel bag and gently pulled back the slide to make sure a round was chambered. The fact that Ben was delusional—perhaps insane—made him dangerous, and Iain hoped he wouldn't have to use the pistol. If he had to, he wanted to make sure the bullet was lethal enough to do the job in one shot, maybe two. So he'd packed the M9 instead of the Sig Sauer. Using a gun would present a whole new set of problems. Disposing a body and erasing a crime scene in the middle of the city would not be an easy task.

Iain clutched the duffel bag and slid into the room, closing the door behind him and relocking it.

Outside, Michael watched for movement in the apartment windows and listened for footsteps nearby, but the area was calm, and nothing stirred behind the dark windows. He hoped that he would not see a flash coming from Ben's window, because that could only mean one thing—a gunshot. It was bad enough they had to exterminate the man, but if forced, he wanted it to be quick and painless. Iain was to slip in, find him sleeping, and inject him with the same narcotics they used with Ethan. No mistakes, no unnecessary fear, and hopefully, no struggle.

Michael sighed.

He did not want to be up there. Being directly involved with the murder was not something he wanted. He was glad Iain ordered him to stay outside. The seconds ticking away on his watch felt like hours, and his legs became restless. He was a soldier, a professional. He'd killed dozens of men in numerous wars and operations. He'd killed men who never saw him coming, with his own bare hands. But this was different. This was not war in any conventional sense; this was corporate war. Consumerism and money were the end-results, not freedom, or necessity. This was murder, plain and simple. There was no way around it. He wanted no part of it.

If he could, if there was any way he could stop this, he would. But he wasn't in charge. He was getting old, grey, and unfit; he shouldn't be involved with such messes any more. Mr. Kalispell had hired Michael to do recon under Iain—his superior officer in Iraq and Afghanistan. His job was to watch business rivals, people of interest, and gather information on them. Take pictures, break a law or two, but nothing as serious as murder. This whole Lucy business was going on for far too long now, and the toll it was taking was beyond appalling. This would be it, the end of the line. He would present his resignation once Lucy went public and disappear to someplace far away.

He had to be careful though, because Mr. Kalispell was not a man to be taken lightly. Michael couldn't be sure how much the man knew about his and Dr. Wulfric's past. That would present an entirely new set of problems.

But he couldn't think about those things now. He had to finish this operation, this *last* operation.

Fifteen minutes passed.

It was hard being the lookout. Not knowing what was going on was maddening. He should have heard something by now.

Two clicks came over the radio, which meant Iain was coming out. A sense of dread washed over Michael. Ben was dead. It was over.

He liked Ben. He was a sad man, a man battling demons, which was something Michael could relate to—something many Special Forces guys could relate to. Ben's demons were different from his own, but all the same, demons come from one place and one place alone—hell.

In the hallway, Iain removed his plastic foot slippers and shower cap, removed the electrical tape from the peepholes, and walked down the stairs and out the front door. He saw Michael across the street and walked around the block to their car. Michael followed. They got in the car, and Iain drove away.

Michael sighed, "Is it over?"

"No, Michael, it's not fucking over. Ben wasn't there. The apartment's empty."

"What?" Michael straightened in his seat. "Where did he go?"

"How the hell should I know? He left his goddamn keys on the counter." Michael saw the veins in Iain's neck grow large, like they had during combat. "I put a camera in his smoke alarm. If he comes back, we'll know. Call the team; get their asses back here. Those fucking morons missed something, and we need to know what."

Michael took out his phone and dialed the comms team.

"Have them watch the front fucking door this time." Iain whacked the steering wheel with his fist. "Fuck!"

Chapter 22

Ben walked to the corner of Shepard and Pratt where he got on a bus going up North Charles. He then waited for a train at Baltimore Penn Station, which took him all the way to New York Penn Station, and from there he bought two tickets going farther upstate.

He exchanged glances with the conductors and passengers when they saw him sitting next to an empty seat, and he was mindful to remain silent to Emily, who sat beside him. She led him from bus to bus, and station to station. It was much easier dealing with insanity now that he *knew* he was crazy. *Just don't talk to her—don't talk to anybody.*

Ben heard the seat cushion creak as she sat down, saw the chair move back on its hinges ever so slightly when she pressed her back against it. She, too, was mindful not to speak, not wanting her Bennie to start talking to an empty chair and wind up in a psychiatric hospital.

The hours of quiet offered Ben time to reflect on a scale that was terrifying.

If you're not really here, he thought, *if you're only a figment of my imagination, then could we speak through our thoughts alone? Can you hear me?*

Emily did not respond. She just sat on the seat beside him with a pleasant grin and a straightforward gaze on her face, as if she could see the end of it all, wherever this crazy trip was taking them.

If you're not real—if this is all a dream, a delusion—then how do I determine what's real and what's fake? Maybe I'm dreaming. Maybe I'm in a coma and can't wake up. I could be lying in a hospital bed, or strapped to a gurney in Dr. Wulfric's office, being experimented on.

Ben's thoughts entered the realm of the macabre:

Maybe the doctor is fiddling around inside my brain, with the crown of my skull neatly cut off and resting on a metal tray, and the dura mater cut neatly from around my brain and draped over my eyes like wet leather. Or maybe I'm dead. This could be purgatory. Everything is fake, a figment of my imagination. Everyone I ever met, everyone around me—my entire life—it never happened
...

Emily reached over and took Ben's hand in her own, squeezing it. His mind slowed and his heart rate dropped back below panic levels.

He rested his head on the headrest, gazing outside the window at the blur of scenery as it raced by. It reminded him of when he was a boy, sitting in the back seat as his foster father drove him for weekend trips and vacations to Lake Placid, and sometimes Vermont. He loved staring outside the window, watching towns race by in dizzying speed—like rapids on a stream. It put him in a trance and calmed his nerves. The absence of people and buildings outside the window, and the increase of trees and wilderness indicated they were now far outside New York City, farther upstate.

He closed his eyes, but when he did, a jumble of words—random and in no logical order—went racing through his mind: *Carbon, carbon copy, absolutely, the significance of maybe tomorrow, and mother, my mother, no, the deadline is whenever.* The words rambled into his consciousness in voices that were not his own, talking all at once, indecipherable.

It was best to keep his eyes open.

He longed to talk to Emily—an overwhelming urge. He had so many questions for her. He had to know what was going on, and he needed to keep the voices he was hearing out of his head. Some sort of reassurance that he was doing the right thing was needed—although he wasn't quite sure what it was that he was doing or where he was going.

It sounded perfectly sane when Emily told him to follow her out of the apartment and directed him to buy the train and bus tickets. When she spoke, when she looked him in the eyes, he was powerless. A fog enveloped his brain that cut off his rational thoughts. It was almost better this way—not having control, just experiencing the flow of bliss as it flooded his body. He would follow her off the edge of a cliff and fly if that's what she wanted him to do.

This silence, these long stretches of being alone with his thoughts, brought trickles of doubt, confusion, and intense fear. He was quite possibly going insane, completely bat-shit crazy. The air in the bus grew thick and hot, and it felt as if the metal walls were closing in on him.

Several miles later, the bus pulled into a gas station and came to a full stop. Ben stood, walked down the aisle with the rest of the passengers, passed the small group gathered at the door to stretch their legs and light cigarettes, and crossed the street. He didn't realize he was leaving; there was never a plan, and he didn't know where he was going, but one thing was for sure: he needed to be far from civilization. If he was close to cracking, he'd rather do it far from where people could see him.

They approached an old diner on the corner, its large plate glass window displaying aged tables and chairs behind dusty sun-beaten curtains. They could see the well-worn breakfast bar with its splintering stools. A few people sat at the counter sipping coffee and eating eggs and pancakes from chipped white plates. The scene was straight out of a Norman Rockwell painting.

Emily said, "Reminds you of Pat's, doesn't it?"

Ben nodded. Just about every town, both large and small, had its own mom-and-pop diner or restaurant. Pat's Diner was Ben and Emily's regular breakfast stop when they lived upstate.

As they passed the old diner on the corner, the air grew fragrant with the smell of fried bacon, and a sweet, smoky smell like maple syrup. Ben's stomach ached, and his mouth watered.

When was the last time I ate? What … day is it?

"Where are we going, Emma?"

"You know where we're going, Ben. You're the one walking."

"I've been following you. I don't know where we're going." But his legs were moving, somewhere. Onward.

The street came to a dead end, and just beyond, in a cluster of trees, flowed a rushing stream. The swells of water foamed white as the waves crashed among the rocks and flowed in swirls among the rapids. They followed the water holding hands, feeling the coolness of water vapor in the air.

"I think I should call Dr. Wulfric."

"We've been over this, Ben. You know you can't do that."

"I don't know." He shook his head, rubbing his temple with his free hand. "I'm going insane; I think—I think I'm crazy."

"No, Ben, you're not crazy."

"I am. I have to be. I mean, this is … you … you're not real."

"Ben!" Her lip curled, and he knew he'd pissed her off.

"I'm sorry, I'm sorry."

"You know you can't trust them. If you call Dr. Wulfric, Iain Marcus will come find you, and you don't want that to happen."

"Why? Why would I care if Iain Marcus finds me?"

She shook her head and exhaled a deep air of disappointment.

"What? Why would I care?"

"Oh, Bennie. You really don't remember, do you?"

"Remember what?"

"The dream you're having. It's all there; it's in your head. You just need to remember."

"Which dream?"

"Drapery Falls, Ben."

He thought about the dream. It was true, now that he thought about it. Dr. Wulfric seemed to act a bit strange when he told him the details. What was it about that dream? As strange as the dream was, it was only a dream. Nothing to be hung up about.

What he *did* remember was vivid: the car driving at night, the sign for Drapery Falls, the cold rain, the man on his knees …

"It's all in your mind, Ben. Just remember."

He played it over and over, repeating each scene. Then, very slowly, the fuzzy gaps began to fill in. He saw himself struggle with the man on the ground, saw and felt his own hand push a syringe into the man's arm. He smelled the smoke as it rose from the pizza box and thought he could even feel the warmth of the fire as it grew.

He became aware that he was not doing these things; he was not in his own body—it was Iain Marcus. He could feel and sense the emotions Iain felt as the events unfolded—the unpleasantness of the cold rain, the rush of adrenaline during the struggle, and the anxiety as he quickly left the scene of the crime. And something else: enjoyment, a sense of pleasure at the thrill of it all.

"Holy shit!" he shouted louder than he anticipated. "I killed someone. I mean, Iain killed someone!"

"What else?"

"I, um …" He let the dream play out repeatedly. "I remember the place going up in flames, and Mr. Kalispell was there with Iain. But Iain is calling him Michael."

Emily nodded. "Well, that's a start."

"Dr. Wulfric, he was involved, too. I don't know how, but he was."

"Yes, Ben, he was. They are murderers. All of them. They are bad people. You can't trust them. We're on our own from here on out. It's just you and me. I'm going to keep you safe, away from these people who want to hurt you. Do you trust me, Ben? Can you trust me?"

He looked into her eyes. Any questions he may have had or feelings of dismay fizzled out of his thoughts. He was mindless—a zombie.

"Of course, my Emma." His eyes felt lethargic. "I trust you."

"They killed that boy while he was working on Lucy. He was doing what you've been doing—testing the serum."

"Are we going to Drapery Falls?"

"We're going somewhere safe. Somewhere far from Iain Marcus and Mr. Kalispell. They are aware that you know too much. They killed that boy without the slightest show of remorse or regret. Murder is nothing to them, just part of the job. Tell me, what was Iain thinking about when he killed that man?"

"Nothing really. He kind of thought he was doing him a favor."

"He felt justified. He thinks murder is justifiable. That makes him a very dangerous man. They know you're having this little, well, this little episode …"

"Crazy. I'm going crazy."

"They know that their secrets are compromised, and that *you* are compromised, and they will do whatever is in their power to keep you and those secrets suppressed. That's why we left the apartment, Ben. That's why we left the city, and that's why we have to keep moving."

"Jesus Christ. Where are we going?"

"A place where we can be alone. You would like that, Bennie, wouldn't you?"

"Yes …" The words came out of his mouth, but he had no control over them. "I'll follow you … anywhere."

Chapter 23

Iain Marcus and Michael Bennet sat in the back of the cramped comms van, pouring over every second of sound and background noise taped from Ben's apartment prior to his disappearance. The air inside the van was rank with body odor and fast food, a disgusting combination that infuriated Iain even further. Still, he kept himself cool and rational. He'd been cramped in tanks that smelled worse.

They were joined by a technician named Aaron Tyler, who actively replayed a blip of sound over and over again, a mumble of words too low and quiet to be easily deciphered. Aaron slowed the recording to a fraction of the normal speed, but it was still incomprehensible. The microphone over Ben's window was badly damaged, and the quality of the recording was compromised. Iain, however, identified a barely audible squeaking sound as the front door.

"Move on." Iain instructed.

Aaron fast-forwarded the recording, focusing on the next blip of sound. Iain took off the heavy earphones and turned to Michael.

"We're missing something."

Michael nodded, removing his own headphones. There was nothing on the tapes. They had listened to each second of the recording maybe a dozen times. It was getting them nowhere.

"We need to think like him, find out where he would go, and why he would go there. What was so pressing that he would disappear early in the morning, without a trace, without his keys?"

"Without his phone," Michael added.

Iain nodded. They'd called his cell phone several times, leaving voice messages in cheerful tones: "Hey, Ben, this is Iain. Listen, we have to meet up. Mr. Kalispell has some good news for you. Call me back when you get this. I'll be in your neck of the woods today, so I can stop by whenever. It will only take a second. Thanks."

It was not until Michael watched the live feed from the apartment, while Iain was calling Ben, that he noticed an illumination from the edge of the couch. Ben left his phone at home, tucked halfway between the couch cushions.

"Do you still think he left for Paris?" Michael asked.

"No, I don't."

They tapped into his bank account and charge cards. Nothing had been purchased. Even if he bought a plane ticket with cash, the comms team would find out. They had every major airline flying out of Philadelphia, New York, and New Jersey cross-referencing his name.

"Where else would he go?"

"I don't know."

"Do you think he went there? You know, to Drapery Falls?"

Iain shot Michael a glance, looking at Aaron who was listening intently to the recordings. He hissed, "Why would he go there?"

"I don't know, maybe he remembered more of his dream. Or maybe he wants to remember more of his dream."

"Without his car? I doubt it." But it wasn't out of the question. It was a possibility they mulled over, but after tapping into Ben's computer and going through his internet history, nothing about Drapery Falls came up. The last conversation they had with Ben, Drapery Falls was still nothing more than only a dream. A phantom town. He had no idea the implications the dream carried. The idea was put aside, especially since his car was parked a block away, and his keys were left on the kitchen counter.

But they were running out of ideas, and possibly time. If Ben was currently experiencing dementia and hallucinations—if he was going crazy—in public, they had to find him soon. Before the police did.

"I guess it makes the most sense." Iain stood in the van, hunched over, and opened the back door. Michael followed. "Aaron, patch the video feed from the apartment to my phone, and don't stop listening to the tapes and checking his charge cards. You hear *anything*, if he buys a fucking cup of coffee in Calcutta, I need to know. Immediately."

Aaron nodded, shielding his eyes from the sun pouring in through the open door.

Michael and Iain jumped to the ground, slamming the door shut behind them. They walked around the block to their car and started the engine.

"Should we get a map?" Michael asked. They wouldn't dare look up the directions on their phones. Digital paper trails were harder to burn.

"I remember how to get there."

In the back of Iain's anxious mind, the image of Ben's phone flashing on the couch, loaded with missed calls and voice messages, gave him concern. If Ben did not return to his apartment—if they found him in Drapery Falls, or anywhere else—he would have to break into his apartment again and destroy the phone.

"It seems fitting if this comes to an end in Drapery Falls, doesn't it?" Michael asked.

"Yeah, I guess so."

"It's come full circle."

They hit traffic as they neared New York, but soon after, the road cleared up and Iain sped along the interstate. He kept his phone on a standing charger, the video feed from Ben's apartment transmitting bright on the screen. The fisheye lens kept a vigil on the entire living room, from front door to kitchen.

Iain looked from the image on the screen to the road, his eyes darting back and forth. His forehead furrowed.

"Shit!" he shouted, startling Michael who was near sleep.

"Wha-what's the matter?"

"I can't believe it! Jesus Christ!"

"What, Iain, what?"

"He's not going to Drapery Falls!" He smacked the steering wheel. "There, Michael! Right there." He pointed to the edge of the video feed.

Michael picked up the phone, squinting, and removed a pair of wire-frame glasses from an inner pocket.

Iain snatched the phone away and dialed into the keypad. It rang twice on speakerphone.

"Hello?"

"Aaron, listen to me, this is important. What's the name of the town Ben used to live in, with Emily?"

"It's umm …" The muffled sound of movement came over the speakers. "One second, It's right here … Sutton Lake."

"Right. That's where he's headed. I need you to find every cabin, every little shithole wooden cabin anywhere in the vicinity of Sutton Lake."

"Yes, sir. But, umm … that's upstate New York? There's got to be thousands of cabins up there."

"Yes, but we're only looking for one. I'll have Dr. Wulfric fax you a picture. And Aaron—keep your eye on the camera."

"Yes, sir."

Iain hung up.

"Aaron is never going to find it. He's right; there are thousands of cabins upstate," Michael went on. "Why are you suddenly certain that's where he's going? I don't see anything to suggest—"

"Look, Michael." He brought the live feed from Ben's apartment back on his phone. "That spot on the wall, right there."

Michael squinted. The wall was blank. "Iain, I don't see anything."

"Exactly my point. There on the wall—that's where he kept that painting of the cabin." Iain pointed again to the live feed. "Right above the shattered mug and whiskey glass, by the door."

"The painting is right there, Iain." Michael pointed to the screen. "On the ground. See it? It's leaning against the wall."

Iain shook his head. "That's not the painting. That's the copy we made for him at the lab. See, it's not framed. The real one is gone. Before he left his apartment, he must have taken it off the wall. It's the only thing he took with him when he left. Not his cell phone, not a jacket, not his keys—nothing. Only the painting. Not only is the painting meaningful to Ben, it's an obsession. His wife painted it years ago. It's come up in his dreams during every test. In his dreams we see him standing atop some hill looking down to a clearing in the woods where the cabin sits surrounded by trees."

"We still can't rule out Drapery Falls."

"No, we can't. However, if Ben did suddenly remember everything that happened in Drapery Falls, and not just the little fragments, he would have gone to the authorities. We would have heard something over the wire; the police would be looking for us. This cabin, that's where he's heading. I don't know why he's going there, but I'm certain that he is."

"Okay, okay." Michael paused to think. "You might be right. Still though, how is Aaron going to find one cabin in all of upstate New York?"

"He may not find anything, but we're not searching all of upstate New York. There aren't thousands of cabins in Sutton Lake. Only dozens, maybe."

"So what's the plan? We're going to drive six hours upstate, and if Aaron doesn't find anything by the time we get there, we're just going to ask around?"

"Look up Sutton Lake. The population is probably in the hundreds. In a small town like that, we have a better chance asking the locals than finding anything on our own. So yes, that is exactly what we're going to do, Michael."

***

Being mindful of the speed limit, Iain and Michael still made excellent time. The sky grew dark as they drove across miles of broad farmlands and homes amidst acres of heavily wooded terrain, until they arrived in Sutton Lake.

The center of town was nothing more than a strip of old and somewhat dilapidated buildings that might have looked acceptable in the '60s or '70s. The popularity of the town plummeted in the late '80s, after the paper mill just outside of town closed, and the population decreased. Most visitors today describe Sutton Lake as *charming* and *quaint*, but Iain didn't see anything charming about the peeling paint on the storefronts, or the slabs of sidewalk moved askew or broken by ever-widening tree roots.

They parked and walked into the first establishment they came to—a dusty old watering hole named Tyson's. After a quick conversation with the bartender and the single patron sitting at the sour smelling ten-seat bar, they moved on.

There were three bars total in Sutton Lake; a very high number, Iain thought, for such a small town. But he doubted the local residents had very much else to do. They walked a few buildings over to the second bar, looking like tired businessmen, which wasn't far from the truth. A number of people were gathered around a sand-filled bucket, smoking—a promising sign. They entered.

On a table by the front door were stacks of local business cards, flyers, and newspapers. Iain glanced them over and picked up a card. They took a seat at the battered wood bar. About a dozen or so middle-aged and older men sat hunched over with their elbows on the spill guard rail, sipping beer from thick mugs and watching the ball game. The regulars looked to have claimed their barstools many years ago. It was exactly the kind of place Iain was looking for.

The bartender walked over, resting his hairy forearms and large belly on the counter. "Gentlemen, what can I do you for?" He tossed two coasters on the bar that advertised *Budweiser* on them.

"I'll have one of those." Iain pointed at a coaster.

"I'll have the same."

"Two Buds." The bartender walked to the cooler.

They paid, then after a moment turned to the old man sitting beside them.

"Yanks tied it up, huh?" Michael asked. "They were down two, top of the inning last I heard on the radio."

"Yep, they sure did," the old man answered.

Iain knew nothing of baseball, so he let Michael steer the conversation. They bought the old man a beer, and they all clinked glasses in cheers.

"Thank you kindly," The old man said with a genuine air of gratitude.

"You live here, in Sutton Lake?" Michael asked.

The man nodded. "Sure do. Born and raised. Guessing you boys are just passing through? There ain't much to see in Sutton Lake."

"How'd you guess?" Michael laughed.

"Actually," Iain chimed in, "we're here on business. We're investors."

"Investors?" The man laughed. "Investing in what, corn? There ain't nothing to invest in around here."

"I wouldn't say that. We have a meeting with this company tomorrow." Iain fished the business card he took from the front table out of his pocket. The man squinted to read the fine print:

Sutton Property
Upstate New York's Premier Real Estate

Iain held his breath. This was the tough part about telling a lie—not getting caught. Did the man work for the company, or did someone else at the bar? Would he know Iain was full of shit? The old man shrugged and looked back at the television. So far so good.

"We buy properties, fix them up, and then put them back on the market."

"Oh, like house flippers. My brother-in-law flipped a few houses in his day. Made some money doing so, but that was ten years ago."

"Oh yeah? Maybe you can help us. We're scheduled to see a cabin tomorrow morning. Got offered a good price. We tried to do a drive-by tonight, but the directions they gave us must be wrong, and there's no one in the office this late. Even the directions the company gave us to get here, to Sutton Lake, were wrong. We got lost twice. I had to stop at a gas station to get a map. You probably know the local roads better than most."

Iain removed a folded piece of paper from the inside pocket of his jacket.

"Here, this is the cabin we're looking for." Iain called Dr. Wulfric earlier, and had him freeze frame an image of the cabin from one of Ben's dreams and fax it over the mobile fax machine in the trunk of the car.

The man studied the picture. "Hmm, is that Frank's? No, not Frank's."

Michael and Iain held their breaths.

"You got an address? A street name?"

"Not one that's right. The address they gave me took us to a dead end."

"Hey, Jim," the man called to the bartender. "This place look familiar to you? These boys are set to buy it."

"Well, we're just checking it out. No decisions have been made."

The bartender walked over and glanced at the picture, stroking his chest-length beard. "Nope, sorry." He shook his head. "Don't think I know it." He went back to watching the game.

"Oh well. I'm sure we'll get there just fine."

Iain took a sip from his beer. For a moment, things had looked promising. They stood to leave.

"Thank you anyway," Michael said to the man.

"Nice meeting you, fellas. Good luck with everything. Thanks for the beer."

The front door opened and another even older man walked in.

"Now wait a minute," said the man at the bar. "Let Stevie here get a look at that picture. He's worked on just about every house there is in Sutton Lake."

Iain stepped aside to let the slow-moving man take a seat at the bar.

"Stevie, you know this place? These boys are looking to find it. They're investors from the city. Got bad directions."

Did I say we're from the city? Iain loved how stories had a way of perpetuating themselves.

Iain unfolded the picture. Steve just glanced upward. "Sure, that's Betty Kruger's old place. She died a few years back; don't know what's going on with it now. Haven't been up there in, gosh, I don't know how long. Fixed the water heater for her, back, oh, maybe ten years or so ago, maybe more."

The blood in Iain's veins pumped like rapids.

"So you know where it is then?"

"Sure, I know where it is. I used to know Betty Krueger, going back, oh, gosh, maybe ten years or so. I fixed the water heater for her back then."

Iain and Michael exchanged glances.

The bartender walked over. "Hey, Stevie." He placed a brownish looking drink on the bar.

"Dewars and soda, Jimmy."

"I know, Stevie; I know."

"Let me get that," Iain said, his hand going to his wallet. "On second thought, I think we'll all have another round."

Chapter 24

Ben's eyes fluttered, and then they opened.

There was no present moment. There was no later and no before. No time or reality. All was black and then it wasn't. He blinked. One eye seemed to go one way, and the other did not quite follow. His eyelids flickered and strained, and he focused until his vision cleared. He was staring at the heavens above. A grey sky. The sun lost behind a sea of clouds.

Where am I …?

The tops of trees swayed in a light wind, and there was a face looking down at him. He opened his mouth but nothing came out.

"Shhh," she said. "Rest."

So he did.

When his eyes opened again, he was staring up at the same sky, only time must have become relevant again, because the grey clouds were now dark with the coming of night—or perhaps they were growing light with the coming of morning. Ben didn't know how much time had passed. The same face was looking down at him: Emily, kneeling by his side. He was aware his head was on her lap. The warmth coming from her legs made him realize the rest of his body was very cold. His feet and hands were numb, tingling with spikes of pain like pinpricks. His fingers felt swollen, like he was wearing thick gloves, and he didn't think he could form his hands into fists.

"Emm …" The mucus in his throat hindered words from escaping. He coughed. The skin around his nose felt tight.

"Emily."

"Shhh," she said. "Relax."

"I don't … I can't get up."

"Yes, you can. Just take your time."

Slowly he did, pushing himself up to a sitting position, and sat there for several minutes as waves of dizziness lapped over him. He coughed hard into his palm, and a ball of mucus came loose. He spat in the dirt and saw blood.

"Emily … what happened?"

"You fell, Benjamin. But you're okay now."

He didn't remember falling. He didn't remember much of anything. One minute he was walking and the next minute he was opening his eyes.

"Is it … am I okay?" He scratched the dry skin around his nose, flaking away pieces of dried blood. "Did I … have a seizure, or something?" Each word caused his head to throb. It throbbed as if he'd just meditated for an hour, or read an entire novel in one sitting. Reality was clouded— seemingly cartoonish—any movement followed by dull aches.

"You're fine now, Ben. Try getting to your feet."

He wasn't sure he was fine; however, he couldn't be sure that he wasn't. He pushed himself up. His legs trembled and gave out, and he fell to his knees.

"It's okay, Bennie. It's okay. Take your time."

The air smelled strange here, thick and awful—like shit; the air smelled like dirt and shit. He gagged and pushed himself up, steadying his nerves and muscles. The world wobbled under his feet.

Emily asked, "How are you feeling?"

"I … don't know."

"Can you walk? We have a lot of ground to cover."

"I don't know." Thinking was hard, and answering questions was even harder. The tip of his tongue felt swollen and too large for his mouth.

Ben looked at the crude path in the woods. The trail was overgrown and long untraveled. People just didn't go into the woods as often as they once had. He took a few deep breaths, listening hard for the stream they were following before he collapsed. Somewhere out of sight, he could hear the gentle flow of moving water.

Breathe in, breathe out. Breathe in, breathe out …

He twisted his body from side to side; his bones and muscles popping and cracking, and he looked off into the woods, through the vertical slats of the dense trees.

"Wait, who's that?" He jumped, pointing behind him. There was a man standing several yards away, nearly invisible through the thicket. "Emily," he whispered. "Emily, there's someone there. Look." The man was facing the opposite direction, walking slowly away. All Ben could see of the man was the back of his head. "Emily?"

She hesitated. "That's no one, Ben. There's no one there. We have to keep going."

"But … am I imagining him? Do *you* know him?"

"It wouldn't matter if I did. Come on now." She grabbed his shoulder and Ben nearly fell over.

"Give me a second." He looked back at the man, who stopped walking and stood staring off. A low noise rumbled through the air at a barely audible frequency, echoing in Ben's eardrums.

For a moment—just a moment—the confusion and fog that enveloped his senses cleared away.

What the hell is going on? Jesus Christ, what's happening to me?

And then a thought popped in his head that he did not know he was thinking:

If only Sophia were here.

He was shocked and guilt ridden that he thought it. And even more shocked that he hadn't thought about her at all since … *how long has it been?* He was further shocked when he realized that he hadn't thought about anything—anything at all—since Emily first appeared. The last few hours, maybe days, weeks, was all a blur.

"Let's go, Ben. Don't look at him." Emily's face was pursed with anger and something else—*fear?* The rumbling in his ears became louder, and slowly, he placed one foot in front of the other, and began to walk in the opposite direction. The rumbling grew in intensity and frequency, and his ears started to ring in pain.

"Jesus Christ!" Ben covered his ears, and dropped to his knees. And just as suddenly as it started it stopped. The ringing went away, and the fog returned to blanket his mind.

"What the—"

"Let's move, Ben."

Ben looked up. The man was gone. Vanished.

"Who was that?"

"It's wasn't anyone, Ben."

Emily turned and looked at him.

Her eyes. There's just something about her eyes.

She touched his hand and they continued walking. He wanted to ask her more questions, but his brain throbbed with exhaustion when he tried to think clearly; it felt swollen and large, as if engorged against his skull. He wanted to know why his face was bloody, and how long he had been unconscious—and *why* he had been unconscious. He wanted to know who the man in the woods was, and why Emily was so quick to turn him away. He wanted to know all of these things and more, but found it impossible to form words into sentences that would convey any semblance of rational thought.

She sensed his confusion and aggravation. "All you have to do is follow me, Bennie. You still trust me, right?"

In a trance he muttered, "Yes … of course I trust you."

Miles passed underfoot, and with them went hours.

"Emma … I'm so tired," he told her again, as he had several times already.

"You can sleep soon, but not now. I know how strong you are. You must keep walking."

The trail rose before him. Large rocks shot out from the earth in massive sedimentary slabs and piles, both jagged and slippery. Emily traversed them with ease, her sharp heels making *clack-clack* sounds upon the hard surfaces, hopping from one boulder to the next. Ben followed, clambering over the slick surfaces on all fours like an animal, sliding down some rocks, and rolling over others. At times, his vision was bright—very bright, feverish— and at other times, it would go dark around the periphery. His clothing was tattered, muddy, and ripped. He fell often, and when he did, he picked himself back up. His labored breath burned his lungs, and his vision throbbed with his pulse. All he wanted to do was close his eyes, succumb to whatever dark or bright void was waiting for him—to finally put his mind at ease.

Then he reached the top of the hill.

And below him was the cabin in the woods.

***

Iain Marcus and Michael Bennet left the bar. They bought the two old men another round, and left them watching the ball game with glassy eyes. They drove past the few restaurants, bars, and a small inn, leaving the center of town behind. The streetlights became less frequent the farther they drove until they seemed to vanish altogether as the town became more rural. The sky was dark as they drove on the desolate road. In the distance, they saw a single streetlight illuminating a crossroad. They approached, barely making out the name: Crawford Pond Road. They took a sharp right. It was just as the old man at the bar had instructed.

Ben should never have vanished like this. Iain's team had proven itself incompetent; now he was far from home, tracking a lead that might not pan out. His grip on the situation was not tight, not tight at all, and he would have hell to answer for if the situation did not start going his way.

Iain had shown his face in town, even showed a picture of the cabin they were looking for to several people in a crowded bar. If they found Ben at this cabin, they would have to remove him. Bury his body far, far away. There could be nothing left behind—no DNA, no traces of their encounter with him whatsoever. This had to be the cleanest job he ever carried out, but at the moment, things were a mess.

Crawford Pond Road was in desperate need of repair. The cracks and potholes were evidence that few people traveled upon it, especially at night. Blowing a tire or cracking an axle was a definite possibility. Occasionally they passed lone mailboxes on the side of the road beside narrow and dark driveways, but they were few and far between. Iain and Michael were far from civilization, secluded even, and that was a very good thing.

They read the numbers on the mailboxes until they arrived in front of number sixteen. They scanned the overgrown driveway for any signs of life. The house, off in the distance, was hidden in the dark woods. Iain killed the lights, turned the wheel, and the car bounced over a mound and onto the unpaved driveway. The overgrown weeds and bushes on either side of the path scraped the sides of the car.

It occurred to Iain that if he had to turn around, he would have to put the car in reverse. A K-turn would be impossible in the dark on the narrow driveway; there was no room for error.

Iain put the car in park and killed the engine.

He reached behind him and turned off the interior lights, then opened the door, stepping out into the night. Michael followed.

They stood motionless, listening. The air was still except for the constant chirpings of an untold number of crickets.

Iain opened the trunk and removed a black duffel bag from the cavity alongside the spare tire. Inside the bag he found a pair of night-vision goggles. Foolishly, it was the only pair they'd brought.

"I'll go up alone to scope it out. Stay with the car." Iain unholstered the pistol attached to his belt, checked the magazine and chamber, and screwed a silencer to the barrel.

***

Only a few steps out from the car, Iain vanished in the darkness, and after a minute, the darkness began playing tricks on Michael's mind. He heard too many noises and felt the need to check his watch way too often. But

Michael didn't move a muscle; he knew the darkness was not something to fear, but something to respect.

Several vibrations emanated from Michael's pocket that nearly caused him to jump out of his skin, and he recognized the feeling of his phone. He remained still and let the call go to voicemail. A moment later, it vibrated again, this time only one short buzz. He cupped his hand over the glaring screen and clicked on a text message from Dr. Wulfric. It was a long message, and he read it fast, aware that the screen was extremely bright and could draw attention. Apparently, the doctor had been calling him all night, but up in Sutton Lake, phone reception was hit or miss. He looked around for Iain, but saw no movement of any kind, and heard nothing but the crickets. He cracked open the car door and slipped inside, closing it as quietly as possible behind him, and dialed the doctor.

***

Ben saw it nestled among thick evergreen trees in the clearing below.

It was the cabin in the woods.

He watched as smoke billowed out from the chimney to be swept away in light gusts of wind. The pleasant smell of wood smoke lingered heavy in the air, along with something that made his mouth water. Food cooking. A pot roast, perhaps, with earthy vegetables stewing in a sauce of red wine and sage. A sweet smell wafted up to where Ben stood, like various fruit pies all baking in the oven at once. His stomach churned audibly, tumbling in its vacant shell.

Without further hesitation, he began clambering down the other side of the hill. He cut through a tangle of branches and vines, cutting his hands and face on sharp thorns, not noticing or caring, until he arrived at the clearing around the cabin.

His breath stopped in his lungs as he took it all in.

The cabin was before him, the stream still flowing over a shallow bed of smooth stones. The pebble driveway was meticulously raked and trailed off into the woods, leading to Crawford Pond Road. A neat pile of wood sat beside a thick stump with the gleaming steel and polished wood handle of an axe firmly planted in it. A cart beside the stump was piled high with firewood, ready to be wheeled to the hearth inside. Light shone from behind the open windows, the lace curtains moving in and out with the gentle wind. The scene overtook his senses, resonated deep within his very soul. A tear rolled down his cheek, leaving a clean streak across his dirty skin.

His vision was clear—exceptionally crisp. Small details of the cabin, such as the gleaming steel blade of the axe, radiated with such clarity and brightness that he was nearly blinded and completely enraptured. His brain was concocting a variety of chemicals, churning them about, and producing pure bliss.

The landscaped flowerbeds and plants circling the cabin emerged from the earth, radiating like blossoming sunrays jumping out from the ground, the blues, yellows, and oranges of the flower petals magnificent beyond belief. The vibrancy was such that Ben had only seen such colors back when he was a teenager and briefly experimented with LSD and psychoactive mushrooms. The center of his body released sensations of pure unadulterated joy that he could not put into words or understand.

Ben fell to his knees, tears covering his cheeks as hot as firewater. Emily stood before him, larger than life, her hand out and open, the sun at her back creating an electric aura shooting out like a halo around her body.

"Come on, Ben. We're finally here."

Ben leaned to rise, but fell back on his ankles.

"I want to sleep, Emily. I'm so tired." The words came out choppy and harsh, lumpy in his throat on the verge of a breakdown. "I'm so tired Emily, I can't … I can't …"

"Shhh." She put a finger to her lips. "I know, baby. You're in pain, but it's just a few more steps. Everything is going to be all right."

She reached down and held out a hand, and he looked up at her. The cabin was before him, and he was powerless to stop the magnetic pull it had on his life—his body, his mind.

He lifted a hand and locked eyes with Emily, offering her, with his last bit of strength, his hand to take, his soul to have if she so desired.

And she took his hand, his soul, his life.

Her body was as bright as the sun as she pulled him up on wobbly feet. Blood rushed from his head, and for a second, everything went dark before returning impossibly bright again.

"Can we go inside?"

"Of course we can go inside; that's why we came all this way. This cabin is ours; it belongs to us. It always has. We're home, Ben … we're home."

All he could do was follow her. The fact that Ben was no longer questioning reality—never questioning Emily—was what made him insane.

They passed the flowerbeds, with the sweet fragrance of jasmine. Emily reached out and opened the door, and a flood of warm air washed over his body. The inside of the cabin was just as Ben had always imagined. The front room was large, sharing the space with the kitchen, where a large fireplace roared with flames. The furniture, floor, and walls were all a light colored wood and smelled deeply of pine. A variety of knickknacks decorated the walls and surfaces: *Home Sweet Home* signs, and freshly cut flowers in vases. An assortment of blue glass jars lined the windowsills on either side, producing various shades of tranquil flowing blue along the floor when the sun shone through them.

At times, his vision became fuzzy, like looking through a piece of smoky glass. Other times his vision cleared to see everything in such vivid detail that the image seemed burned in his retina, and grew brighter with his pulse. The sparkling array of dazzling colors spread to the periphery of his vision, slowly encompassing everything he saw. The colors were jagged, with patches of grey and black, and soon he wasn't sure if he could count his fingers if he held his hand before his face.

Just as his vision dulled, it popped back with an unbelievable crispness that was beyond anything he could comprehend.

Then he saw the man and jumped, his back hitting the door.

"Jesus!" he shouted.

The man in the woods was there, in the cabin, in the corner of the living room, sitting on a wooden chair beside the cast iron stove. He sat rigidly upright with his back to Ben, his spine straight as a board and his palms resting on his knees.

Emily's face contorted. "Ben, I need you to—"

"BEN," the man's voice boomed.

The words seemed to emanate from the room itself, vibrating the very rafters and foundation of the cabin. The man did not move, did not budge. Dust particles in the air were stagnant around him, as if he sat in a bubble where time did not exist.

Ben let out a groan and fell over. His back slid down the front door. His hands covered his ears. The words of the man resonated so deeply, with such an echoing force, that his eardrums throbbed on the verge of bursting, like grapes pressed between two fingers.

"BENJAMIN."

"F-F-Fuck!" Ben sputtered. His eardrums rang, and he wasn't sure if he felt blood on his palms.

Emily didn't move. She stared at the man through narrow eyes. "What are you doing here?"

The man didn't answer.

"Ben," she looked down at him with his head tucked between his knees. "Ben, look at me. You have to make him go away."

He looked up at her with huge bloodshot eyes. "I … can't. You …" He spoke, but the ringing in his ears made his words sound muffled.

"No, Ben, I can't; but you can. You have to get rid of him. Now!"

***

When Iain returned, Michael was standing outside the car, just as he had left him.

"The cabin is desolate. There's no movement whatsoever."

"Are there any cars? Anything?"

"Nothing. The place looks vacant. The front door is open just a crack."

"Did you go inside?"

"No."

"What's the plan? Do we move in now or wait until morning?"

Iain didn't hesitate. "We move in now."

Michael grabbed the duffel bag and walked closely behind Iain. Their shoes crunched the gravel underfoot, sounding deafeningly loud in the stillness of the night. The walk was short, and soon Michael could see the outline of the cabin bathed in the moonlight. He wished they had packed a second set of night-vision goggles.

They approached the side of the cabin and crept up to one of the windows. Michael looked in, but couldn't see anything.

"It's vacant." Iain whispered, and motioned to the next window.

They circled the house, looking in every window. Two of the windows were shattered, the floor covered with broken glass and matted with shriveled, rotten brown leaves. They stopped a few feet from the front door.

Iain, with his night vision goggles, whispered to Michael that the inside of the cabin was desolate of furniture or any semblance of a functioning home. It was an old and dilapidated wooden shell of a former house. Many of the walls were covered with graffiti, and thin sheets of wallpaper hung from the walls like decomposing flesh. Empty liquor bottles, food wrappers, and cigarette butts littered the corners of the rooms. Michael feared they might encounter a group of drifters.

"Let's go in," Michael said. "If he's not here—and I'm starting to think there's no reason for him to be here—we have a long drive home, and a lot more searching to do."

Iain nodded, and they moved to the door. Iain tightened the leather gloves over his fingers and unholstered his silenced pistol. Michael did the same with his pistol, clicking the safety off.

Iain nudged the door open and stepped inside. Michael followed. After only a few steps, Iain came to a halt, putting his fist in the air. Michael stopped mid-stride. Iain motioned to the corner of the room. Michael squinted, leaning forward.

My God.

He could just make out the shape of a male body lying among broken beer bottles and rotten leaves, facing the wall. A dirty matted blanket—tattered and weathered—lay draped over his body.

They moved forward, one step at a time.

The person did not stir, did not move.

Iain leaned over the body. "It's him," he whispered.

Christ, Michael thought. *I'm too late.*

Was this really Benjamin Walker huddled on the floor? There was no backpack nearby, no jacket, no gear, no possessions—nothing. Just a motionless man in the corner of a cold room, seemingly part of the clutter and debris, covered with an old blanket and laying on a bed of decomposing leaves.

Iain knelt down and took the glove off his left hand, pressing two fingers to the side of Ben's neck. "He's alive," he said. "Barely."

Michael let out a sigh, careful not to be audible.

"Stay here," Iain whispered. "I'll check the rest of the house."

Michael listened to the floorboards creak as Iain left. The boy was so still—too still. Michael wanted to scoop him up and run.

When Iain returned, he said, "There's nobody here," and fished three glow-sticks out of the duffel bag. He bent them in the middle to snap the vials of hydrogen-peroxide inside and shook them to mix with the diphenyl-oxalate and fluorescent dye. He dropped them on the ground. They illuminated the room in fluorescent green, enough light for Iain to remove the goggles. He turned back to the body on the floor. It was Benjamin Walker all right.

"Iain, I—"

"It would be simple," Iain cut him off, "just to leave him here. A drug addict found dead. Simple. Easy. However, we've shown our faces in town, and people know we asked about this cabin. We could bury him nearby, but if someone reports him missing, and say, a security camera happened to spot him at some stage of his journey, and the police start asking around and following his trail—well, that wouldn't be good for us."

"Iain, listen—"

"We have to take him far away. But, first things first: we have to give him the injection. Michael." He turned to face the man eye to eye. "Why don't you get the hypodermic? I think you should be the one to do the honors."

"Iain, it doesn't have to be this way."

"Doesn't have to be this way?" Iain looked incredulous, the green light from the glow-sticks casting bizarre shadows over his face. "This is the only way it can be, Michael." He snapped.

"No, Iain, it isn't. It wasn't the only way back in Drapery Falls, and it isn't the only way now. We've made so many mistakes—too many mistakes. We don't have to kill him. He doesn't deserve to die like this. We can save him. He's an innocent man."

"Innocent? Is that really what you think? Are we talking about the same person here, or has your mind become so warped as to believe—"

"Iain!" Michael startled even himself. "There *is* another way, and if you would just listen for one goddamn second!"

Iain shut his mouth.

Michael took a deep breath, composing himself. "There is another way. I've been talking to Dr. Wulfric, and—"

"When did you talk to Dr. Wulfric?"

"Over the last few days, and just now back at the car. He called when you left to check this place out."

Iain's stare was unflinching, like stone, but Michael knew the man well enough to decipher the tiny nuances in his persona: the veins pulsing in his neck, the glazed look in his eyes—genuine, unadulterated, anger.

"Dr. Wulfric has a solution. He can make a serum that will flush the Nano out of his body for good. A cure. It will be gone forever. There's still hope for Ben; he can have a new life, a fresh start."

"We tried that already with Ethan, and look how that turned out."

Michael didn't say anything.

"Jesus, man." Iain scoffed. "Do you think I don't know? Do you think Mr. Kalispell doesn't know?"

"What—"

Without a moment's hesitation, Iain swung a heavy right hook, cracking Michael square in the jaw. Michael's knees buckled, and the pistol he was carrying slipped from his hand. He dropped to the floor and his head bounced on the ground.

***

Ben sat hunched over, looking up at Emily. The air in the room was becoming still, the roaring flames in the fireplace slowing to a fraction of their speed, and then the flames froze in motion, like a snapshot. Emily stared at him—into him.

Then he blinked and the room wasn't there anymore.

He was on his feet, standing in a … a … cave? A breeze and plenty of sunlight came in through an open passageway leading outside the mountain, infiltrating the cave with dry cool air. The ground and walls were solid rock, and the cavity was spacious. A battered man sat before him in a chair, wearing tattered cloth robes. He was screaming and crying out long words in a language Ben couldn't understand. Next to the man was a pile of bloody hair. The man's scalp and face looked as if fistfuls had been cut away with a blade.

Another man stood with his back to him, an assault rifle slung over his shoulder and a sidearm attached to his belt. The man wore a mixture of military fatigues and dust-covered robes and scarves. He turned.

"Michael, are you sure you—"

Ben looked down, rather his head moved without his control, and he saw his thick hands—hands that were not his own—covered in tight, fingerless gloves, resting on an automatic rifle slung over his chest.

His body moved fast. He felt the cold metal of a knife handle on his fingers as his other hand gripped the little hair left on the man's head. The man cried out in a squeal, and the blade of the knife sunk deep and sliced from one side of the man's throat to the other. The cut was calculated and precise, and hot blood sprayed over Ben's hand and forearm. Ben stared, watching the man gurgle and foam at the mouth. A few moments went by and the man no longer moved. Red saliva dripped from his lips and trickled down to form pools in the hollows of the rock floor. Ben tore a piece of cloth from the man's robe and turned his back while cleaning the blade of his knife.

He walked to the opening of the cave, scanning the clear blue horizon cut jagged along the mountain range far in the distance. Down at the base of the cave opening, the rest of the team had finished searching the slaughtered guards and were busy disposing of their bodies. They buried the corpses under rocks and stuffed them into crevices, where they would decompose to dry bones among the dust and sand and sunbaked reptiles, never to be seen again. The desert was a thirsty beast, never satiated over the blood of men.

The soldier in the cave with him, a young Iain Marcus, gathered his equipment and joined him at the mouth of the cave. "Let's roll," he said, and just as Ben's assumed body began to move out of the cave, everything changed.

He was no longer in the mountains; he was in an operating room. There was a person strapped to a gurney before him, and two men wearing white lab coats stared intently at a computer monitor beside the bed. His body felt different, not as spry as before. Ben tried to move but couldn't. He was not in control of this body. He stood behind the two doctors.

His mouth opened and spoke, "How is he?"

One of them answered. "Hear those beeps?" Ben could hear beeping coming from the heart monitor. "That means he's alive," the tired voice said.

"BENJAMIN!"

He was back in the cabin, his hands clawing at his ears. Time had not changed, had not moved on in his absence.

"What ... what's happening! Oh Christ, what do you want? Who are you?" Ben yelled at the back of the man's head.

"Don't talk to him, Ben! Don't listen to a word he says! He's a liar if he speaks!"

There were other sounds in the room now, mumbled words and shoes dragging over the plank floor. Ben looked about, but saw no one. The voices were far off, muffled shouting; a scuffle had broken out.

"SHE'S GOING TO KILL YOU BEN! SHE WANT'S TO KILL US BOTH!"

"Ahhh, fuck!"

The whole room vibrated and shook. One of the blue bottles on the windowsill fell to the ground and shattered. Ben leaned over, gagging, swallowing back stale bile. "Who—who are you?" He jumped to his feet, moving fast to the man in the chair.

"SHE'S GOING TO KILL YOU BEN."

His body trembled with the words, electrified, the force of the reverberation moving him backward, but he pushed through the pain and moved one foot in front of the other.

"No, Ben!" Emily shouted.

Ben braced himself and ran to face the man, only the man's body did not move or change as Ben circled about him, and somehow his legs turned without moving. Ben still faced the back of the man's head no matter where he stood.

"No!" Ben shouted, circling the man. "Who are you? Who are you?" No matter where Ben stood the man's back remained before him, his legs stretched out away from him, his palms resting on his knees. It was as if the man were spinning in the chair, only he never moved an inch. It was impossible; an optical illusion that the human mind was not able to comprehend. It belonged to some other dimension, another world.

Ben reached out to touch him, but his hands disappeared through the man as if he were made out of air. "No! No, no-no—NO!"

He spun around and around, stumbling over his own two feet.

"What are you? Leave me alone!"

He saw flashes of Emily standing by the door as he spun in circles. "Yes, Ben, yes! Make him leave. Make him go away!"

Ben collapsed on a wide cushion on the window seat beside the man's chair. He was out of breath, wheezing. Strings of saliva dripped over his lips as he sucked in air. His head went down to his knees.

A voice next to him spoke. "He's gone."

He jumped to see Emily sitting beside him. He looked to the chair. It was facing him, and it was empty. He looked back at Emily, who was smiling with the radiance of pure sunshine. She cupped his cheek in her palm. His face contorted and quivered as tears streamed down his cheeks and dropped off his chin.

"You did it, Ben. You did it."

"I … can't … do this anymore …," his voice croaked. Somewhere in the room, or from the room itself, muffled noises resumed: low-pitched commotion, hazy crashing and yelling sounds. The ground was creaking and things were shaking. The vases trembled on the tables, and some fell to the floor, crashing on the ground in broken splinters of glass and spilled water, sending the flowers bouncing across the floor.

"Rest now, my Bennie. You can finally rest."

"I don't understand. I don't understand." He was bawling. She pulled him close, and he rested his head on her lap. His vision was fading into an all-encompassing and pulsing aura.

"I'm so tired … Emily …"

"Close your eyes."

"But—"

"Shhh."

She held him tight, stroking his hair and humming a tune he recognized as an old lullaby his mom used to sing to him, only Emily wasn't singing the words, just humming the melody.

She's trying to kill you, Ben.

The words weren't loud; they were soft and calm. They spoke to him from deep inside his own mind, and yet it wasn't he who spoke them. It was the voice of the man.

Ben, wake up.

Why would she want to kill me? Ben asked in reply.

Emily was humming and caressing his hair. Each stroke of her hand drove him further down into the pits of darkness.

Because she believes it's the only way to save you.

I don't want to … live anymore. It's so … very hard …

You're sick, Ben; you've been sick for a long time. But you don't have to be sick anymore. There are things that you don't remember, things deep down inside of you. A portion of your mind has been corrupted, turned to darkness. Reclaiming your brain as a whole will help you fight away this poison that's coursing through your veins. You can remember if you try—if you want to try. Together, we can flush away the serum that Lucy has poisoned you with. We can remember the things from your past, and we can do it together, but you have to want to try. You can't give up.

I ... don't know how.

Somewhere, very far away, Ben could feel Emily caress the hair on his head and hear her melodic hum.

Yes, you can, Ben. The first part is going to be the hardest ... you have to say goodbye, Ben ... you have to let Emily go.

No, I can't do that! She's just come back to me after all of these years—these years filled with torture and anguish! I can't go back to the pain of not having her. It's too much to bear. I'm finally happy.

You're not happy, Ben; you're dying. She's not real, but the grip she has on you is. You have to let her go. Not just this projection of Emily that your mind created—the Emily that brought you to this cabin—but the real Emily. The Emily you hold in your heart, the one you fell in love with and married. The one you miss more than anything in the world. You have to let her go.

How do I do that?

Accept the fact that she's dead. Realize that you can't move on with your life until you accept that she's gone. Put behind you the nights of drunken debauchery, the nights of wallowing and crying to the heavens for her to come back to you. You gave up on everything—your life, your career, everything. You've been unable and unwilling to accept her loss, and this is where your attachment has brought you. You're dying, Ben. Let her go. Remember that there is another person in your life who can make you whole again. You will never be able to love this person if you don't deal with your crippling attachment to Emily.

I ...

Reality was fading before his eyes, the colorful aura becoming incredibly white, and the feeling of Emily's hand on his head was only a tickle.

Sophia Lorenz, the voice said.

Sophia's a ghost—she doesn't exist.

It's this memory of Emily you're clawing at that doesn't exist. You don't know for sure if Sophia exists or not. You have to search yourself—your heart and mind. The truth is inside you.

Sophia … Ben tried to come out of the fog, but his mind was lost. *How do I remember?*

Your brain thinks the only way to stop this disease—the Nano particles inside your body that are destroying your mind—is to kill you. Your body is confused. Your mind is jumbled. You've been taking too many drugs for too many years; you've spent too many nights connected to electrodes, depriving yourself of sleep and medicating yourself on alcohol and despair. Your mind created this image of Emily to help you kill the disease, and the method it has selected is to kill the host—which is you.

There is a glitch somewhere in the fabric of your very being—death goes against the very nature of survival. You have the power to kill off the Nano yourself, and I can help you do it. There are parts of your brain that were corrupted a long time ago—made void—and the disease is using these dark areas to operate without your knowledge. Your body doesn't know how to respond.

These Nano particles are weak. All you have to do is remember. Fill in the areas of your brain that aren't functioning, and your body will do the work for you. We can get this disease out of your body. But first, the only way to make your mind right and remember the past is to deal with the present.

How do you know all of this? Ben was so confused.

I've been through this before, and I've been following your life very closely.

Drapery Falls suddenly flashed across his mind. The dream played out in choppy increments, and the man on the ground … his face, it was blurry, but …

The man in my dreams, the man Iain killed … that was you.

Yes, Ben. That was me. It's time to say goodbye to Emily, Ben. It's time …

I … don't know if I can … Emily, my Emma …

Like small bubbles coming to the surface of water and popping, Ben's mind saw snippets of Sophia, and he felt emotion—real emotion—and felt a sense of sanity. It was far away, but it was there. His dates with Sophia: they felt so real. They had to be real; he had to believe that they were real. Did he really want to die? Or was the poison speaking for him—was it the poison that made him give up? He suddenly wanted to see Sophia again more than anything, feel her hand, touch her skin, kiss her mouth …

… but there was also Emily.

Please, God, don't make me leave her!

It was his own voice that answered, *But she's not even here. She's dead, Ben, and you have to move on.*

As the blackness in his mind became all-encompassing, he pictured Emily alive. The real Emily; not this projection of her that his mind had created.

He saw her when they got married by the town mayor, her in the wedding dress that she bought second hand and sewed herself to fit. Her young face was radiant and scared as they exchanged solemn vows in shaky voices, her nervous smile and blue eyes framed by her bouncing curls. He saw her walking into their bar for the very first time, terrified, with the keys still fresh in her hand.

He saw her taking forever to put on makeup in front of the bathroom mirror while he waited patiently on the sofa, the air growing fragrant of Dolce and Gabanna, and him looking at his watch every five minutes.

He saw them arguing over where to put the sofa and TV while moving into their new home. Both of them were exhausted from moving boxes and hungry waiting for the deliveryman to bring them the Chinese they ordered. They would eat that night sitting on the floor with a box as a table, tired, dirty, and miserable. The handkerchief she'd tied over her hair wet with perspiration. And yet they were happy—happy beyond what words could describe.

He saw her smearing paint on his face from her nose when they kissed, then hugging him tight, laughing so hard, and the two of them rolling on the floor with laughter.

He saw her in the studio standing before the easel, her reflection in the glass window, face stern, deep in thought, forehead crinkled, freckled with paint …

Emily, my love, my beautiful girl … I have to let you rest now, Emma … I have to say goodbye …

He heard her humming in the distance.

And then the humming stopped.

His head fell to the cushion and his eyes darted open. The darkness in his mind cleared. He sat up, rigid. The cushion next to him was empty. He looked at the chair. The man sat quietly, watching, their knees almost touching. Ben didn't startle, didn't flinch. The room was still—dust motes didn't move from where they hovered in the air, the flames in the fire were frozen in place. His brain was fizzing and buzzing in his skull. He thought he could hear it coming to life again, flushing new blood into the folds and grooves, fixing itself like the cracking of knuckles.

"Hello, Ben."

"Hello, Ethan."

"I've been waiting a very long time to see you again. So very long. Do you remember me?"

Ben nodded.

The man across was young, maybe twenty. Ben could see his face clear as day.

"Ben, do you know what's going on?"

"Yes," he said. "You are not Ethan Moore. I am Ethan Moore."

The man nodded. "We have so much to catch up on."

***

Michael's eyes darted open and he stared, disoriented, at an old wooden ceiling. He was on his back and his jaw was killing him. The confusion cleared and he remembered where he was and what just happened. He jumped to his feet, still limber for an old man. Seeing that Iain was still standing only a foot away made Michael realize he'd only blacked out momentarily. The fact that he was still alive meant he was either lucky or Iain wasn't done with him yet.

"You still have a wicked right hook, Iain."

"And you still have a glass jaw, Michael.

Michael rubbed his chin. Iain was wearing those damn leather 'sap' gloves, with lead powder sewn in the knuckles. His jaw hurt like hell, but pain was something he could tolerate.

"So, it's come to this," Michael said. "Our true feelings are out in the open. You need to come to terms, Iain. There was hope for Ethan Moore back then, and you failed to give him a chance. You *wanted* to kill him."

"Bullshit," Iain said. "I was following orders. You should have been doing the same." Iain began pacing to Michael's side, circling. "Since we're putting everything on the table here; I've known all along that it was *you* who helped save Ethan. He obviously didn't wake up and crawl to safety that night in Drapery Falls all by himself, high on heroin. I'm well aware that Dr. Wulfric was in the vacant room across the hall, and you helped him save the boy. I know you switched the needle in the bag with a lower dose and a concoction of tranquilizers that the doctor whipped up. I know Dr. Wulfric broke into the room to save the boy and nearly killed himself dragging him through the flames. All of this I already know. Mr. Kalispell had a separate comms team stationed across the street. They saw everything. But hey, that's what you do for family, right?"

Michael didn't know this, but he kept his expression stoic. "We gave the boy a fresh start. Dr. Wright wiped his memories clean, let him begin a new life with a new name and no memories of Lucy or any of us. We even forged him a birth certificate. He met Emily, and even she never suspected a thing. The doctors did a flawless job of transplanting memories, both real and fake. Ben had no memory of living in Drapery Falls after his grandmother died; he thought he moved straight to Sutton Lake."

"Yes, and Ben—or Ethan—sure fucked that life up. He would've been better off if we had killed him back then. Look what's become of him!"

Michael looked at Ben on the ground. He might as well have been a corpse.

"What do you think Mr. Kalispell will do to us if we let Ben live a second time? Hmm? If we fail and jeopardize the program again?"

"So what if we fail him again? Who gives a shit what he orders us to do? He's a corporate bigwig, not our commanding officer—and we're not at war. None of this is important, Iain. Who the fuck is Mr. Fucking Kalispell to give us a kill order?"

"You want to know who he is, Michael? You want to know who Mr. Kalispell is? He's a person with a lot of power, a lot of resources, and a lot of money. So many resources, so much money, and so much power, that he knew all about you and Dr. Wulfric saving Ethan this entire time, and did nothing but sit back and watch.

"You tried to make it look like an accident, like Ethan somehow made it to his car and drove to the lab, but you failed. You wanted us to have no other choice but to proceed the way Dr. Wulfric wanted and use that crazy program that Dr. Wright had just finished. I think all along you've known that Mr. Kalispell's been onto you. You can feel it when you're in the room together, you can see it in his eyes."

The blood in Michael's veins pumped hard, and his cheeks felt hot.

Iain continued, "Mr. Kalispell was suspicious of you from the beginning, and his suspicions turned out to be correct. Your phone's been tapped, and still is. So is mine. So is everybody's. We know you and the doctor were in it together. Fuck, Mr. Kalispell was so upset that he ordered me to dispose of Dr. Wulfric following the wipe on Ethan's mind. He's lucky to be alive. The only reason that he *is* still alive is because Lucy can't exist without him. It's a good thing for him that he accepted my offer to come back; otherwise, I was instructed to eliminate him at his house when I spoke to him by the pond."

"And me?"

"What about you?"

"Were you ordered to dispose of me as well?"

"Michael." Iain sighed. "This is your last chance. You can make things right. Get the syringe from the bag, and stick it in Ben's—or Ethan's—arm. Whatever you want to call him. That's an order."

"The syringe isn't in the bag; I threw it in the woods. I don't have to take orders from you, Iain. This isn't the army. At some point you went astray. You think murder is acceptable. What we did in the army—what we *had* to do—was different. Maybe some of the things weren't right, I don't know. The things I've done—the things I've seen—have tortured me over the years, given me countless nights of anguish, and I know deep down that what we're doing here is far worse. Murdering an innocent man is not acceptable. The fact that you think it is acceptable makes me believe that you're no longer fit to be leading this operation. I'm taking over as team leader, and my first order is for you to stand down and help me get Benjamin Walker out of here. Alive. This is *your* last chance, Iain."

Iain laughed.

Michael's hands formed into fists as the gap of silence between the two men thickened. He knew Iain wasn't going to stand down, and he also knew that there was no way out of this. Even if he did kill Ethan, Mr. Kalispell would still dispose of him as well. Maybe not today, maybe not tomorrow, but sometime soon, he would be a dead man. He was a loose end that had to be cleaned up.

Michael's eye twitched, and Iain raised his silenced pistol, but Michael was quick and grabbed Iain's arm, twisting it to the side. Iain moved his body in the direction of his twisting arm to avoid getting pinned. Michael grasped Iain's wrist. They struggled on their feet, their bodies close together.

With his free arm, Iain tried pressing his elbow into Michael's throat, but Michael kept twisting Iain's right arm back, causing too much pain for Iain to get any leverage. They went around and around in a circle, their arms locked, until Iain's back hit the wall. Michael used the extra weight he had on Iain to pull him back, and then smash their bodies back up against the wall, repeatedly. Iain's grasp on the pistol weakened and the gun fell, clattering over the floor. Iain was able to twist his arm free and the men jumped apart, the gun between them. They froze, staring into each other's eyes.

"Here, Iain. You forgot this in the car." Michael dug in his pocket and tossed Iain's cell phone on the ground.

"So what?"

"I saw your phone light up when I was reading the text Dr. Wulfric sent me. You left it attached to the charger. It lit up with the same text message I just received, only you didn't get the message from Dr. Wulfric—you were having all of my calls forwarded to you, personally tapping into my line. I went through your call log, and saw the messages from Mr. Kalispell. I know you were ordered to eliminate me if need be. Tonight. I should have killed you outside, but I didn't. I wanted to give you a last chance—a final chance to redeem yourself, be the man that you once were, back when you had honor."

"Get over yourself. I was giving *you* one last chance to redeem *yourself*, be the man that you should be now, and do the right thing."

"Do the right thing? Christ, look at yourself. Look at what you're doing! Look at what you've become—look at the monster that you've turned yourself into!"

They circled the room, the gun in the middle, both men fully aware of each other's formidability.

In a blink of an eye, they both leaped at each other, meeting in the middle and crashing to the floor. They twisted, grabbing at each other's throats, eyes, ears—punching, kicking, kneeing.

Iain got on top of Michael, his forearm wrapped around Michael's throat, and he pulled his body back, his legs wrapped around Michael's torso. The air and blood traveling between Michael's head and body stopped, and he felt as if his head would explode.

Michael bucked his body, pulling forward with all his might, and he threw Iain off. They both scrambled to their feet, facing each other again. Iain's nose let out a trail of blood that soaked the front of his disheveled shirt, and Michael took a deep breath of air into his lungs. Blood trailed down into his eye. He must have been cut, but he felt no pain.

They were both out of breath. They weren't as young and limber as they had been in their army days. Iain began taking off his suit jacket with deliberate moves, and Michael did the same. They circled each other all the while, eyes locked, tossing the coats to the side, and loosening their shirt cuffs and ties. Buttons were already missing, and Michael's shirt was torn down the side.

Iain lunged first, going for Michael's throat, and they locked up, still standing, grabbing, pulling, and pushing with all of their strength for an advantage. Michael slid his hand in his pocket and removed a cylindrical device, trying to keep Iain's eyes away from glimpsing the shimmering metal near his face. It was the syringe. Michael had lied about throwing it in the woods, and now he used all of his strength trying to press the sharp needle into Iain's neck, but Iain's arms were locked with Michael's, and he was pushing him back formidably.

Their faces were close enough to touch, when Michael suddenly head butted Iain at the bridge of his nose, hitting him with such force that Iain saw a flash of bright light, and blood poured from his nostrils. The needle jumped forward, missing Iain's neck, but sinking into the flesh at the edge of his forearm. Michael pressed the plunger at the same time, unaware that the point of the syringe had passed through the skin to the other side, sticking out in the air.

Iain let out a roar, twisting his body with all of his might, throwing them both against the front door. The door broke off its hinges, and they crashed to the ground outside. Michael fell heavy on his back and rolled, the air knocked out of his lungs. The needle broke and flew off in the grass. Iain got to his feet and ran back inside to grab the dropped pistol.

He turned, pistol in hand, and fell to a knee, grabbing the doorframe for support. His vision was vivid and pulsed in concert with the quick beating of his heart. The darkness all around him seemed brighter. His arm was warm with blood and covered with wet heroin.

The needle … must have gotten some … in my blood …

He rose to his feet. He was on the verge of total disorientation and was trying desperately to stay conscious. There was a lot of heroin in that needle; he had no way of knowing how much made it into his body.

When he got back outside, Michael was on his feet, hobbling away from the cabin with a piece of splintered wood sticking out from above his right kneecap.

Iain aimed, and pulled the trigger.

The silenced pistol made a whooshing sound as it fired, but the shot went wild, thwacking into the ground several feet away from Michael. But Michael fell all the same, grabbing the leveled edge of an old tree stump for support. His leg was bleeding fast; the jagged piece of wood had gone straight through the fleshy part of his thigh and scraped the bone. He thought it might have hit an artery. He turned and tried to stand, but he fell, his back against the side of the stump.

Iain approached, his steps wavering and unsteady. He blinked long blinks, trying to shake away the flashes of light going through his mind. His head felt like a balloon that was rising into the sky, soon to get away from him.

Michael grasped the wound above his knee. *I've lost. I tried my hardest, but I've lost. I'm so sorry, Ethan … I tried.*

Iain stood over Michael, the gun so close that Michael thought he could reach out and grab it, but knew he shouldn't try. The long barrel wavered before his face as Iain steadied himself, squinting one eye down the sights on the barrel.

Michael grabbed at his injured leg, squeezing the flesh above the jagged piece of wood to slow the bleeding. He felt something under his other hand, buried in the grass, heavy like a stick. He traced his fingers over the splintering shaft, feeling the cold-rusty metal at the end. He knew what it was, and without a moment's hesitation, he grabbed and swung the old axe from his sitting position. The still-sharp blade crashed into Iain's hand, sending the gun along with a chunk of Iain's thumb and a part of a finger flying through the darkness. Iain could only stare dumbly as his drug-numbed mind tried to process what just happened.

The axe handle splintered in Michael's grip. Pieces of the wood flew off with the swing, lost with the gun and Iain's fingers. Michael pushed himself up on his good knee and swung the axe again in the opposite direction. The blunt end crashed into the side of Iain's head making a sickening *crack* noise. The wood splintered completely and the metal head broke free. Iain's body twisted in an awful and unnatural position and he stumbled backward, but did not fall.

Blood poured from various openings on his head and face, turning his features a slippery red and making him look crazy in the moonlight. Michael tried to level himself, but the swing had taken all of his strength, and he fell to his side. Iain's eyes were wide, the blood dripping down his face looked black as ink in the night, and he was wild—insane. The adrenaline counteracted the euphoria from the heroin, and Iain's left hand groped for something on his belt or in his pocket: a knife perhaps, or maybe that old Taser of his. Michael turned onto his back to face Iain. He probably couldn't ward off another attack, but he would try.

Iain made a snapping motion with his wrist and a black-steel telescoping baton expanded in his hand. Michael looked at him. Iain was smiling—actually smiling—with blood pouring out from open wounds. This would be it—the end of the line for Michael Bennet. This smiling, laughing, crazy, drug-fueled man would have his kill. He would whack away, and the metal baton would break through the feeble piece of wooden axe handle Michael clutched before him like a shield. It would break the bones in his fingers, hands, and forearms, and then reach his skull, where it would continue to bash away on his face until the metal end hit dirt. Michael could only hope it would be quick, just a few blows until his arms were worthless, and hopefully, he would be unconscious as Iain continued to slaughter him.

Iain stepped forward, his grip on the baton tight—when the unmistakable crack of a bullet echoed.

It happened so quickly that Iain didn't even know what hit him. His body twisted and crashed to the ground, looking as if a car had slammed into the side of his body.

"Jeeesus!" Michael's voice scratched out. He shielded his face with his forearm, hoping that would be the only shot. He pushed himself up on an elbow and saw a ragged man in the doorway of the cabin, clutching the wooden frame for support. "Ben, is that … is that you?"

Ben's hand went limp, and the pistol fell to the ground. It was Michael's own pistol, lost when Iain had punched him in the jaw.

"Stay right there, Ben." Michael's throat was still constricted from being choked, and his words strained. "Don't move, Ben … I'm coming."

Michael pushed his back against the old stump, using the broken axe handle for support. "Ben! Stay with me Ben." His breathing was fast and labored. Ben fell to his knees in the doorway then toppled over sideways.

"No! Stay with me, Ben! Stay with me!"

Michael got his butt on the stump, and sat there heavy for a minute catching his breath.

"I'm coming, Ben," he said. "… I'm coming."

Chapter 25

There were footsteps coming down the hallway.

After spending two hours alone in silence, Michael could easily make out the slight creaking of floorboards and the shuffling of shoes against carpet as the man stopped before the door and slipped a key into the lock.

A moment later the man was inside, closing the door to his office behind him and locking it.

He didn't see Michael right away. First, he turned on a light switch, illuminating the room in a dim, tranquil light. The man was halfway to his desk when he saw Michael out of the corner of his vision. He stopped in his tracks. Slowly, he turned to face him.

Michael was sitting on a leather couch on the side of the room. Mr. Kalispell just stood there, his briefcase swaying in his hand, his suit freshly pressed, and his hair and face neatly groomed.

His expression was hard to read, but Michael was good at deciphering the tiny nuances, the micro-expressions, in a person's persona. Mr. Kalispell was at first frightened at seeing someone in his locked office, although he did not react. Then he saw Michael, and being the smart man that he was, his mind immediately processed why Michael was sitting alone in his office, alone in the dark. Michael knew he wanted to ask, 'What are you doing here? Where's Iain?' but he knew the answers to those questions.

Instead, he nodded to Michael and said, "Good morning, Michael."

"Good morning, Mr. Kalispell." Michael gestured for Mr. Kalispell to take a seat.

Mr. Kalispell went to his desk, put his briefcase down and loosened his tie. "So, here we are," he said.

"Indeed."

"I suppose it would be of no use explaining to you the consequences of your recent actions."

"You would be correct in your assumption."

Mr. Kalispell put his feet up on his desk, leaning the chair back as far as it would go and let out a deep breath. Involuntarily, Mr. Kalispell's eyes flicker to the middle file drawer, only inches from his hand. When he looked back up, Michael was shaking his head. Michael had already searched the desk and found the Walther P22 pistol tucked in the back.

"So then," Mr. Kalispell said. "Let's talk,"

"Yes, let's talk. Would you like to go first?"

Mr. Kalispell shook his head. "You already know what I'm going to say."

"All right then." Michael sat back in the couch, crossing his legs, careful not to bump his stitched-up thigh. "Let's go back, back a few years, to when Lucy was in development. Back when we recruited Ethan Moore. The boy was troubled, quite troubled. He made some bad choices, and the consequences of his actions were detrimental, to say the least. However, there was a time, before his actions went too far, that you were willing to work things out with him—bribe him and let him go on with his life."

"Michael, if you're thinking that's even a remote possib—"

"No, Mr. Kalispell, I don't think a bribe is a *willing* possibility."

"I would like to remind you that I have enough information connecting you and Peter Wulfric to this experiment that the authorities will have no problem throwing the two of you in jail for the remainder of your years."

Michael shrugged. "At this point, jail beats many alternatives."

Mr. Kalispell's forehead furrowed. "Excuse me?"

"Sure, you have information on us. So be it. We've known that was a possibility this entire time. So, after you sent Iain to coerce Dr. Wulfric at his home, the doctor and I came up with a plan."

"And what plan was that?"

"We gathered our own information; copies of *every* shred of paperwork, all the notes, experiment results, signed release forms—everything."

Mr. Kalispell mulled this over. "Maybe so, but I had Iain sign all of the paperwork relating to Lucy. Hell, even this property is under a false company name. It would take more than just paperwork to tie me to the project, or to Ethan Moore."

"Maybe so. Maybe so." Michael smiled. "Here, I have something for you." He dug into his pocket, producing a small USB flash drive. "Catch."

He tossed it across the room, and Mr. Kalispell jumped to catch it.

"What's this?"

"Audio recordings. You can keep that copy; I have plenty more. I made that one for you. Do you want to plug it in and have a listen?"

Mr. Kalispell was silent.

"I've been wearing a wire ever since you threatened Dr. Wulfric. I had a sneaking suspicion that if you were willing to eliminate Dr. Wulfric, you would also be willing to do the same to me. Was I wrong in my assumption?"

Mr. Kalispell remained silent a moment longer, but realizing there was no use in denial, he said, "No, you're not wrong."

"We also planted video cameras on your property. I know where all of *your* cameras are, so it was easy to stay undetected while we installed our own. We have hours of footage with you on the property, at the lab, talking to me, Dr. Wulfric, and Iain Marcus."

"I see. You do realize that this spells certain disaster for us all."

"This project has been a disaster from the get-go, and the doctor and I are through playing games. If we are left with no other alternative, Dr. Wulfric and I are willing to go down with this sinking ship called Lucy. However, drowning isn't good enough when imminent demise is on the horizon. If need be, we'll blow the whole fucking boat to smithereens."

Mr. Kalispell placed the USB drive on the desk. "I see." He sighed. "So, what now?"

"All of the information we've gathered—the audio recordings, video, paperwork—has been encrypted to digital files. The files are ready to be sent to every major news organization in the United States, as well as the attorney general, the FDA, a few dozen politicians, and human rights organizations that would love to get their hands on this. Dr. Wulfric, Dr. Wright, Benjamin Walker, and I must enter a code in our computers three times a day; otherwise, the files will be sent automatically. Just think about the shame you and your company will endure. Kalispell industries may not be destroyed, and perhaps you will even avoid jail time, but your name will be forever tarnished. Your father's portrait in the hallway will look down on you with shame and disgust."

"Right. I see where you're going. Let's cut to the chase—what do you want?"

"What we want is simple: to walk away. We don't want *anything* to do with Lucy or your company. We want the freedom to live out our lives without fear of retribution. We'll even make a promise to you: we will never share the information we've gathered; we will deny any knowledge of your business proceedings to anyone who might ever come asking. We will disappear. You can go about your business however you see fit.

"We don't care what you do; we just don't want to be a part of it. All we want is to walk away. You were once willing to allow Ethan to do just that. Won't it be easier for us all? We part company and never speak to each other again. That is our demand. I ask you this, is that something you can live with? Never seeing us again? Or should we gear up for war?"

Mr. Kalispell stared at the wall.

He spoke deliberately, "Michael, it seems fitting that we cut our ties and go our own separate ways. I will *not* promise that I'll stop keeping an eye on all of you, but that is something I think you already know. However, I can promise that none of you will ever be put in danger as long as you maintain your end of the bargain and never speak of our involvement together. You can go about your lives as you see fit. Essentially, you are all fired."

Michael slapped his knees. "See? Now, that wasn't so hard, was it?"

"No, indeed." Mr. Kalispell looked grim.

Michael stood, grimacing as he clutched his stiff leg. "Oh," he said, "there's just *one* more small thing."

Mr. Kalispell looked up at him. "And what would that be?"

Chapter 26

There was light.

So bright that he couldn't keep his eyes open, so he closed them and time passed.

When his eyes opened again, the world was a blurry mess—unrecognizable. He strained to focus on something—anything, to make sense of where he was, who he was. There was a person standing above him, and then the same bright light flashed in his eyes, going back and forth, like a … flashlight?

Muffled voices spoke.

He closed his eyes.

When they reopened, he was able to focus on the textured ceiling high above. A face appeared above him.

"Ben, are you awake? Can you hear me?"

Ben's raw throat felt as if he'd swallowed large pinecones. He nodded. The flashlight appeared again, and Dr. Wulfric leaded in close, studying the dilation of his pupils.

"Can you speak? Don't push yourself."

Ben swallowed and cleared his throat. "Yes." His voice was choppy and hoarse, like the words themselves were cut by glass. "I can speak."

"Good, Ben. That's good." The doctor smiled. "Oh, that's so good, Ben."

Dr. Wulfric left and came back, holding a Dixie cup filled with ice chips. He fed Ben a small spoonful of the crushed ice, letting it melt on his tongue before feeding him more. The cold water blanketing his raw throat issued swells of soothing relief.

"Makes you appreciate the little things." Dr. Wulfric patted Ben's knee and fed him some more. The Doctor's eyes were wet. "You need to rest now, but you're fine, Ben. You're going to be just fine."

Ben did as the doctor ordered and went back to sleep. The next time he awoke, he was calm and felt a pleasant lightheadedness, as if he were drifting on a raft, floating on a tranquil sea, the rough waves long behind him. He was warm and comfortable beneath a sheet and comforter with two soft pillows under his head.

"Are you feeling any better?"

"Yes, Doctor. I am." He sat up in bed.

"I want to keep you connected to the IV for a while; you're still dehydrated. You must be starving. Michael went across the street to get you some soup. Do you have much of an appetite?"

He was starving, but felt like he might throw up at any given moment. "I am, I think. I'm nauseous too."

"We'll start slow; just a few sips of broth. Here, a sip of water might help also." Dr. Wulfric poured a cup and handed it to him.

They were staying in a hotel room, a not-so-great-looking hotel room, with two double beds facing a TV, a small circular table under a picture window, and a bathroom around the corner. The blue carpet and white walls were drab and outdated, and the television was a product of the 80s. The wall on the far side of the room was stacked high with cardboard boxes, several of which were open. Files were spread over the small table in chaotic array. An open briefcase sat on the empty bed beside him, full of medical supplies—bandages and gauze, a stethoscope, an ophthalmoscope, and various containers with pills and needles. The sheets and blankets on the other bed were carelessly thrown over the mattress, and the pillows were tossed to the side.

"Where are we?"

"Monticello."

Ben nodded. He had passed through Monticello many times when he lived upstate.

"Ben … we need to talk." Dr. Wulfric looked away, rubbing the bridge of his nose. "I don't even know where to begin …"

"You don't have to explain yourself."

"No, Ben, I do. I do. There's plenty I need to explain. Jesus … this is my fault—everything is my fault."

"No, Doctor. It isn't," Ben pushed a pillow farther behind his back, "and I forgive you."

Dr. Wulfric looked at him. "What do you mean?"

"This wasn't your fault. I know you always had the best of intentions. I know you saved me—not once, but twice. I know you pulled me out of my apartment in Drapery Falls while it burned to the ground. I know you laced the needle Iain stuck in my arm with drugs to lower my heart rate, to make it appear to Iain that my heart had stopped working completely. I know that you and Michael are responsible for saving me again."

"My god, Benjamin, how …"

"My name is Ethan, correct? Ethan Moore."

Dr. Wulfric's mouth was agape. "How do you know all of this?"

Three loud knocks came from the door, followed by three faster, rhythmic taps and one last hard one. Dr. Wulfric got up to open the door. Daylight streamed into the curtained room, and two figures entered, closing and locking the door behind them. Michael carried a paper bag from the diner with chicken soup for Ben, and sandwiches for himself and the doctors. He saw Ben sitting upright, awake and alert, and smiled.

"He's awake!" said the man with Michael. "Ben, you're awake!"

"Hello, Stuart."

Dr. Wright rushed to the side of the bed. He felt his breast pocket for a penlight, and then looked to the bag of medical supplies when he realized he wasn't wearing a lab coat. Dr. Wulfric put a hand over his wrist.

"He's fine, Stuart."

Dr. Wright sat on the edge of Ben's bed. "How are you feeling?"

"I'm fine, Stuart. I'm all right."

"Ben … we have so much to talk about."

"He knows," Dr. Wulfric said, shaking his head. "I don't know how, but he knows everything."

"What—"

"Dr. Wright, you don't have to explain yourself. None of you do."

"What do you mean, Ben?"

"I believe he would like to be called Ethan," Dr. Wulfric added. "It's time we gave Ben back his rightful identity."

Ben shook his head. "Call me Ben. Whatever life I had before, it feels like a dream. I can remember things—my past—but it doesn't feel like I lived any of it. I might have been named Ethan Moore once, but I've become Benjamin Walker."

"How do you remember?" Dr. Stuart Wright felt a great wave of shame. He was guilty of writing the software that changed Ethan Moore's memories and identity to that of Benjamin Walker. The program, along with an altered version of the Nano serum, allowed Dr. Wright and Dr. Wulfric to view and alter Ethan's mind and memories while connected to Lucy.

Essentially, the software caused Lucy to work in reverse. Instead of recording Ethan's mind and sending the information back to Lucy, the doctors had Lucy supply the information, and send it to the Nano, where it was then broadcast to the neurons in his brain. Immediately after, the doctors destroyed all of their work, vowing to never re-create that specific program or serum again. Playing God was not something they wanted to be a part of, but it was the only way they could save Ben's life.

"Please, Ben," Dr. Wulfric went on. "Tell us how you remember?"

"Because of him." Ben pointed to Michael, still standing by the door. Everyone turned to face him. Michael nearly dropped the bag of food.

"Me?"

"Yes, you. Let me start at the beginning." Michael pulled up a chair, and they sat in silence, listening to Ben explain in detail the events as they unfolded. He told them about Emily and his journey from his apartment, between a train and busses, and his trek through the woods. He told them about his *fall*—which Dr. Wulfric believed to be a mild seizure. He told them about the faceless man and the cabin, and the conversation he had with, essentially, himself.

"That's when things started becoming clear to me. Whatever part of my memory that had been blocked suddenly began breaking free. I could remember being Ethan Moore, back when I was young. I remembered being recruited for the Lucy project shortly after my grandmother died, and I remembered you both—Dr. Wulfric and you, Stuart, working for Mr. Kalispell at the lab outside Drapery Falls."

"That's amazing, Ben. It shouldn't be possible for you to remember any of this." Dr. Wright looked stunned.

"I think I had to remember. It was either I remember or I die." Ben continued the story. "Strange things started happening when I entered the cabin. I began seeing things through someone else's eyes, like when I had the dreams of Drapery Falls. I didn't know who's eyes I was seeing things through at first, but then I realized it was Michael, or rather, *I* was Michael in the dream.

"I saw you guys working on me, fixing me, after I was dragged from the burning apartment. I saw you put me under Lucy, back when it was still a prototype, and write the software that allowed you to make adjustments to my memory. I could feel … I could feel what Michael was feeling, his emotions and sensations. I felt his tension when he disobeyed Mr. Kalispell. I felt him worry that I might still be in danger, and that you were all in danger—serious danger. I know that you made a deal with Mr. Kalispell that you would wipe my memory in exchange for my life. It was the only option he entertained. I know the terrible stress, guilt, and disappointment the three of you felt, and I know you put your own lives on the line to save me."

They were quiet. Then Dr. Wulfric said, "That's just remarkable."

Ben continued, "It was the software, the program that told the Nano particles how to behave, that blocked and changed my memory. This software allowed the new serum to do what it did. The dark areas of my brain—the areas I couldn't access or operate—was where the serum survived, keeping itself alive without my mind being actively aware.

"When I began hallucinating, when my mind created the image of Emily, I truly believed she intended to kill me. I think my body's response to rid itself of the Nano was to eliminate those dark spots of my brain, the corrupted neurons. The thing my once-rational mind did not comprehend—although it should have—is that eliminating the dark parts of my brain would also wipe out everything else. Mutually assured destruction.

"Ethan explained that the visualization of him that I was seeing came from the blank parts of my mind that were actively becoming aware, to stop my impending death. Slowly, I began remembering my past, and allowing my own immune system to begin eradicating the Nano, as it should have done to begin with. I woke up around that time, but I don't remember much. My past was still coming to me, bubbling up into my thoughts little by little.

"I woke up with a migraine—a very bad migraine. I vomited when I tried to move, and I saw a pistol lying next to my head. I heard a gunshot so I picked up the gun. I tried to yell, but I couldn't. I crawled to the doorway, and through the almost blinding lights of the aura migraine, I saw Iain aiming a gun at Michael's face. I knew from my dreams, or hallucinations, that it was Iain who killed Ethan Moore—at least Iain thought so at the time—and he had no regret doing it. I also knew that Michael saved me back then, and that if I didn't help now, Iain would kill us both. We would all be dead—all of us. So, I did what I had to do. I aimed the gun as best as I could and pulled the trigger."

Ben finished speaking, and everyone was silent. He thought about explaining the cabin, the way it appeared to him when he entered, the knick-knacks and roaring fire in the hearth, and the heavy smell of food cooking—but that memory wasn't for them. It was special to Ben, real or not. He may never be certain *why* he went to the cabin to begin with, why Emily had taken him there. But now, it was clear in hindsight that he knew all along where his feet were taking him. It was his own subconscious that took him there, the part of his mind that was forever consumed with the painting of the cabin.

Perhaps he had to be in the cabin to properly say goodbye to Emily, to his old life and his old ways. Or perhaps Emily—or the Nano— knew it was the one place he was guaranteed to follow her to, so she could get him alone, where no one could save him. The cabin was the one spot he held in his heart more than any other.

Dr. Wulfric broke the silence. "That's fucking amazing!" he said. Ben laughed, and then they all started laughing. Dr. Wulfric continued, "When we got you here, to this room, your blood was still coursing with the serum. As the hours progressed, the numbers steadily declined until the Nano was gone altogether. Your own immune system did the work; it flushed the drugs out of your system. I knew it would, it just needed a little time. The Nano, when it mutated and progressed, could be partially responsible for its own demise. I believe the mutated Nano fixed some of those blank spots in your memory, although in doing so, it let your immune system flush it out from your body."

"How …" Michael interrupted, his words stammered. "How did you see those things? You said you saw things through my eyes, like you were in my body?"

Dr. Wulfric answered, "Because you were sleeping here next to Ben in this room after we fixed your leg, and you told us that you were briefly unconscious in the cabin after Iain punched you. He must have read your thoughts, just like he did with Iain back in Rome."

Michael looked Ben in the eyes, and then turned his gaze to the floor, rubbing the side of his jaw. Ben would never mention all the things he saw through Michael's eyes: the war, the countless bodies that fell before him. He felt Michael's stress, regret, and the feeling of loss he held in his heart. The years of torment had not been easy to deal with. Ben felt nothing but sympathy for Michael.

"The only thing I don't understand," Ben said, "is why you brought me back to the project?"

No one wanted to answer. Dr. Wulfric looked to Dr. Wright and Michael, and they both stood up. Dr. Wright said, "I think this is a conversation you and Peter should have alone."

"No, Stuart." Dr. Wulfric waved them back to their seats. "We're all in this together. You and Michael should stay." He sighed, and continued, "We tried to do the experiment without you. We tested several other participants, but no one could adapt to Lucy to the extent your mind did. We tested over a dozen subjects—fourteen to be exact—and none of them could achieve the level of lucid dreaming that you are able to achieve.

"We knew about your personal life, about Emily and how tormented you'd become over the years. We were generally afraid for your health. We didn't want … well, anything to happen to you. We wanted you to have a happy, long life. You deserved it after your ordeal in Drapery Falls. We knew you were unhappy, that you were drinking too much, becoming financially unstable, and incredibly depressed after losing Emily. So depressed that we were concerned you would either hurt yourself or lose your job and be tossed on the streets. Worst of all, we didn't think you would care if something bad *did* happen to you. You were giving up on everything. That's why we supplied the jobs with Dr. Wright over the years, so we could keep tabs on you and give you some money while doing so."

"So, you brought me back because you thought it was for my own good?"

Dr. Wulfric paused, then continued, "No. It wasn't like that." Ben could see Dr. Wulfric's eyes getting wet. "Mr. Kalispell wanted—demanded—that you be brought back on the project. He threatened that he would bring you back whether I liked it or not, and that if I disobeyed, he would have me removed from the team. Which meant either jail or death. Mr. Kalispell has some information on me, some, well, damaging documents that show I used certain illegally obtained drugs during my time at Johns Hopkins. I'm not proud of this, but it's the truth. I lied to the school board, and forged reports. I felt at the time, and to this day, that the drugs I used were safe, but they were not approved.

"Mr. Kalispell told me that he *allowed* you to live after the wipe on your brain, but he wanted you back on the project. I had to accept you back. I had to get you back on Lucy, otherwise Mr. Kalispell would have found some other scientist to take my place, and no one but Michael would have been left to ensure your safety. We tried to make the whole experience as pleasant as possible for you. At least it would give you a purpose again, a job. Once again, offer a chance at a fresh start. It was never supposed to be like this; we had it all worked out. You were going to have a wonderful life: trips around the world, plenty of money. The serum was different; it never should have behaved the way that it did. I tested it on myself."

There was uncomfortable silence in the room.

Dr. Wulfric put his face in his palms and said, "There's something else you need to know."

Dr. Wright straightened up in his chair, looking over his shoulder at the door.

"The reason you met Dr. Wright back when you were a child, the reason you did all of those early experiments before joining Lucy … was because of me."

Ben looked at Stuart, then back at Peter. "I don't understand?"

"Let me start way back, when I was young man. I was twenty or so, and I met a girl when I was in grad school who I fell in love with. She was a few years older than me. There was a diner across from campus where I ate after evening classes. She was a waitress there, and we got to talking. One thing led to another, and I eventually worked up the courage to ask her out on a date.

"She was a wild-child, we couldn't have been more opposite, but we had a real connection, something I can't logically explain or put into words. She drank too much and partied all the time. I didn't mind back then, when I was a young man and didn't know any better. We got engaged after dating for seven months. A year went by and we started fighting regularly. Her drinking was becoming a problem; she lost her job and would have lost her apartment as well if I had not been hired at Johns Hopkins. We were just scraping by. She suffered regularly from migraines, just like you, minus the aura. She spent days locked up in her room with the curtains drawn, and when she felt better, she would celebrate by getting drunk for a week. We still had plans to get married when we decided—*she* decided—that we should spend some time apart."

Dr. Wulfric took a sip of water, and then continued. "For a year she wouldn't see me. She rarely answered my calls, and refused to meet me face to face. She was … a complicated woman. I've been told that you can never truly understand the reasons why you love someone the way that you do, and I believe that to be true in my case. I loved her with all of my heart, even though she was bad for me; she tortured my very soul without the slightest care.

"A year later, we got back together. She was weak and sick looking. She was different somehow. She was very apologetic and affectionate, and we decided to get married later that week at the borough hall. A month into our marriage she made a confession: she had been pregnant during our one-year separation, and she gave the baby up for adoption. She said she wasn't fit to be a mother, that we were too young to have children, that she needed the money the adoptive family paid her for food and rent during the pregnancy. She said my career would have been ruined, and that I should be thanking her. My heart was broken. I demanded to know where our child was—*my* child. She refused to tell me; she said she didn't know. But she did.

"I searched for my child on my own, but to no avail. We weren't married at the time of the adoption, so I had no immediate legal rights. She told the agency that she didn't know who the father was. This is hard for me to admit … but maybe I could have tried harder … I gave up looking because I didn't want to upset my wife, who objected at trying to find my daughter.

"The next few years together were consumed in strife. We split apart often, and in the end, we were just friends who would see each other now and again. Although we remained married until her last days, we lived in two separate houses and had two separate lives. Seven years passed, and one day, while things were good between us, we went out to breakfast. She drank several Bloody Mary's, then told me she wanted to do something different, something new—she wanted to go roller skating. So we did.

At the park there just so happened to be a birthday party ending for a little girl when we arrived. The girl skated by me. I even waved to her. After the party left, my wife told me to sit down. She told me that I had just met my daughter."

"Dr. Wulfric," Ben interrupted. "Are you—"

"I'm your grandfather, Benjamin."

The room was silent. Dr. Wright fidgeted in his chair, looking again at the door.

Dr. Wulfric sighed. Tears were rolling down his cheek. His voice was shaky and timid when he spoke again. "Your grandmother didn't want me to meet her, didn't want me to get attached. She didn't want me to meet my own child. She thought it would only make things more complicated.

"We briefly lived together again around the time when you were born. She, your grandmother, was a very sick woman. I know that now, although at the time I was in denial. Her headaches progressed rapidly as she aged, and she would sometimes spend weeks locked in her room. I was resigned to the fate that I would never meet my daughter; never know what she looked like as an adult, or what type of women she had become.

"Then out of the blue, my daughter—your mother—showed up one day at our front door. She was an adult now. She was able to track us down through an agency, and she was holding you in her arms. I was speechless. We spent the first hour getting to know each other, talking and crying. It was lovely, beautiful. I can't even tell you … but your grandmother … before you and your mother arrived, was already on her second glass of wine. By dinner, she was on three, and as the night continued, so did her drinking. We got into a fight. Whatever it was about, I don't remember. My only guess is that she simply didn't want a family. She wanted to be alone. She wanted everyone to go away so she could drink and be miserable, alone. I'm only telling you this story because I think you already know."

Ben didn't say anything.

"I saw it in several of your dreams, when I re-analyzed the recording from France, only your dream was blurry and the facts slightly off. You dreamt of your grandmother scolding you, telling you that you were a failure. That was true. She did say those things; only she wasn't talking to you, she was talking to me. Your mother was in the bathroom, and you were in the kitchen as your grandmother's mood went from borderline to aggressive. She was pouring a glass of wine when she turned to me, letting the wine pour freely from the spout. You were playing on the ground, and the wine poured all over you.

"When your mother came out of the bathroom, she was frightened to see you in my arms, dripping with wine and sobbing uncontrollably, as your grandmother went off on a tangent that was barely comprehensible. She took you from my arms and left. In due time we would have made amends, but a month later I found out that she had been killed in an accident."

"So why didn't you tell me you were my grandfather sooner? Why did I end up living with her, and not you?"

"I ..." the tears were now running down his cheek. "At first, after the event with you getting covered in wine, I knew—or thought I knew—that perhaps my wife was correct: you would be better off not knowing us. We were not fit to be parents or grandparents. I thought you were better off not getting involved in our life."

"I ... don't know what to say."

Dr. Wulfric continued, "I learned from that one dinner that you were suffering from migraines, just like your grandmother. After your mother died and you were given to a foster family, they decided to keep limited communication with your grandmother. We were no longer living together, or even trying to rekindle our relationship, so it was easy for her to keep me in the dark. However, I learned that your migraines were getting severe, so I introduced you to my colleague, Dr. Stuart Wright. That way, I could keep a better eye on you without interfering. As far as you living with her, I was kept unaware of that until after you moved in. We rarely spoke at that time. She told me you moved in with another foster family. It was Dr. Wright who told me the truth, but by that time, it was too late to do anything about it.

"I got you involved with Lucy as a way to make up for all the years. It was supposed to pay you, and pay you well. Set you up to have a wonderful life. I was going to reveal to you my identity then, but … I kept putting it off. I couldn't work up the courage to tell you. Your grandmother was right, we would have made horrible parents. I'm so sorry … for everything. Never … never, in a million years, would I have brought you into this if I knew how things were going to turn out. I'm … a horrible person; I've failed you in so many ways—so many times."

Ben cleared the lump out of his throat. "I'm so sorry."

"Ben, my boy, you have nothing to be sorry about. My God. You've done nothing wrong."

"You're a good man. I know you are. You didn't deserve to deal with all of that, and I'm sure you would have been a great father if given a real chance. If it's any consolation, I forgive you. I forgive you for everything you might feel guilty about, and I would like … to get to know you."

Dr. Wulfric took Ben's hand, patting it with his palm, "I may not be much, but I *am* your family, and I'm all that's left. Why don't I tell you all about myself."

Dr. Wright stood, "I think it's time for you two to be alone. Michael?" Michael stood, and they walked to the door.

***

"I have one more question for you—all of you." Stuart Wright and Michael Bennet were back in the room after a long drive. Everyone turned to Ben. "What do we do now?"

"That's a good question," Dr. Wulfric said. "Michael went to see Mr. Kalispell this morning."

"You met with him? Face to face?" Ben's eyes went wide. "Are you crazy? He could have killed you right then and there!"

"He would never do that." Michael shook his head. "He hates getting his own hands dirty. If he was going to have me killed, he wouldn't be present while it happened."

"We gave him an ultimatum," Dr. Wulfric cut in. "Here in this room, we have all the essential documents on Lucy." He went on to explain to Ben all of the information they had gathered on the project, and Michael told Ben about his meeting with Mr. Kalispell that very morning.

"So, we're blackmailing him," Ben said.

"Yes, essentially."

"Still, what's to stop him from simply killing us and destroying the data—or at least trying to destroy the data before we enter in our codes? I don't know if blackmailing him is the best option."

"Actually," Michael said, "blackmailing him *is* the best option. I swore to Mr. Kalispell that all we want to do is walk away. We don't want to go public. We don't want anything to do with Lucy. We don't want fame or glory. We don't want to see him behind bars, and we most certainly don't want to go to prison ourselves. We just want out. I've been working for Mr. Kalispell for many years now, and I know he's rather comfortable with bribes and blackmail. He'd rather *not* have additional deaths on his hands to worry about, if there's a way around it. If Mr. Kalispell genuinely wanted us all killed, we would all be dead by now. The fact that we are still alive right now is a blessing. As long as we stay quiet and go our separate ways, we'll be all right. I think I've convinced him that we have no desire to go public."

"What about Lucy? Or Dr. Egan?"

Dr. Wulfric answered, "Lucy is dead. I took all the important files from the lab, and without me, the project can't continue." He poured himself a glass of water from the pitcher on Ben's nightstand. "Unfortunately, Dr. Egan was fired, but that's a risk he knew he was taking when he took the job. He'll be fine. He's a bright boy and we've kept him in the dark about Drapery Falls all of these years, so there's no threat to his safety."

"So what now?"

"Well," Dr. Wulfric said. "I have an idea …"

Chapter 27

The loudspeakers in the airplane made a crackling noise, then a pleasant female spoke in French, followed by English:

"Ladies and gentlemen, we will now begin our descent. The captain has put on the 'fasten seatbelt' sign. Make sure your trays and seats are in their upright positions, and turn off all electronic devices. The outside temperature is 72 degrees, and sunny."

Ben filed out of the plane with the rest of the passengers, holding his carryon.

He retrieved his bag at the baggage carousel and left the airport. He had with him all of the possessions that he currently owned. Back at the hotel in upstate New York, Ben had called his landlord and worked things out so he would pay two months' rent and lose his security deposit, but he would be out of his lease. The man was upset, but Ben had been a good tenant.

Ben didn't return to the apartment. He left everything behind.

He signed his car over to Dr. Wright, who promised to sell it and wire Ben the money. Not that it mattered. Money would never be an issue again. His suitcase was full of it.

Before leaving the hotel room, Michael gave Ben two duffel bags. One contained Ben's own money that Iain had taken from his apartment when he broke in. The other duffel bag contained his share of the money that Michael had blackmailed out of Mr. Kalispell. There were so many crisp stacks of cash in numbered bands that Ben felt dizzy when he unzipped the duffel bag. Mere pennies to Mr. Kalispell, but enough money for a regular guy like Ben to get by for many years. Maybe he'd open another bar. Maybe.

Dr. Wulfric drove Ben to the airport, and on the way, he handed him a thick manila envelope.

Ben looked at the folder in his hands. "What's this?"

"Just open it up. I'll explain."

Over a dozen or so black and white photographs were stacked inside. They ranged in time from their trip to Paris until the day before Emily showed up in his apartment.

"My god," Ben said.

There she was, clear as day. The beautiful Sophia Lorenz. Ben felt a rush of relief. She was real, and he longed to hold her tight, smell her clean hair as it pressed against his face. A few tears came to his eyes, but he held them back. The pictures showed them having drinks at The Metro, eating dinner at Steaks and Capitol. It showed them talking at the Paris airport when they first met and walking hand in hand in Rome. Then there were the pictures at the end of the stack …

Dr. Wulfric pointed to the photographs, not taking his eyes off the road. "Those were taken after our trip to Rome, when the serum had mutated." One showed Ben driving to the airport in Baltimore—alone. Another showed him walking through the parking lot toward the airport entrance holding nothing but air in his hand.

"She wasn't there."

"No. She wasn't. Not that time."

Ben put the photos away, and left them in the car. He did not want to see them ever again.

A cab took Ben from the airport to the Euro Alliance Institute, in Paris, France. He removed his luggage and waited near the front door. He stood on a small bridge overlooking a thin stream that he wondered might be a tributary of the Seine.

He waited there watching the water, and looking at the faces of the people as they left the building. An hour passed, and as he stood leaning against the ornate guardrail of the bridge, he envisioned tossing into that moving water the one possession that he still owned. He stroked it gently in his pocket. He envisioned it caught up in the current, floating away to be lost on the horizon.

And then he saw her.

She did not see him. She walked wearing a backpack, her hair tied high in a ponytail. Sophia was within arm's reach on the bridge when she saw him.

"Ben!" She was taken aback. "Oh my God!"

She reached out and hugged him. He squeezed her tight. Her hair smelled of vanilla, and he stroked the side of her head, feeling the softness of her hair in his hand.

"Ben! What are you doing here? Are you okay? I've been calling you for days, where have you been? I've been so worried."

She took a step back and looked at his face. "Are you okay, Ben? Are you sick?"

His mouth was trembling, but he wasn't sad.

"I … I think we need to talk. I have a lot to tell you—I have to tell you everything."

"Of course, Ben. Of course."

She led him away, off the busy street, toward her apartment. She held his elbow, her body against his.

At that moment, Ben had everything he could ever want or need: the girl that he loved, his sanity, plenty of money, and the one possession that Dr. Wulfric found folded into a square in his pocket when Michael brought him unconscious to the hotel room.

The painting of the cabin in the woods.

Epilogue

-From the 'Journal of Science Tomorrow,' *December:*

In what is being described as the most groundbreaking, if not controversial story of the century, the scientists who created the much-talked-about *Lucy*, or the Frequency Responding Lucid Transmitter, are set to give a press conference later this week.

The machine that goes by the casual name 'Lucy' made international headlines last week when lead scientist, Dr. Charles Egan, made his announcement to the world that yes, they have created a machine capable of reading and mapping out thoughts and images created during a person's sleep cycle in great detail. No further statements were provided to explain how the machine operates.

In response to these claims, human rights activists from around the globe have raised their voices in protest, stating that the machine is in direct violation of personal rights and privacy. Eugene Rhymes, a spokesperson for *Empowering Rights*, issued the following statement:

"A person's thoughts—their dreams—are a personal matter. They do not belong to a room full of scientists and government officials. One's mind is private, and should remain that way. How do we know the government will not use this machine to read people's thoughts while they are awake? If they have the technology to monitor a dream, then they have the technology to read thoughts, and that is the beginning of a true police state. A person's mind deserves the freedom to remain private."

Empowering Rights is just one of the many groups threatening to sue Kalispell Industries if Lucy is made available to the public.

In a response, lead scientist Dr. Charles Egan made this comment: "We anticipated there would be a share of negative response to Lucy. Our objective has never been to read anyone's minds, or unwillingly monitor their thoughts. The positive scientific ramifications of this device are astounding. In a clinical setting, Lucy will be used to help cure a plethora of mental disorders, the list of which only time will tell. In a private setting, Lucy will give a person the ability to witness his or her own dreams firsthand. I truly believe this device will enhance our understanding of our very selves, and lead us into a new age of awareness. Lucy is essentially the thing dreams are made of."

Lucy was funded in private by Kalispell Industries, which has met harsh scrutiny from local and city officials, along with the scientific community at large, regarding the secretive manner in which they conducted their research, leading many to believe there might have been some unethical practices during the device's development.

In response to these claims, Kalispell Industries spokesperson, Iain Marcus, was quoted as saying; "I assure the general public that no laws were broken during any stage of development and research. It has been a long, hard road for our scientists, but at no point did we not comply with local and statewide regulations and laws. Our records are immaculate."

The president and CEO of Kalispell Industries, Mr. Timothy Kalispell, gave this short statement via email when asked to answer questions pertaining to any unethical proceedings, "I have the best—the smartest—group of scientists, lawyers, and advisors working around the clock on this project. Their hard work and dedication should be praised, not scrutinized. I have complete faith in my employees to answer all questions during the press conference."

The press conference is scheduled Friday at 4 P.M.

We'll be bringing you all the news and updates as they happen live.

Acknowledgements

As mentioned in the dedication, I cannot thank my wife enough for her constant support and dedication to our family. Special thanks is also deserved of the two people who helped me more with this project than they could ever know. Finnbar and Nicole, thank you very much. The same goes with my parents, Hal and Natalie Zenner, for their advice and suggestions.

About the Author

Brandon Zenner was born and raised along the coast of New Jersey, just a stone's throw away from the beach. When not writing, his wife, daughter, and two dogs keep him well entertained.

If you enjoyed this novel, the best way you can support the author is by taking a minute to leave a review on Amazon. Short and sweet works fine.

Visit http://www.BrandonZenner.com to learn more about Brandon's work, and join his email list to be informed of future publications and promotions. Or follow him on any of the social media sites listed below:

https://www.facebook.com/brandon.zenner
https://twitter.com/SlapstickII
https://www.google.com/+BrandonZenner

Thank you for reading The Experiment of Dreams. And thank you for still reading, down to the very last line.

Sincerely,
Brandon Zenner